THE DARK DOOR

Award-winning science fiction author Kate Wilhelm has entered the field of mystery and suspense with equal skill and excellence. *The Dark Door* is a brilliantly crafted novel featuring detectives Charlie Meiklejohn and Constance Leidl, who race to find the cause of a strange force that's sweeping across the country, leaving madness and murder in its wake.

"WILHELM IS IN TOP FORM AS THE THRILLER PLOT RACES ALONG AND THE CHARACTERS TEETER OVER AN ABYSS OF SANITY!"

—Publishers Weekly

ABOUT THE AUTHOR

Kate Wilhelm has won the Nebula Award for short fiction for the past two years. Her numerous books include *The Hamlet Trap* (another Charlie & Constance Mystery) and *Where Late the Sweet Birds Sang,* winner of the prestigious Hugo Award. Kate Wilhelm lives in Eugene, Oregon.

KATE WILHELM

THE DARK DOOR

TUDOR PUBLISHING, INC.
NEW YORK CITY

A Tudor Book
Published by special arrangement with St. Martin's Press

March 1990

Tudor Books published by:

Tudor Publishing, Inc.
276 Fifth Avenue
New York, NY 10001

This is a work of fiction. The characters, names, incidents, places and dialogue are products of the author's imagination, and are not to be construed as real.

Printed in the United States of America.

THE DARK DOOR

□ PROLOGUE □

THE PURSUIT OF KNOWLEDGE WAS THE ONLY ENdeavor worthy of intelligence, the master had taught, and the student Kri believed without question. As time passed, the student Kri achieved high status, not yet a master, but already an associate, and together he and the master developed and launched the first probe for life among the stars.

The tiny cylinder passed through interspace and back as programmed, but in the messages it now sent were streaks of clashing colors, wavery mud-gray splotches, even a black spray that swelled and shrank, appeared and vanished. With regret the master shadowed the self-destruct panel. The fountain of multihued lights that recorded the probe's existence dimmed and faded. The messages ceased.

The second probe, much altered, did not send any messages after its passage through interspace, but now a column of blackness marred the fountain of lights. This black column did not waver, nor did it grow; however, it shifted, first here, then there. It persisted despite all their efforts to remove it. Again the master shadowed the self-destruct panel; the column of darkness continued to lash within the fountain of lights. No messages were forthcoming.

Reviewers were appointed to examine the work, test the equations, study the methods; they could find no flaw, yet the fountain of many colors remained disfigured and hideous, marred by darkness that had become the darkness of ignorance, and then the shadow of fear.

"We cannot find the probe," the master said at the review hearing. "Once it passed through interspace, it was lost to us. We know it still exists somewhere. We know it is seriously flawed, perhaps fatally flawed. It will pass out of the galaxy eventually, and until it does, it poses a problem, perhaps even a threat to any life form it locates. It is beyond our ability to stop it or to correct it. We have tried to no avail."

The reviewers gazed at the marred fountain of light, a pale, sad flicker here and there the only visible reaction among them. After the adjournment, the master's own lights dimmed and faded; before the associate could follow his example, the reviewers intervened.

"Associate Kri," the master of reviewers said, "the pursuit of knowledge is to the academy the highest order of intelligence, second only to love and respect for intelligence itself. You and your master have brought dishonor to the academy, and a threat to life. However, in doing so, you have also alerted us to the dangers of unknown hazards that lie in interspace. We thought ourselves ready to travel among the stars, and we find instead that we must be resigned to roam no further than the reaches of our own star system until we have solved the problems your probe has revealed. Because the good you have brought to your own race is overshadowed by the evil that you may have brought to other life forms, it is the decision of this review panel that you must complete the project you have begun. Until the lights of the probe fade, you will monitor them, for however long the probe continues to exist."

Kri's own lights dimmed and flickered. "May I," he asked in a low voice, "continue to work on the probe in order to try to solve this mystery?"

"Yes, Associate Kri. That is the only task you will have for as long as it exists."

□ □ □

The cylinder emerged from interspace in the star system of a primary with five satellites. One by one it orbited the satellites until it found life. When it completed its examination of the planet, it left behind a trail of destruction—death and madness. Associate Kri prayed to the intelligence that ruled all life to destroy it, but the fountain of many lights remained undiminished; the blackness at its heart continued. It did not respond to shadowing of the destruct panel; it did not send any messages.

□ □ □

On the planet Earth fur-clad hunters pursued shaggy mastodons across the ice sheets to the steppes beyond, and some kept going south, always south. They came in waves, seeking better hunting, more hospitable territory, and then the ice crashed into the sea, and the retreat vanished.

□ □ □

In time, Kri's people launched an interspace starship, then another, and another. Some of them even searched for the tiny cylinder, but they could not find it in the immensity of space. Kri continued to monitor the fountain of lights with the blackness of evil at its core. He knew exactly when it emerged from interspace, when it reentered. He could not know what it did in the intervals. He no longer saw the multihued lights; all he could see was the blackness, the dark door of evil.

□ CHAPTER 1 □

JUNE 1979. CARSON DANVERS KNEW HE WAS BEing overly cautious, getting insurance quotes for all four places he was considering, but he had time, and it was better to be cautious before the fact than have cause for regrets afterward. Although River House was fourth on his list, he and Elinor had already decided this was the one they really wanted. Half an hour out of Washington, D.C., through lush countryside with gentle hills and woods, a tiny village a few miles past the inn, it was perfect. He would keep the name, he had already decided. River House, a fine gourmet restaurant for the discriminating. He glanced at Elinor's profile, caught the suggestion of a smile on her lips, and felt his own grin broaden. In the back seat his son Gary chatted easily with John Loesser. Gary was seventeen, ready for Yale in the fall; it was time to make the change if they were ever to do it. He suppressed the urge to laugh and sing; John Loesser would never understand.

Carson pulled off the Virginia state road onto a winding blacktop driveway and slowed down to navigate the curves, several of them before the old inn came into sight. The grounds were neglected, of course—rhododendrons thirty feet high, blackberry brambles, sumac—and the building had the windows boarded up. But even so its air of regal affluence was unmistakable. Three stories high, with a wide antebellum porch and beautifully carved pillars that reached to the third level, it bespoke the graciousness of the century past.

"We'd keep the upper levels for our own living quarters," he said over his shoulder to John Loesser. "A main dining room downstairs, several smaller rooms for private dinners, a lounge, that sort of thing. I'll have to do a lot of remodeling, of course, but cheaper than trying to build at today's prices."

"If it's structurally sound," John Loesser said in his precise way.

He did not have stars in his eyes, and that was all to the good, Carson thought. One of them should stay practical, add up the pennies, add in insurance costs. That was John Loesser's department, assessing the insurability of the place. He stopped his Buick at the front entrance. As soon as they left the air-conditioned car, the heat of late June in Virginia assailed them. Carson pulled off his coat, and after a moment John Loesser did also. Elinor was sensibly dressed in a cotton shift and sandals, her legs bare, and Gary had on shorts and a tank top. Only the businessmen, Carson thought with some amusement, went through the motions of suits and ties. And after he bought River House, made it the restaurant he had long dreamed of owning, he promised himself never to wear a necktie again in his life, or a coat in the summer.

"I have flashlights," he said, opening the trunk of the Buick. "I loosened some of the boards on the windows last week, but the basement's like a cave." He handed John Loesser a large flashlight, took another for himself, and saw that the other man was staring at two rifles also in the trunk. "Gary's going to get in some practice while we're going over the building." He closed the trunk and tossed the keys to his son.

Elinor watched the three men remove some of the window boards, then go on to the next bunch and take them down. How alike they were, she thought, surprised, all three over six feet, all blond. Of course, Gary was still somewhat frail-looking, having shot upward over twelve inches in the past year; it might take him three or four years to fill in the frame he was constructing for himself. Seventeen, she found herself marveling. A sharp image superimposed itself before her eyes, eclipsing for a second the three men: an image of herself walking with Carson, with Gary in the middle swinging from their hands, laughing. Yesterday. Ten years, twelve years ago. She shook her head and turned to the front door of the inn, put the key in the padlock, and opened it. When she entered, she left the door wide open to admit air and more light.

On one side was a wide sculpted staircase sweeping up in a graceful curve. They would have a women's lounge up there; permit the customers to fantasize briefly of being the lady of the house, making a grand entrance to a crowded, suddenly hushed ballroom, glittering with the wealth of the Virginia aristocracy. Elinor smiled to herself. That was her fantasy. The area to the right had held the registration desk; nothing was there now. A closed door led to a narrow hallway and small offices. To the left of the entrance stretched a very large room with a centered fireplace built with meticulously matched river stones. She could visualize the palm trees, the velvet-covered lounges and chairs, low, ornately carved tables, brass lamps. . . . Only faded, rose-colored flocked wallpaper remained. She moved through the large open space toward the back of the building. Suddenly she stopped, blinded by a stabbing headache; she groped for the doorway to steady herself.

An overwhelming feeling of disorientation, of dizziness, swept her, made her catch her breath and hold onto the door frame; her eyes closed hard. The moment passed and she could feel a vein throbbing in her temple, a knife blade of pain behind her right eye. Not now, she moaned to herself, not a migraine now. She opened her eyes cautiously; when the pain did not increase, she began to move again, through a corridor to the rear of the inn. She unlocked another door and threw it wide open, went out to another porch to lean against a railing. She took one very deep breath after another, forcing relaxation on her neck muscles, which had become like iron. Gradually the headache eased, and by the time Carson and John Loesser moved into sight, it was a steady throb, no longer all-demanding.

Carson saw her leaning on the rail and felt a familiar twinge of pleasure. Standing like that, in profile, as trim and as slender as she had been twenty years ago, she looked posed. She looked lovely. "Are you married?" he asked John Loesser.

"My wife died five years ago," Loesser said without expression.

"Oh, sorry." Loesser was already moving on. Carson caught up again. "Here's the back entrance. We'll have a terrace down there, and tables on the porch overlooking the river. The property extends to the bank of the river. I want it to be like a garden, invite strolling, relaxing."

They went through the open back door, on to the kitchen, which would need a complete remodeling, walls to come out, a dumb waiter to go in. Carson was indicating his plans when John Loesser suddenly grunted and seemed about to fall. He reached out and caught a cabinet, steadied himself, stood swaying with his eyes shut. By the time Carson got to him, he was pushing himself away from the cabinet. A film of perspiration covered his face; he looked waxy and pale. Carson's first thought was *heart attack,* and with that thought came the fear men his age, mid-forties, always suffered. Loesser was that age, too, he knew. He took Loesser's arm.

"Let's go outside, get some air. Are you okay?"

"I'm all right," John Loesser said, pulling free. His voice was faint; he sounded puzzled, not afraid. "A dizzy spell. Could there be some gas in here? Bad air?"

Carson looked at him doubtfully. "How? I've been all over this building three times already. Elinor, Gary, we've been in every room, and that was with the boards on the windows, before we were allowed to open it up at all."

Loesser drew in a deep breath, his color back to normal, a look of irritation the only expression Carson could read. "Whatever it was, it's gone now. I have a bit of a headache, maybe that's to blame. You understand any figure I come up with is a ball park figure, contingent on many other reports. A termite inspection, for example."

Carson nodded and they wandered slowly

throughout the other rooms on the main floor. Something was different, he thought suddenly. It was true that he and Elinor and Gary had prowled through the building three times, but now something was changed. He felt almost as if something or someone lurked just out of sight, that if he could swivel his head fast enough, without warning, he might catch a glimpse of an intruder. He had had a violent headache ever since their arrival. Pain throbbed behind his eyes. It was the damn heat, he decided; maybe a storm was building, the air pressure was low. Or high; it felt as if the air was compacted, pressing against his head. He and Loesser went up the wide, curving staircase to the second floor, where he began to outline the plans for a women's lounge.

Suddenly he heard Elinor scream, a piercing shriek of terror, cut off by a gunshot. He turned and raced through the upstairs hallway to the rear stairs. John Loesser ran toward the stairs they had just ascended. Before Carson reached the first floor there was another gunshot that sounded even louder than the first. He tore out to the porch, pounded to the far end of it, and saw Elinor crumpled on the floor.

One of her sandals was gone, he thought distantly. How could that have happened? He touched her face. One eye was open, as blue as the dress twisted about her thighs. The other side of her face was gone. He touched her cheek, whispering her name. He started to gather her up, to lift her, carry her inside, straighten out her dress. . . . From a long way away he heard a man's anguished wail. Angered by the noise, he jerked up, snapped around, and saw his son Gary leveling the rifle at him. He was still moving when the gun fired, and fired again. He was flung backward by the momentum, stopped briefly by the porch rail. Then he toppled over it to fall to the thick underbrush below.

□ □ □

He came awake slowly and did not know where he was, why he was sleeping in the shrubbery. He tried to rise and fell back to the ground. Someone sobbed; he listened to hear if the other person would say something. An insect chorus crescendoed. He tried to roll to one side and prop himself up, but found that one of his arms had turned to lead. There was no pain. Something was wrong with his vision; he wiped his eyes with the hand that worked. Sticky. Suddenly he really looked at his hand and saw blood; memory returned, and pain swamped him. He heard the distant sob again and knew this time that he was making the noise. Elinor! Gary! He began to work at pulling himself up, rising first to his knees. Then, fighting dizziness and nausea, he got to his feet. He staggered, fell, and rested before starting again.

Falling, crawling, staggering, pulling himself along with his good hand grasping the brambles and scrub trees, he hauled himself to the building, then up the stairs to the porch, where he collapsed again. After many minutes he started to inch his way to Elinor. The entire end of the porch was awash in blood. Elinor was not there.

A wave of pain took his breath away; he pitched forward and lay still. When he could open his eyes again, he saw her footprints, one shod, one bare. She must have gone for help, he thought clearly, and in his mind the vision of her destroyed face and head swelled, dwindled, and swelled again like a pulse. He forced himself to his feet.

For the next hour he followed the bloody footprints, sometimes on his knees, sometimes staggering on his feet. At the bottom of the curved stairs there was a bigger pool of blood, more prints. He picked up a wallet. Loesser must have dropped it, he thought distantly, the way Elinor lost her sandal. He put the wallet in his pocket and pulled himself up the stairs, resting more and more often now; sometimes he slept a little, woke to hear his own groans. Slowly, he moved on upwards.

They were all around him, he realized during one of his rests. The intruders he had sensed before were still here, everywhere, watching him, surrounding him, pressing against his head, waiting. He came to the rifle and rested by it, moved on. Then the prints stopped. He lay with his cheek on the floor and knew one of the bloody trails was his own. Straight ahead was a closet with an open door; the bloody path ended there. He sighed tiredly and lifted his head, tried to see past a blackness that filled the doorway from top to bottom. Inky blackness, nothing else.

He rested. They were here, everywhere, he thought again, from a great distance. Waiting. Suddenly he jerked awake. Waiting for him to bleed to death. Waiting for him to die! Slowly he began to retrace his trail. He rolled most of the way down the stairs. He found himself at the Buick and fell onto the front seat and rested a long time. It was getting dark. Key, he thought. He had tossed his keys to Gary. Without any thought or plan, he found Elinor's keys in her purse on the passenger seat. He got the car started, and aimed at the state road. When he reached it, he slumped forward and slept.

□ □ □

He heard a soothing voice, felt hands on him, tried to return to the drifting state that was not sleep, but pleasanter because it was dreamless oblivion. The voice persisted.

"Can you hear me? Come on, Mr. Loesser, wake up. You're safe now. You'll be all right. Wake up, Mr. Loesser."

He was being pulled back in spite of himself.

"A little more, Mr. Loesser, then you can sleep again." The voice changed slightly. "He can hear you and answer if he wants to."

A different voice spoke. "Who shot you, Mr. Loesser?"

He opened his eyes, realized that only one seemed to work, and reached up to feel a bandage that covered most of his face. He remembered being awake earlier, remembered wanting, being denied, a sip of water, being allowed to sleep again.

"Who shot you, Mr. Loesser?" The speaker was out of focus, thin-faced, sad-looking.

"Gary," Carson said and heard it as a croak.

"Did you say Gary? You mean Gary Danvers?"

"Gary," he said again and closed his eye. "My wife—"

"Yes. Your wife? What about your wife?"

"Dead," he said in his strange croaking voice.

The other voice came back, the soothing one. "Go back to sleep now, Mr. Loesser. Your wife died a long time ago. Remember? That was a long time ago."

"What's that all about?" the sad man asked.

"He's confused. Shock, trauma, loss of blood. His wife died in an airplane accident more than five years ago. Let him rest now. You won't get much out of him until the Demerol wears off, anyway."

"Okay. Okay. I'll drop in tomorrow."

Carson Danvers drifted and thought that if he were John Loesser, he would have grieved for his dead wife a long time ago. He slept.

□ CHAPTER 2 □

"MR. LOESSER," DR. MCCHESNEY SAID, "GO back home. Don't hang around here. I can recommend a doctor to oversee your convalescence now. You need to be with friends, relatives, people who know you and care for you. All this brooding about what you might have done is pointless, Mr. Loesser. I've talked to the detectives, and they all agree that there was nothing more. In fact, it was very brave, perhaps even foolhardy, for you to try to help at all."

Carson Danvers sat on the side of his bed. His face was swathed in bandages. A bullet had grazed his cheekbone, had torn away most of the flesh on one side. He would need plastic surgery. His right arm was in a cast. A bullet had gone through his shoulder. His torso was bandaged. They had gone in and removed part of a rib shattered by the third bullet. The rib had deflected it, sent it back outward through a second hole. Except for the plastic surgery, he was repaired, healing, ready to be discharged from the hospital.

Dr. McChesney stood up. "If you decide to stay around here, I can recommend a rooming house where they'll take care of you, and I'll have my nurse set up an appointment in my office next week."

"That's what I'll do," Carson said. Talking hurt; he kept it at a minimum.

"Okay, I'll make the arrangements. Your company will pick up the bill, they said. You're on sick leave for the next three months and we'll evaluate your situation then. Nothing to worry about on that score." He regarded his patient for a moment, then put his hand on Carson's shoulder. "I don't know how the hell you dragged yourself up those stairs, either. God knows, John, you did more than was human as it was. Don't torture yourself. I'll send in the nurse for you."

Carson knew he had to tell them the truth about who he was, but not yet, he thought. Not yet. Elly's parents, her sister, his parents. . . . How could he tell them Gary had gone crazy and killed his mother? Even trying to form the words it would take to tell them brought a long shudder and made his eyes sting with tears. Not yet.

The strange thing was the ease with which he was getting away with being John Loesser. They had found a wallet—Loesser's wallet—in his pocket; Carson's things were in his coat left in the Buick that day. Even the man the company sent out had accepted him. Of course, he had not known Loesser personally, but he had seen him a time or two. Carson had not been expected to talk then, and the bandages had concealed his identity further, but even so, he mused, even so. The few times he had started to explain, he had gone dumb, started to shake, lost control. Twice they had given him an injection to put him to sleep again, and the last time they had sent in a new doctor whose name had already escaped him. A shrink, he had realized after a short time. Guilt, the shrink had stated ponderously, was the most debilitating emotion of all. He had talked on, but Carson had stopped listening. Guilt of the survivor, he realized, was what the shrink assumed he was suffering from. And he was, he was. Guilt over doing something so horrible to Gary that he had turned on his own parents with a gun. Guilt over not being able to help his dead wife. Guilt over not being able to help his child. Guilt, guilt, guilt. But as John Loesser the guilt was abstract, distant. He would tell them later, he had decided that day. Much later.

Two weeks after leaving the hospital he flew to Richmond and let himself into Loesser's apartment. He still had bandages on his face, would have them until plastic surgery did its magic. People he met averted their gaze, and that was fine with him. The apartment was scrupulously neat—almost obsessively so—with good paintings, good books, good furniture, good stereo and television. Money, he thought bleakly. Loesser had had money. He had not given it any consideration until then. He went through the apartment carefully, getting to know his host, not liking him, but reassured because it became more and more apparent that Loesser had had no friends or relatives. Had he become a recluse after his wife's death, or had the trait always been there? There were names in an address book; he recognized a few from cards he had received—impersonal, duty cards—while he was still hospitalized. He found the financial statements. There was real money. Mrs. Loesser's insurance had been half a million dollars, a traveler's policy that anticipated the worst scenarios, and now and then paid handsomely. He found her picture, a pretty woman with a small mouth, upturned nose, blue eyes. A forgettable face. The picture had been put away in a closet in a box of mementos, along with her college diploma, and medical records dating from childhood up to the time over five years ago when they had ceased to matter.

He spent the weekend there, learning about Loesser, learning about money, about stock holdings, bonds, certificates of deposit. No one challenged him. The building superintendent knocked on the door, and when Carson opened it on the chain, the man hardly glanced at him. He had heard, he said; what a hell of a thing. If there was anything he could do. . . . He went away.

Carson sat in the darkening room on Sunday and suddenly was overwhelmed with grief that shook his frame, made his cheek hurt with a stabbing pain, made his chest tighten until he feared—and would have welcomed—a heart attack. He had to call her parents, he knew, but not yet. Not until they found her, found Gary. No bodies had been recovered. Not yet.

He drove Loesser's Malibu back to Washington, and collapsed into bed as soon as he arrived at his rooming house. He could get an apartment, he thought, staring at the ceiling, a good apartment with a view, and there he would wait until they found her, found Gary, and then he would call her parents. The next day he drove out to the inn.

Someone had come and boarded it all up again, exactly the same as it had been the first time he had seen it. He walked around the building and stopped at the back porch where he had found her. Although it had been scrubbed clean, in his mind the blood was there, her body was there, one sandal missing. Where had it gone? He almost went down the stairs to the tangle of briars to search for it. He clutched the rail with his good hand and rubbed his eyes with the other. He remembered rising, seeing his son with the rifle. Suddenly, cutting through the memories, there was the other thing again, just as it had been the last time. Something present but out of sight. Carson did not move, held his breath listening. No sound. But something was there, he knew without doubt. Something. Slowly he turned, and now he closed his eyes, concentrating on that something. He felt as if he had moved into an electrical field vibrating on a level that did not affect muscles and skin, but was active deep inside his head, making it ache. For a moment he swayed, but the dizziness passed quickly and all he felt now was a headache that was growing in intensity. Like a hangover, he thought from a distance, spacing himself away from it, the way he had learned twenty years ago in college. Pretend it isn't there, think yourself away from it, and let the damn thing ache all it wants. Cholly's advice. Cholly, his college roommate whom he had not thought of in years. The headache became manageable and he opened his eyes with caution, as if afraid of startling away that something that was there with him. He could still feel it; he felt surrounded by it, pressed from all sides. Moving very slowly he started to back away, backed down the steps to the overgrown path, walked deliberately around the building to get inside his car, Loesser's car. It was still there with him. He turned on the ignition, and then it was gone.

That night he stood naked before his mirror and regarded the long ugly scar that started somewhere on his back out of sight, curved under his arm and went up to just under his nipple. The scars on his shoulder were uglier, bigger. The skin and bone grafts would blend in, the doctors had said, but it would take time. His face was the worst of all. Hideously mutilated, inflamed, monstrous. Plastic surgery would hide it all, they assured him. He was an excellent candidate for the kind of reconstruction they were capable of now. His gaze traveled down his body and he was mildly surprised to see how thin he had become. He had lost nearly forty pounds. The doctors had been amazed that he had lived through his attack, that his recovery was going along so uneventfully, so quickly. He had been amazed at the same things, but now he knew why he had been spared, knew what he had to do. He had been spared because he had to kill the thing in the inn.

He moved the next day to a bright, airy apartment with a view of the Potomac that looked lovely, inviting. He thought of the river below the inn; was that where the bodies had been hidden? He knew even as he wondered that that was wrong; they had been taken behind that darkness of the doorway. This time no tears came. He began to think of what he would need. Crowbar. Flashlight. Gasoline. He already had decided he had to burn it out, let fire consume and purify the house. Matches. How terrible it would be to have everything ready and no matches. After a thunderstorm, he decided, when the woods would be wet. He did not want a conflagration in the woods, did not want to hurt anyone, or chance having the fire put out before its work was done. An interior fire that would be out of control before it could be spotted from outside, at a time when no one would be on the road to call a fire department. He made his plans and the next day began to provision himself. There were thunderstorms almost every afternoon; he was able to pick his night.

□ □ □

He felt *it* as soon as he stopped the car at the inn. It was three-thirty in the morning, an inky black night, the air heavy with leaf mold and forest humus; earthy smells of the cycle of life and death repeated endlessly. He could smell the river, and the grass. He circled the inn to the back, where he forced open the boards on several windows. He climbed in and opened the door, then went back to the porch. Carefully, he poured gasoline where her body had been, followed her invisible tracks through the house, one foot shod, one bare, both bloody; no traces remained, but he knew. He covered the trail with gasoline. Up the curving stairs, through the hallway, to the door where the bloody prints had stopped, where the abyss still yawned. That was where Elinor and Gary were, he knew. They had been taken into the abyss. He sprayed the walls with gas, soaked the floor with it, then finished emptying the can as he retraced his own trail from that day, down the back stairs, to the porch. It was done. A distant rumble of thunder shook the air. The things all around him, pressing against him, vanished momentarily, then returned as the thunder subsided. Now and then he found himself brushing his hand before his face, as if to clear away cobwebs; his hand passed through emptiness, and they were still there, pressing against him. The dizziness did not come this time, but his head was aching mildly. He struck a match and tossed it to the gleaming wet gasoline where she had lain. The porch erupted into flames that raced through the building, following the trail he had made, through rooms and halls, up the stairs. There was a whoosh of flame from the upper floor. He had not closed the back door; belatedly he wondered if he should have knocked boards off in the front to admit a cross draft. He stood watching the flames blaze up the kitchen wall, and he knew he had done enough. Slowly he turned and walked to the car, taking the *something* with him, oblivious of the death he had planned for it. He got in and turned on the ignition; as before, it fled. He drove away without looking back.

□ □ □

Over the six months he had more surgery on his shoulder, plastic surgery on his face. A scar gleamed along his cheekbone. They could fix that, they told him. Give it a few months first. He did not go back. He learned to use his right arm all over again; the bank, lawyers, no one questioned the changed signature. They all knew the trauma he had suffered, the difficult recovery he was making. He took from Carson Danvers very little. Carson had been a master chef, and the new person emerging equipped his kitchen with the best cookware available and bought good spices and herbs, but he used them very little. John Loesser had been obsessively neat; the new man liked neatness more than he had realized, but not to such an extreme. Carson had been outgoing, friendly, talkative. He had liked people, liked to entertain people, kid around with them. The new man knew no one; there was no one he wanted to talk to, no jokes, no stories worth repeating any more.

He spent many hours in his darkened apartment in Washington watching the lights on the river, watching the patterns of light in the city, thinking nothing. He spent many hours reliving his past, going over scenes again and again until he knew he had recaptured every detail, then going on to other scenes. At first the pain was nearly intolerable, but over time it lessened and he could even smile at the memories. Their first date, how awkward he had been, how afraid he would offend her, bore her, even frighten her. He had loved her from the very first, and had declared his love much too soon, long before she was ready to consider him seriously. He had been so dumb, tongue-tied with her, and adoring. The pain diminished, but the emptiness grew.

The company sent someone out to see him again, and for the first time he suggested that he might never return to work. He talked to the man—Tony Martinelli—in a shadowed living room, making certain he was hidden by shadows. Martinelli did not press him, was probably relieved. They would wait, he had said; there was no rush, no quick decision to be made. But no one had urged him to mend quickly and return. Loesser had had no real friends in the company; no one would miss him. In time they sent papers; he hired a law firm to represent his interests, and paid no more attention to any of that until one day when he received a letter asking politely if he would mind sending back certain records, certain computer information. He went to the study where he had John Loesser's computer, records, files, books—all boxed. He had not looked at any of it. That afternoon he unloaded one box after another and examined the contents. He got out the computer manual and connected parts to other parts as directed, but he did not know what to do with it. There were books on the insurance industry, on computers, on statistics and rates and liability schedules; there were actuarial tables. At last he had something to do, something he could not ask for help with; Loesser was supposed to know all this. It had been weeks since he had called the police to enquire about the missing bodies, weeks since he had thought about revealing his own identity. That night he realized that Carson Danvers was as dead as Elinor and Gary Danvers.

He learned how to use the computer, learned how to copy the disks, use the modem. He took a large folder to a Xerox machine and copied everything in it, then reboxed the originals. He sent the company the information and was finally done with them. He could not have said why he wanted copies; there was no real reason other than it was something to do. Without pondering further, he gradually learned the business through John Loesser's accumulation of records and notes and his modem connections.

He had been startled one day when, following John Loesser's directions, written in the man's precise, minute handwriting, he had found himself accessing a mainframe computer that apparently held data from the entire insurance industry. Fascinated by the information available, he had scrolled through categories. Liability claims: flood damage in Florida, starved cattle in Montana, wind damage in Texas. . . . Accidents in supermarkets, on city buses, in neighbors' yards and houses. . . . Medical claims for hernias, broken bones, hysterectomies, bypasses. . . . He was appalled by the automobile claims, then bored by them. He learned how to ask for specific groupings: shark attacks, bee stings, food poisonings. . . .

His fingers were shaking when he keyed in

the request for hotel fires. There it was, his River House, followed by *Arson—unsolved.* He was shaking too hard to continue. What if they had a way of tracing who looked up information like that? What if they came back to him? The next day he registered as a public insurance adjuster, making his use of the computer data appear more legitimate. Why? he asked himself, but he did not pursue it. He looked for a list of closed hotels and marveled at the number. Carson Danvers would have liked seeing what all was available, he thought.

Some days later it occurred to him to look up instances of sudden madness and homicides, and again he was appalled. He scrolled the list and went on to something else, then stopped. Camden, he thought. He had seen something about Camden, Ohio, in the papers recently, and there was one of the abandoned hotels in Camden. He went back to that list and found it. Dwyer House, built 1897, closed 1936. Forty-two rooms. Used as an office building from 1938 to 1944. In litigation from 1944 to 1954. Owned by Gerstein and Winters Realty Company. Insured for forty thousand. It sounded almost exactly like the inn that Carson Danvers had been looking for. Wrong place, but right building.

In his mind's eye he saw the wide back porch, Elly's body sprawled, the bloody prints that led up the handsome, curved staircase. And he felt again the unseen presence that had swarmed all around him. Saw again the vacant, mad look on Gary's face, the look of homicidal insanity. . . . He turned off the computer and went out for a long walk in the city.

The next day he looked up Camden in the library newspaper files. He was no longer shaking, but instead felt as cold and hard and brittle as an icicle. He found the story that had caught his eye, the match his mind had made. Mildred Hewlitt had gone mad and slaughtered several patients in a nursing home on Hanover Street, where she worked. She had vanished, and so had one of the victims. The hotel, Dwyer House, was also on Hanover Street. That was what had stopped him. He walked home and looked up the computer listing for the claim that had first sent the hairs rising on his arms and neck. Two weeks earlier, a college boy had gone mad and run his car through a pedestrian mall; he had fled on foot and vanished. One of the victims had filed a claim; the mainframe had recorded it. That day Carson Danvers packed a suitcase and left for Camden.

He stole an Ohio license plate from a parked car in a shopping mall, and put it on his car the morning he reached Camden. He checked into a motel outside town, read the local paper from the past two days, walked downtown. He chatted with a waiter, the motel desk clerk, several others. He did not go to the real estate office. He went to the shopping mall where the clerks were all ready to talk about the terrible accident.

"He came in over there," a woman said,

standing outside a Hallmark shop, pointing to a stretch of pavement that was barricaded now. A row of wooden planters had been smashed, store windows were boarded up. "He revved up and came in doing maybe fifty, sixty miles an hour, screaming like a banshee. My God, people were flying this way and that! Everyone screaming! Blood everywhere! And he got out and ran. No one tried to stop him. No one had time to do anything, what with all the screaming and the blood. He got clean away."

Carson shook his head in disbelief and walked on to a Sears store, where he bought a crowbar and heard the same story, embellished a little because this time the salesman relating it had not actually seen what happened. He put the crowbar in his car and went to a K-Mart, where he bought a gas can and flashlight. Then he found his way to Hanover Street. It started in town, went straight through a subdivision, and then became a country road very quickly. The nursing home where Mildred Hewlitt had worked was a few blocks from the subdivision; after that there was a small store and gas station combined, and then farmland and sparse woods. A four-lane highway had been built three miles to the south; business had followed, and Hanover Street was left to the truck farmers. The same as River House.

He drove slowly until he reached the driveway to Dwyer House. There was a chain across it. The hotel was not visible from the road. The woods had invaded the grounds, deciduous trees with new April leaves not yet fully developed—ash trees, maples, oaks, all scrawny and untended. High grasses and weeds and hedge gone wild filled in the understory. There was a path through it, well trod, evidently in daily use. He drove another hundred yards and came to a turn on the side of the road of the hotel and drove onto it. It was dirt, rutted and unkempt, but passable. A service entrance? Why no chain, if so? And why would Mildred Hewlitt have come back here, and the boy, and the four or five others he had read about? Mystified, he kept driving slowly until he came to a clearing, an old parking lot maybe. He could see the hotel from here: three stories, a frame building ornately decorated with cupolas, balconies, porches with handsome rails and fancy posts. It was boarded up, but he could imagine the stained glass windows it must have boasted. Inside there would be the paneling, the carefully dovetailed joints, the elaborate patterns in the walnut floors. He felt as if he knew this building intimately; it was so like the ones he had investigated a long time ago, looking for a place to create a fine restaurant. So like them. He stopped and turned off his engine, and he felt *it* again, and that too was the same. A pressure, a presence, like cobwebs with an electrical charge. This time the headache was slight, a distant throbbing. He got out and stood by his car door, looking around, and now he understood why people came here. Lovers' lane, a place to park out of sight of the road, beyond the sound of passing cars or the inquisitive eyes of anyone. That explained the ages, he thought, not moving away from the cobwebs, brushing at his face now and then. One girl of eighteen, a suicide. The college boy, twenty-one. Mildred Hewlitt, twenty-five. Another young man of twenty who had been apprehended smashing windows at the elementary school. When seized, he had collapsed in a catatonic state from which he had not recovered. Others, mentioned in whispers, with puzzlement, just weird things, the desk clerk had said in a low voice. Weird, you know? Carson Danvers stood brushing away electric cobwebs that were not webs at all, and he nodded. He knew. He got in the car again and turned on the ignition, and was alone again. He drove out.

A fine rain had started to fall, soft, promising spring growth, smelling of newly sprouted seedlings and fragrant earth. Spring, Carson thought, warmer nights, couples in cars with engines turned off, mayhem. Back in his motel, he set his clock for three-thirty and lay down, but did not sleep. When it was time, he drove to the hotel parking lot and turned around, so that his car faced out. He ignored the webs that found him instantly, and unloaded his equipment methodically. He pried open a door in the rear of the building, dropped the crowbar on the porch, and entered cautiously, flashlight in one hand, gas can in the other. This time there was no need to make a trail, to obliterate the past with fire. He made his way through the blackness, following his narrow beam of light, moving with great care, not wanting to fall through a rotten floorboard, or trip over an abandoned two-by-four. He found the stairs and climbed them, testing each step. The building was solid, filled with real cobwebs and dust and mold. He was disoriented momentarily at the landing on the second floor, but closed his eyes and drew a mental map, then continued down a hallway to where he judged the center of the hotel was. Many of the doors were open; none was locked. He opened more of them and then began to splash the gasoline around the walls, through the hall. He brushed away webs and shone his light around to make certain he had soaked the place thoroughly, and then went back downstairs, dribbling out gas as he moved. He tried to find a spot roughly under the gas-soaked area, and emptied the can, spilling the last drops on a handkerchief he had knotted around a rock. He looked about with the flashlight one more time, then went to the back door he had forced open. There he lighted a match, touched it to the handkerchief, which blazed instantly, and heaved the handkerchief to the bottom of the stairs to ignite a trail of fire. He could feel the webs all around him, pressing as he picked up the crowbar and returned to his car. He put the empty gas can in the trunk, brushed away webs, got in his car, and turned the key. It fled. He drove out carefully. No sign of fire was visible when he drove past the main entrance. The rain was falling, more like a mist now, settling gently with great persistence, as if a mammoth cloud were being lowered to earth. He got back to his motel, back to his room, and fell into bed—and sleep—without undressing.

It was one of the very few nights of the past nine months that he was untroubled by dreams, that he awakened feeling refreshed and vital.

□ CHAPTER 3 □

OCTOBER 1985. CONSTANCE LEIDL DROVE HOME happily that October afternoon. The two-year-old Volvo still smelled of apples; a stack of books from the university library added its own peculiar, comforting odor, but the dominant fragrance was of fall, of wood stoves, frosts to come, and burning leaves. "The world is draped in the glory of autumn," one of the patients in the hospital had murmured to her. A hopeless schizophrenic, wandering in a world of poetry and surrealism. Constance shook her head, then smiled, remembering Charlie's complaint as they had picked apples over the past three days.

"Honey, I don't get it. Why do we tend all

these damn trees and then just give away the apples?"

"Do you want strangers in here picking them?"

"Come on!"

"Well then. . . ."

"It's not one or the other," he had said indignantly.

"We could sell off the hillside."

He garumphed at her grin. "Okay. But tell me why we are doing this." A cold breeze had colored his cheeks as red as the apples they were picking. He had stopped working and was regarding her with a mutinous expression.

"Well," she had said with what she considered great practicality, "because."

"Ah," he had said, illuminated, and they had returned to the chore of picking apples.

Today she had delivered three bushels of them to the hospital. There were twenty bushels on the back porch, some to be called for, some to be delivered. She hummed under her breath. Just because. She loved this section of the drive home from the hospital she had visited. On one side of the blacktop county road stretched a pasture graced by three sorrel horses that struck poses whenever traffic was present. A white fence completed that picture. On the other side, the side she lived on, a two-hundred-year-old farmhouse marked what she thought of here as her stretch. The old house was of stone and wood and bricks, with a slate roof; the Dorsetts lived there. They said

Dorsetts had always lived there, would always live there. She believed that. Next was a tall, cedar-sided house with a southern face constructed mostly of glass. The Mitchums lived there. They had four sons, all husky football types. Two of the boys had come over to complete the apple-picking, and had taken away two bushels of apples for their labors. Sometimes Constance fried the special Swedish cookies that Charlie loved more than any other sweet, and gave most of them to the Mitchum boys. She had explained that, also. If she kept them in the house, Charlie ate them, and at his age—fifty plus—he did not need all those calories. The boys did. When he asked if she couldn't simply make fewer, she had said no.

Everywhere maple trees blazed and cast red light on the world. Autumn had been benign so far. Its progress had been gentle, with a few early hard frosts, then a mellow Indian summer, and now more frosts. There had not been a tree-stripping windstorm, or slashing rain. A long expanse of pasture—the Mitchums kept goats—and finally her own house appeared. The lowering sun turned the maples in her front yard into welcoming torches. It fired the chrysanthemums that edged the driveway with a carpet runner of red, rust, glowing yellow, and white. There was a silver Mercedes parked in the center of the driveway in front of the garage door.

Constance scowled at the other car. The drive was wide enough for two cars, but not if one that size took the center. And, she thought with irritation, she'd be damned if she would run over the chrysanthemums. She stopped behind the Mercedes and got out. As she walked toward the house she saw that Charlie and an unknown man were in the garage. From the roof of the garage the gray tiger cat Brutus glared at her with slitted yellow eyes.

Charlie came out to meet her. He was wearing jeans and a plaid shirt that emphasized his huskiness. His hair was crinkly black with enough gray to look distinguished, and, since moving out in the country, he had turned a rich mahogany color. She thought he was extraordinarily handsome and often told him so. He liked that. Now he kissed her and murmured, "The mountain has come to Mohamet."

Where he was dark, she was fair, her hair pale to nearly white, her eyes light blue—some thought gray—her skin a creamy ivory, touched so lightly with color it was as if she seldom spent time outdoors. Yet she was out even more than he was. She was tall and lean; she would be a stick of an old woman, she sometimes said, almost regretfully. They walked together to the garage where the visitor waited, looking ill at ease. A gray man with a tight mouth, she thought coolly, a city man who should stay there alone where he belonged.

"Honey, Mr. Thoreson," Charlie said. "My wife, Constance Leidl."

"Oh, ah, Mrs. Meiklejohn, or is it Ms. Leidl? How do you do?"

She had known his handshake would be limp, she thought, still very distant and cool, if proper. "Either, or both at times," she said. "Shall we go inside?" She watched with clinical interest to see if he would unconsciously wipe his hand on his trouser leg. He did. A gray man, with a gray, fearful soul. Sixty, sixty-two. Gray hair, sallow complexion, gray suit, discreet maroon tie. She started for the front door.

"Honey," Charlie said, "we can talk here."

"I apologize for parking like that," Thoreson said almost simultaneously. "Cats were running everywhere. I thought it best simply to stop."

Just then Candy, the orange cat with butterscotch eyes, approached Constance with a melting-legs walk, meowing. Constance started to pick her up, but she slunk away, looking nervously at Thoreson and Charlie, complaining.

"Charlie, what's been going on?" Constance demanded.

"Nothing, not really. I opened the door and the cats all ran out just when Mr. Thoreson pulled in, and I came out to meet him, and then you got home."

She watched him, wondering what he was hiding, and then turned to enter the house. The front door stood wide open.

"We'll just wait here," Charlie called after her.

When she glanced back, he grinned his most engaging smile, and Mr. Thoreson looked more uncomfortable than ever. Cautious now, she entered the house and immediately choked on the thick, sharp smell of burning chili peppers. Her eyes teared, and she groped for the door and backed out again, coughing.

"Charlie," she cried, "why didn't you warn me?" She continued to cough, fumbling in her purse for a tissue.

"You would have wanted to find out for yourself," he said reasonably. "I was going to make Hunan chicken. It starts with frying ten chili peppers."

Thoreson looked from him to Constance, back to Charlie. He examined the garage with disdain, then said, "Mr. Meiklejohn, is there some place we can talk? Phil Stern assured me that you would at least listen."

"I suppose it gets worse on in the house?" Constance asked.

"Sure does," Charlie agreed. "Kitchen's uninhabitable. I turned on the exhaust fan and opened windows."

"Mr. Mieklejohn! Damn it, I drove all the way out from New York to see you! I apologized for not calling ahead of time. Stern promised he would call and explain the situation to you."

"He didn't call," Charlie said. He looked at Constance. "Benny's?" At her nod, he turned to Thoreson. "There's a roadhouse down the road, four, five miles. Let's go have a drink there. And you can talk. I'll listen."

Thoreson's lips had drawn into a thin line.

"You'll have to follow us," Constance said and started back to the Volvo. She did not look to see if Thoreson was dismayed by the lack of hospitality she and Charlie were showing. City man, go home, she thought, and take your problems with you.

□ □ □

"Who is he?" Constance asked, in the car with Charlie driving now.

"Hal Thoreson. He said he was supposed to come with Phil's recommendation, but Phil never got around to it. Actually Thoreson called a week or so ago, wanted me to meet him in New York, but I knew you'd think I was trying to duck out of picking apples." What Thoreson had done, although Charlie did not say this, was order him to a meeting.

"I don't like him," she said.

"Uh-huh."

"He's an *insurance* man!"

Charlie laughed. "So's Phil."

"That's different, and you know it."

"Not where business is concerned." He had known Phil Stern in college, and they had remained friends over the many years since then. When Charlie took an early retirement from the New York City police force, Phil had turned to him for a private investigation, then another, then several more. What Phil had bought was not so much Charlie's expertise as a detective, although that had been important, but rather his unmatched knowledge of arson. Charlie had been a fire department investigator for years before becoming a city detective. It was Thoreson's fault, he thought aggrievedly, that he had burned the peppers. The damn cookbook said you could do the preliminaries early and in less than ten minutes turn out the dish. Hah! He had wanted to surprise Constance, had heard a car and had gone to look out the front window; the chili peppers burned, and he ended up with the sourpuss Thoreson. It had not been a good day, he brooded, parking at Benny's. Thoreson's silver Mercedes was right behind him. He caught up with them before they entered the roadhouse.

Benny's was virtually empty that afternoon. It was not yet six. A man in a leather jacket sat at the bar talking to Ron, the spindly bartender who would leave as soon as Benny arrived. Two women were talking in low voices in a booth at the rear of the room. Charlie and Constance waved at Ron and took another booth; they sat side by side, Thoreson opposite them. Ron slouched over, took their order, and slouched away again. No one spoke as they waited for the drinks to arrive, but the moment the drinks came, Thoreson began, as if the service were his cue.

"Two weeks ago there was a conference of

underwriters in Dallas. I attended, as did Phil Stern. I have known him for many years, of course. During one of the informal meetings a startling fact was unearthed. When I mentioned the matter to Stern, he suggested that I might discuss it with you. I have been trying to do so," he said with some bitterness. "I know that I am not an engaging man, Mr. Meiklejohn, Mrs. Meiklejohn."

He had rehearsed it in his silver Mercedes, Constance realized with interest. First the teaser, then his abject self-abasement, and now he would reveal the startling fact. She glanced at Charlie; he appeared engrossed in spearing an onion in his Gibson.

"I seldom have to deal with the public, and never have had to deal with a matter of this delicacy, and, frankly, the thought of hiring a private investigator for such a . . . a discreet matter is abhorrent to me."

"You have your own investigators," Charlie suggested.

"Of course. However, we feel that there may be a leak somewhere. Phil thought, and I agreed ultimately, a private investigation would be more to the point."

Charlie got the onion and ate it with evident satisfaction. He smiled at Thoreson. "Why don't you cut the bullshit and get to the point."

"That is precisely why Phil was supposed to talk to you," Thoreson said in a plaintive voice. "He knew I would bungle it alone."

He actually sighed. Constance felt Charlie nudge her leg, and she looked away to keep from smiling.

"It came to our attention that there has been a series of hotel fires," Thoreson said. "So far, three insurance companies have paid out a million dollars in claims. That's one of the reasons we thought an independent investigation would be wise."

"It just came to your attention," Charlie murmured.

"Yes. They are widely separated geographically, and span a period of five years."

"How widely spread?" Although he still sounded lazy and not very interested, Constance knew from his voice that Thoreson had finally said something that worked.

"Vermont, Ohio, North Carolina, California, Idaho, and Washington State."

Charlie shook his head in disbelief. "A serial arsonist working from coast to coast? I don't believe it."

"Were there casualties?" Constance asked, almost in spite of herself.

"None. In fact, each hotel was closed down, out of use when it burned."

Charlie looked blank, rather dull. "You need the ATF or a national organization to investigate something like that. Spread over five years? There won't be anything to see anyway. It's probably coincidence."

"Phil said he would tell you the *modus operandi*—is that the phrase? It's the same in each case. We know there have been at least six deliberate fires, probably three more that we aren't so certain about. In each case, the fire started in an interior room and burned outward, and by the time the fire departments arrived, the buildings were practically gutted already. Always between two and five in the morning. Almost always when it was either raining or snowing, the exceptions being during a dense fog in one instance, and following a week of rain in the other. Every one was considered arson at the time."

Charlie was shaking his head. "And you think someone in one of your companies must be in on it? Why?"

"Not in on it, not that way. But maybe feeding information to someone else. Information about where abandoned hotels are, what the coverage is for them."

Very kindly Charlie said, "Mr. Thoreson, go home. If you suspect a conspiracy to commit a crime tell the FBI. If you suspect arson, notify the ATF. Let them take care of it." He glanced at Constance, who nodded. ATF, the Bureau of Alcohol, Tobacco and Firearms, had a national arson investigative team.

Thoreson's lips had tightened again. He had not yet touched his scotch and water. Now he put it to his mouth, then set it down sharply. "That's about the last thing we want to do. There certainly would be a leak then, maybe publicity. Do you know what it would mean to have this publicized?"

"Copycat fires," Charlie said. "But the ATF can be very quiet about what they're up to. Very discreet."

"And they solve three percent of all arson cases they investigate!" Thoreson snapped. "We decided to keep it private. One person, you, asking questions, looking into this matter, would not attract undue attention. A flock of men asking questions? How long would that remain concealed? Mr. Meiklejohn, the insurance industry depends on discretion. Without discretion there would be no insurance industry." He picked up his drink again, and this time he downed it all. "We are prepared to be very generous, sir. What we are most afraid of is the possibility that someone has started a new service, a syndicate, if you will, that has a task force composed of people knowledgeable in the business of arson. With inside information about where the old buildings are, if they're insured, they could approach the owners, make a deal, and light the fires. Mr. Meiklejohn, this matter has already cost three of our companies over a million dollars!"

"And what if I look into it and decide that it was all coincidence, after all?"

"That would be the absolutely finest report any of us could hope for."

Charlie was gazing at him fixedly, his eyes narrowed. "There's something else, isn't there, Thoreson? What is it?"

Thoreson drained a few drops of melted ice into his mouth, then, keeping his gaze on the glass, he said, "In those firm cases I mentioned, each time, the fire department—volunteer departments in every case—seemed to delay fighting the fires. Almost as if they deliberately let them burn past saving before they went into action."

Regarding Thoreson with near indifference, Charlie lazily held up his hand to catch Ron's attention. In a moment Ron appeared with a tray of new drinks. Only then did Charlie speak. "So you think the various volunteer fire departments are in on the conspiracy, too?"

"I don't know what to think," Thoreson admitted. "A million in claims, Mr. Meiklejohn, that's what I really think about. Old abandoned buildings, good for nothing in most cases. And there must be hundreds more just like them scattered around the country. Hundreds!" He rubbed his eyes. "With your experience, you could go to some of those places and talk to the people in the fire departments, find out what they know, if they know anything. Find out if they really did delay taking action, and if so, why. Stern showed me the manual you wrote, the bible for volunteer fire fighters, he said. Those people would talk to you. You could say you're gathering data for a new book or something. They'd talk to you."

Constance wanted to shout, No! He won't work for you! Go away! She wanted to hold Charlie and whisper, not this one. Not this time. No more fires. No more arson. No more burned-out buildings with rotten timbers ready to fall on you, floors ready to cave in, walls ready to crumble down. "Charlie," she said, touching his arm. He turned his face toward her, but she knew he was not seeing her, not now. His eyes had gone flat, like chips of coal, ready to flare, ready to burn. "Charlie," she said again, more insistently. The light came back to his eyes. "We have to go to San Francisco in ten days, remember? And then a couple of weeks in Mexico. Remember?"

He blinked, looked back to Thoreson, and shrugged.

"Let me leave the reports with you," Thoreson said, in near desperation. "I have them all here in my briefcase. Don't decide right now. Look over what we've managed to get together first. We wouldn't expect you to drop everything and concentrate on just this matter. After all, it stretches out over five years as it is. But if you can look into it in the next few weeks, the next few months . . ."

He means he'll be sure to have Phil call, Constance wanted to say, and drank her Irish coffee. Charlie thought the same thing, but he said mildly that he would read the reports, study the claims, and be in touch. Thoreson was so relieved he would have signed a blank check, Constance thought.

"We asked Phil Stern to handle the details," he said. "Since you've worked with him in the past it seemed appropriate. His company is one of a consortium, as is mine. We're equally responsible, but he will be the liaison, if that is agreeable." He tasted his second drink and stood up. He did not offer to shake hands with either of them.

"If you can let me know in the next day or two . . ."

"By Friday," Charlie said, also not offering to shake hands. He did not rise. Thoreson looked from him to Constance, his lips a tight line; then he nodded and left.

"Charlie, this is insane," she said as soon as Thoreson was out the door of the roadhouse. A few new people had drifted in; voices and music were rising to a routine volume. "What can you possibly do five years after the fact? Do you really intend to spend the next few years traveling from Vermont to California to Ohio, and wherever else he mentioned? Alone?"

He grinned at the threat. "Nope. I'd hire Tom Hoagley to do some preliminary research for me while I stay home and pick apples, and then go to San Francisco and listen to you on your panels."

She felt a chill. Was that the reason he had not tossed Thoreson out? She had written a series of articles on xenophobia and its impact on everything from the behavior of elementary school children to national foreign policy, and as a consequence had been invited to participate in a national psychology symposium. She had assumed he was looking forward to going to San Francisco for a week with the same enthusiasm she felt.

Although in theory she was retired, in practice she was as busy as she ever had been, giving papers, writing books, doing research, consulting. The only thing she had dropped was teaching. Also in theory Charlie was supposed to be using his time in writing a definitive book on fire investigative methods; the manual Thoreson had mentioned was the only product to come out of his efforts.

"An assistant," Charlie said with a nod. "Tom Hoagley. Let someone else find out things, like were there unusual strangers in the areas before the fires? Any repetition of any unusual behavior? Developers casing the places? Offers to buy the properties? Unusual newspaper subscriptions before the fires? Owners showing signs of unusual wanderlust in the past few years?" He was gazing thoughtfully at the room, filling now with the usual weeknight customers. "If a stranger showed up in our little community and did anything weird, how long before everyone in this place would know, do you suppose?"

"The next day," she said. "Charlie, are you going to take this case?"

"Not sure yet. Like I told him, I'll go over the reports, then decide. See who investigated, for instance. Some pretty good guys out there prowling about, you know. What really gets me is that he said the fire departments let the places burn. Not that I believe him. He's an asshole. But there are some pretty good people out there poking about in the ashes. I wonder if that's what they're saying."

She looked shocked. "You don't believe that!"

He had been thinking out loud and now regarded her soberly. "I don't believe or not believe it. But if it turns out to be true, I sure as hell want to know why. Let's have dinner here. Hungry?"

They made their way to the dining room a few minutes later and he looked at her with horror when she ordered sweetbreads. A shudder passed over him.

When they got home that night the acrid smell of burned chilis was nearly gone, but the cats acted as if an invading army had moved through the house. They went from room to room sniffing warily and jumped when Charlie dropped Thoreson's briefcase.

During the night Constance came awake to hear a howling wind savaging the trees in the yard. The long mellow autumn had come to an end.

□ CHAPTER 4 □

"YOU LOOK LIKE HELL," CHARLIE SAID TO PHIL Stern, who was in bed in his Manhattan apartment. "Why'd you send Thoreson out cold like that? Is it serious? Should I keep my distance?"

"It is serious," Phil said darkly. "If it wasn't serious, I wouldn't have to be in bed, right? Since I am here, it must be serious." He grunted when he shifted his position. "Keep your distance. Flu. What are you doing here?"

"Helping Constance deliver apples." He shook his head. "It's a long story."

"So you met Sore Thumb."

Charlie felt blank. "Sore thumb? I give."

"Thoreson. Halbert Thoreson. Those of us who know and love him call him Sore Thumb. If he made it, you know why."

Ah, Charlie thought, the man in pain, with the tight lips. He nodded. "You up to talking? Shouldn't you be quiet? Rest, or something?"

"I'm resting. I'm resting. Up to my gills in dope, swimming in dope and resting. Sore Thumb's a pain in the ass, but he's probably onto something. I'm surprised he showed up. The thought of scandal scares him more than the bogeyman."

Phil repeated much of the story Thoreson had told. He thought the number of arson fires was probably closer to ten, or even twelve, but some of them were doubtful. "Look," he said a few minutes later, "Thoreson's company has been hit harder than anyone else in this mess—one reason they abhor publicity. Thoreson's name's not even linked to any of this, that's how cautious he is, how careful about his company's reputation. I'm fronting. Me and the company," he added. "Not that old man Boyle's happy about it, but that's how it is. So you decide, and we send out the contract, except I'm taking off for Bermuda as soon as they unlock my door here. Sick leave," he added, too smugly. "I have good insurance."

Charlie spread his hands and said, "Then there's no case at this time, not until you're back in harness."

Phil started to shake his head and grunted again. "That's one of the things I shouldn't do yet," he said after a moment. "You're on, Charlie. If you'll look into it. God, we've got more than forty of those white elephants on our books! We haven't been hit yet, but I'm afraid we will be."

"Usual terms?" Charlie asked.

"Whatever you say. Sore Thumb complained about the amount, but I said you don't work cheap. We'll have a check mailed tomorrow. Give yourself a raise. I'll initial it. A reasonable raise, that is."

Charlie leaned back and surveyed his friend critically. "Must be a hidden head injury, brain fever. Okay. Meanwhile, Bermuda's a good idea."

"Yeah, I know." Phil closed his eyes. "I'm tired. You talk. What's this bullshit about apples?"

□ □ □

Over on Houston Street Constance was regarding her old friend Patrick Morely with affection. "It really is about ten bushels," she said. "But we couldn't pack bushels very well, so we scrounged up the liquor boxes instead. "You'll just have to explain the best you can how you came by ten liquor boxes, my friend."

Father Patrick Morley, executive director of the children's home that occupied most of the block, laughed with delight. "And you say there is no independent good or evil! Come along inside and let me give you a cup of coffee. Where is Charlie?"

Two adolescent boys appeared and started to

unload the boxes of apples. One of them kept looking at Constance with a shy smile. Patrick led the way inside the massively built school. A few more children peered at them from a doorway; the door closed softly when they drew near. A faint grin played on Patrick's face, the only indication of his awareness of his charges' interest in the visitor. Everywhere the building needed repairs—paint, new woodwork, a window. . . . It was scrupulously clean. They went into his study and sat down near a low table that held a few mugs and a thermos. He righted two of the mugs and opened the thermos, inspected the contents, then poured. "I probably could find some sugar and cream," he said without conviction.

She shook her head. "Charlie's visiting an old friend. We'll meet for lunch. How are you?"

"Well," he said, dismissing the subject. He looked dreadful, too thin, pale. He was dying of leukemia. Looking at him, aching for him, Constance could almost admit to the evil that he believed had an independent existence.

Somewhere a bell rang, and the quiet beyond his study door was broken by young voices, footsteps, doors opening, closing. Patrick's smile widened. Constance sipped her coffee. It was very bad coffee. Why are you sacrificing your life? she had wanted to ask him many times, though she never had, and never would.

He was regarding her again, his eyes calm, serene. "Do you remember the game we played in school?" he asked suddenly. "Someone in the back row tapped the person in front of him and whispered, 'Pass it on.'"

She nodded, grinning now. "By the time it got to me it was more than just a tap."

He laughed. "Exactly. The multiplier effect. Good is like that. A good thing happens to you, you pass it on, bigger, better than you received. It multiplies." The smile left his face, and with its absence he seemed suddenly very old, very aware. "Evil's like that, too, Constance. People like you, so basically good, call the good you do reasonable. You call the evil you see irrational, evil behavior done by people who need help. In that context even evil becomes reasonable. Your own rationality is dangerous, Constance. It can be a trap more deadly than you can conceive."

"What a terrifying world you live in," she said softly, chilled by his death that seemed too close now, too imminent.

"For me there is no terror," he said, and she believed him. His personal serenity was unshakable, his faith beyond question. "You see my world as terror-filled because I admit to absolutes—absolute good and evil, absolute faith and belief. I see your world as even more terrible, Constance. You can't measure good and evil with a relative yardstick. When you see absolute good you have to search for hidden motives, puzzle out a compensation system, even if the good is your own. I'm afraid that when you are confronted with absolute evil, you will find your rationality gone, and without reason or faith, you are truly lost. Then you become a tool of evil, no more than that; or you die."

"I'm not afraid of death," she whispered. "That isn't evil. Death is part of all life. You know that."

"We pass on our knowledge of death, our fear if it's present. Some feel it as a tap, others as a blow. But when that death is brought about by a confrontation with evil, what we pass on can be a fatal blow and those we leave behind feel it that way. Some recover. Many don't, and they in turn pass it on, ever harder, ever more insistent, ever stronger with the force of evil behind it. It multiplies its effects until someone is strong enough to deny it again, to quell it for the time being. It doesn't die, it waits for a new victim to start the game again."

Constance stood up abruptly. "I have to go. I'll be late."

Patrick rose also. "Remember when our paths crossed over twenty years ago? How outraged you were that I had become a priest. You told me very firmly that if I ever tried to convert you, our friendship would end. I never did, did I?"

"Of course not," she said coolly. "Nor I you."

He laughed and took her hands. "Good-bye, Constance. Thank you for the apples. For all your goodnesses." He did not immediately release her; his hands were hot.

"Why did you talk to me like this now?" she asked, making no motion to draw away.

"I don't know. Ever since you called, I've had a darkness in my mind about you. My dreams are . . . troubled these days, dreams of old friends, people I have loved, people I must speak to, people I must ask to forgive me for injuries so old they seem to belong to someone else. People I must warn. At least one person I felt I must warn. You." He studied her face, then kissed her on the forehead. "I feel that you're in grave danger. I'm sorry."

□ □ □

Whenever Charlie and Constance got to town together they had lunch at Wanda Loren's restaurant on Amsterdam, half a dozen blocks from the apartment they had lived in for so many years. The neighborhood never changed yet was always different, Charlie thought, as he strode briskly, half an hour late. One shop vanished, was replaced with another not very different. Fondue was out, yogurt in. Sushi houses had appeared; the Italian restaurant that used to serve the world's best veal in marsala was gone. An Indian restaurant was there instead. The crowds were exactly the same people, he felt convinced, just wearing different clothes. Suits for men and women were in; casual jeans and tee shirts out. The air smelled the same, a poisonous mix of exhaust fumes and metal and people. The noise level was the same, five decibels above tolerable. He ducked into Wanda's.

"Hey, Charlie, how are you, for Chrissake! She's here already."

Wanda greeted him with a hug. She was four feet ten inches, weighed too much to talk about, she always said, and had a beautiful face, a cameo face with perfect lines, almond-shaped eyes, and not a blemish or touch of makeup.

"Wanda, if I weren't such an old man I'd sweep you off your feet," Charlie said and kissed her on the mouth. "You've lost a couple hundred pounds."

"Twenty, Charlie. Just twenty so far. But thanks."

He joined Constance and saw with surprise that she had a bottle of wine in an ice bucket and was already drinking it. Before he could comment, she asked, "You're taking the case? Tell me what you've been up to. Okay?"

He put his hand over hers for a second, then poured wine for himself and started to recount his morning's activities. He knew about Patrick, knew it must have been bad. Later she would talk about it, he also knew, but now he would fill in the silence.

Afterwards, he thought that if it had not been for Patrick's approaching death and his warning that had so disturbed Constance, everything would have been different. She would have been sharper with her questions; he probably would have turned over more of the investigation to Tom Hoagley. Aware that the very fine food Wanda served them was being wasted on Constance, that she was deeply abstracted, he found himself including her in his plans, assuming a partnership, taking it for granted that she would allow herself to become involved. Anything, he thought, to wipe that blank look from her face, to make her refocus her eyes on the here and now, not on some vision Patrick had implanted. He would need her help in reading the newspapers, he said, and she blinked finally and looked at him.

"Tom is going to get newspapers together from the communities where the fires broke out," he explained again. "It's going to make quite a stack, I'm afraid. I'll need help in going through them, searching for anything that might link one area to another. Okay?"

He had intended to have Tom Hoagley do that, but saying it this way made him aware that he wanted to do it himself, with Constance helping him. Together they might spot relationships that someone like Hoagley might not see, although he was quite clever.

"You really think all those fires are related, make a pattern?"

"Yes," he said without hesitation; until that moment he had reserved judgement. Even then it might not have been too late if she had pressed him for a reason, pressed him to defend his position. He could not have done it then, but it might have made a difference.

□ CHAPTER 5 □

CHARLIE PAUSED OUTSIDE THE PARTLY OPEN door to Constance's study. She was talking: ". . . and the children who remained in the environment until adolescence never did develop a recognizable form of xenophobia. Instead, what they manifested throughout their adult lives was an attitude of acceptance, empathy, and curiosity about other people. God damn it to hell!" Something slammed onto a table. He glanced inside. She had banged her notebook down. She glared at him.

"Sorry," he said. "Lunch. If you want some."

She got up, carefully pushed her chair under her desk, her motions exaggerated, the way she moved when she was mad, then left her room. "That idiot! That damn thick-headed idiot!"

"Waldman?"

"You know what he told me on the phone? Ten minutes! Because Isaacson wants on the panel, they're cutting our presentation time to ten minutes each!"

They went to the dining area in the kitchen and he ladled soup for her, then himself. "You have to condense your presentation?"

She tasted her soup, nodded, then nodded more vigorously. "Good soup. Let me try it on you. First I'll start with definitions. Derivations. Xeno from *xenos*, an old Greek word that was derived from an even older word, *xenwos*, of unknown origin. The word means *strange, stranger, foreign, alien*. That sort of thing. As far back as language has existed and been recorded there has always been a word for the others. Okay. Phobia from *phobos*, Greek again, meaning *fear, flight, panic*. That derives from *bhegw*, and *phebesthai*, and means again, *panic, to flee in terror*. So that gives us xenophobia—a panic reaction to flee from the stranger. Now Isaacson and his gang are claiming that xenophobia is innate, and they use animal studies to prove it. You know, the chicken is born with an innate reaction to a chicken hawk, or any outline that vaguely resembles the real thing. I say we're not chickens and the world isn't made up of chicken hawks. And there is this study of a group of children who were collected as infants in England during World War II. A real mixed bag of kids. The study that was done on them was looking for neuroses. You know, kids taken from parents, that sort of thing, but it works beautifully to prove that no one taught them to fear each other, or strangers in general, and they didn't, then or later. Nonxenophobic. They don't see the same world that other people do, where every skin variation means a threat. That's the point I want to make in my initial presentation, and I simply can't do it and make the other points I need to make in ten minutes."

He listened to her, served himself more soup, and watched the changing expression of her face, the way the light from the late afternoon sun caught her hair. Even he could not tell where it had started to turn white and where it was simply the very pale blond hair that he had loved for more than twenty-five years. When she paused, he said, "Honey, what would happen if you ran over your allotted time? What if you talked for thirteen minutes instead of ten? Would they turn off the lights? Pull the plug on your microphone? Stage a walkout?"

She looked at him in speculation and suddenly grinned. Presently she chuckled.

When they were finished with lunch she went with him to his study and looked at the map he had taped to the wall. It was the United States, and there were pushpins here and there.

"Red for the hotels that were stripped first, then burned," he said. "Blue for those intact. White for the two without collectible insurance."

"Stripped?"

"Yeah. Sometimes, before an unexpected and unfortunate fire breaks out, it happens that the owners sell off paneling, or fixtures, or flooring, stained glass, that sort of thing." His voice was dry, noncommittal. "The builders included features that were the ordinary affluence then and are nearly priceless now. Sometimes they get sold before the fire."

"Did they start in the Northeast, move west?" she asked, studying the map.

"Nope. The first one, in this series, anyway, was in Ohio, then North Carolina, Vermont, on over to California, Idaho, then Washington."

"This series," she murmured. "If Phil was right and there were twice this many, there may well be others that no one suspects, so many that you probably won't be able to find a pattern, even if there is one."

He conceded the point; the phone rang and she drifted back to her work while he went to answer it. It was Stan Kraskey, one of the investigators who had inspected the ruins of the hotel near Longview, Washington. Stan had been a rookie under Charlie's tutelage fifteen years ago in New York City.

After the pleasantries, Stan said, "Jesus, Charlie, you know you can't prove anything like that, but twice in a row? No way. It was the same down in California, the Orick fire. Look, the Longview fire was twelve miles from the station house. Those guys are pretty good up there, lots of practice during the dry season running to forest fires, and for them twelve miles should have been a snap. It had been raining a couple of months steady, the way it does up there in the winter. Supersaturated everything. And the joint burned to the ground. They knew it was set, and I knew it was set, but that's not the point. The point is they could have put it out, everything in their favor, and they didn't. They were late in getting there, trouble with a hose, trouble with a pump, low pressure, not enough water in the tank. Jesus! The guy I talked to looked me straight in the eye and lied in his teeth and knew, by God, that I knew he was lying."

"Why?" Charlie muttered. "What was in it for them?"

"Not a damn thing I could figure out. If I'd had a clue about why, I'd've nabbed them for it. Not a clue."

"Local stories about the place? Bad reputation?"

"Charlie," Stan said aggrievedly. "Come on."

"Yeah." There were always stories about an abandoned building, especially a big one that had been famous to any degree at all. "But was it more than usual there, or down at Orick?"

"If it was, I couldn't dig it out of anyone. I had to give up on both of them."

"Any sign of usage on either of them? You know, drugs, transients, anything of that sort?"

"Nope. One of the reasons the fire crews gave

for their delay was the state of the access roads in both cases. And they had a little bit of a point, not enough, but a little. They weren't in use."

Charlie asked a few more questions and finally hung up, more dissatisfied than ever. "Fire fighters don't just let buildings burn to the ground, damn it," he muttered.

The next day they flew to San Francisco. On Sunday they had a dim sum brunch, and Indian *tandoori* chicken for dinner and Charlie began looking forward to the week ahead with more enthusiasm than he had been feeling. He planned to attend only the two panels that Constance would participate in, eat very good food at frequent intervals, go out on a fishing expedition, visit a couple of his old friends, and in general relax. Instead, on Monday he decided to drive up the coast and visit the scene of the Orick fire.

He decided at the Embarcadero, where the symposium was to open in a few minutes; he was watching Constance mingle with people he did not know and had no desire to meet. There was a long spread of coffee and pastries, fruits, juices, even a champagne-orange juice punch. A man standing at his elbow was saying: "Of course, considering the many ramifications of the overt behavioral systems manifested by the inner-city inhabitants, it is necessary to concede that without proper psychological evaluations starting at birth and continuing throughout childhood, those children are simply enacting the predetermined roles that have been designated—"

"Excuse me," Charlie said and put his glass of punch down carefully on a railing and walked away. The man seemed oblivious; he continued to talk.

Charlie started to wend his way to Constance and overheard snatches of different conversations. "First we have to provide an environment which will permit the actualization of the potential—"

"You see, there was this parcel of land, seven acres, for heaven's sake! and I got this idea. Most of the patients really need physical activity in addition to psychological counseling. Don't you agree?"

Charlie looked at that woman with awe. Farm labor bringing in a hundred plus an hour? He moved on. Another couple was talking about the impossibility of landing a teaching job anywhere. "The old fogies just hang on and on," a handsome young man said mournfully.

"Hi," Constance said close to his ear. "You look lost."

He turned to greet her. "I thought I was tougher," he said, "tough enough to stand it for a few days. Wrong. I want a gun and a high spot already and the meetings haven't even started yet. It's still get-acquainted-and-share-a-sweet-roll time and I'm going berserk."

Laughing, Constance took his arm. "I know. You'd rather talk about water pressure per square inch and hose material and if the new chemicals released in today's fires are really worse, or do you just know more about them."

"Damn right," he said fervently. A man standing at her other side was watching with amusement. He had a light brown beard neatly trimmed and short, and brown eyes and hair; he was dressed casually in a sweater and slacks.

"Okay," Constance said. "Before you stage a spectacular break, I want you to meet Byron Weston." She made the introduction.

"We met before, didn't we?" Charlie asked as they shook hands, then followed it with a denial. "No, television. I saw you on television."

Byron Weston nodded, still amused. "Do you mind if I use you to demonstrate something, Mr. Meiklejohn? Would you cooperate?"

Charlie glanced at Constance who looked too innocent. "Sure," he said.

"What I want you to do is close your eyes, and then answer some questions for us. That's all." Charlie closed his eyes. "How high is the ceiling of this room?"

"Thirty feet."

"How many people are in here?"

"Two hundred forty, including seven hotel service people, three plainclothes detectives, and one hotel detective."

Constance felt more than a little awe as Charlie answered a few more questions of the same sort, each time without hesitation. When Byron thanked him, she squeezed his arm.

"That was the demonstration?" Charlie asked. "It only proves how effective thorough training is. It becomes second nature to notice the things important to your line of work."

"That is exactly my point, Mr. Meiklejohn. Your wife and I were talking about the team I'm training to handle postcrisis effects. Sometimes people appear fine immediately after a crisis, only to have their own crises months later, even years later. Hostages, victims of gunmen on towers, innocent people threatened by bank robbers, even survivors of natural catastrophes. There is some resistance to prophylactic therapy, but we're trying to win converts."

Charlie nodded thoughtfully. "We see it with fire victims," he said. "At first you think it's just the immediate shock of nearly dying in a fire, but sometimes I think it's more like guilt. The guilt of the survivor. If a fire fighter enters a building without being suited up, and sometimes you have to, the guilt increases for some reason. As if the protective gear, the helmet, the equipment reassures them that they really couldn't have done anything, after all."

A discreet chime sounded and people began to return to the long table to get rid of cups, napkins. Byron Weston glanced toward the doors with annoyance. "Mr. Meiklejohn, that's exactly the sort of thing I've been looking into. Could we have dinner, tonight maybe?"

"Sorry, don't think I'm going to be around."

He turned to Constance. "I thought I'd go up to Orick and get a firsthand account, spend a day or two there."

Byron laughed. "How about tomorrow night? It just happens that I'll be in Orick tomorrow night."

Charlie shrugged. "Why not?"

"I'll be at the Seaview Motel, a few miles south of town. Leave a message where you are and we'll get together. Wonderful, Mr.—Charlie. Thanks." The chimes echoed again and somehow managed to sound a bit impatient. He made a face and said. "Gotta go. See you tomorrow night, Charlie." He nearly ran as he left.

"Well," Charlie said, watching him move out of sight. "He must not want to miss opening ceremonies."

Constance smiled ruefully. "Darling, he *is* the opening ceremony. He's the keynote speaker. I have to go too."

He kissed her. "I'll call tonight." He watched her walk away quickly, and then wandered through the emptying room that he had described accurately to Byron Weston, although he could not remember making any particular effort to notice any of those details.

□ □ □

That evening Charlie watched sunset from the broad windows of Sam's Fish House, ten miles south of Orick, California. Sharing his table was J.C. Crandle, thirty-five, ex-FBI, and presently the chief of police of Orick. J.C. was heavy-set and very tanned. His hair was thinning, pale brown, sun-bleached nearly blond in front. His eyes were dark blue, without warmth.

"You can ask all the questions you want," J.C. was saying. "It just won't do you any good. It's in the report, exactly the way it happened, and there's nothing more to add. That's how it is."

"You weren't on the police force then, were you? How can you be so sure it's all in the report?"

J.C. drank his beer and waved his hand for another. A young woman in red slacks who doubled as server and bartender sauntered over, winked at them both, and took away the empty bottles.

"It's there," J.C. said, scowling not so much at Charlie as at the rest of the dining room, the other half-dozen people in it, the gaudy sunset beyond the windows. "I know it's all there because no one gave a shit about that goddamn fire."

Charlie ordered a bucket of steamer clams and they went to work on them and a loaf of hot bread that was included. Neither spoke for several minutes.

"Look, Charlie," J.C. said then, "the insurance guy who came down after the fire, he was a jerk, you know?"

Charlie shrugged. "Actually he's pretty good.

He's got a nose for arson."

"Maybe so, but he's a jerk. That was too soon after all the trouble here. People who could talk just wanted to talk about the trouble. People who couldn't talk about that just plain couldn't talk about anything. He thought they were being evasive. Evasive, hell! They just didn't give a shit."

"What trouble was that?" Charlie asked and knew immediately that this was what J.C. wanted to talk about, *all* he wanted to talk about.

"See? That's how you're different from that other one. People'd bring it up and he'd close his notebook, say thanks, and go away. It was in the papers. You probably saw it and forgot already. They haven't forgotten here."

His voice had become low, almost menacing. He looked up from his bowl of clam juice and bread, cast a quick, wary glance about the room, and lowered his voice even more. His story was interrupted repeatedly by the busboy removing shells, the woman in red slacks bringing more clams, other customers who greeted him, the arrival of more beer, his own long silences as he pondered what to say or stopped to eat again. It took him over an hour.

Two sisters, Beth and Louise Dworkin, had moved to the coast ten years ago, he said. Beth was fifty-three, Louise forty-three. Neither had ever married. They had been schoolteachers in Sacramento until they moved to Orick to start their own boarding school for children up to the sixth grade. Some children were left with them for a week at a time only, some for a season, some a year.

"They hired a music teacher, another teacher to help out, a bus driver for field trips—just like any school. And they made out like bandits, that's for sure. Then the trouble started." J.C.'s dark blue eyes looked black and dull.

"Around Christmas most of the kids went home, but a bunch of them stayed on up there over the holidays. A week before Christmas, four years ago, one of the little girls, eleven years old, was found wandering in the woods stark naked and crazy as a bedbug. Gibbering, screaming. A bunch of college kids spotted her. Two of the guys took off after her. She was really crazy, fighting, screaming. Anyway, she got loose and ran to the cliff and went over the side."

The college kids had gone to the police, and about the same time the Dworkin sisters had called to report the little girl's disappearance. Their shock at hearing about the death was complete, and they talked about sending the rest of the children home and closing down the school for a while, or maybe even forever, but people talked them out of it. Other children were acting strangely, but the doctor called it hysteria. Beth had developed severe headaches, and he said that was stress-related. With Christmas at hand, sick kids, a sick teacher, it was more than the doctor could cope with, and he was due for a couple of weeks in Hawaii, so he tended to dismiss all the symptoms as hysteria, effects of the unfortunate death that no one was responsible for. It would pass, he reassured Louise, as soon as the new term began and things got back to normal, and he left on his planned vacation. Another doctor in Orick was on call for the school, but no one knew him well, and somehow no one ever got around to calling him. Christmas came and went; the disturbances continued, maybe got worse. From then on the entire affair was too cloudy to make sense of, J.C. said.

The young teacher the sisters had hired returned, the music teacher came back, children began arriving for the new year, and to all appearances things were getting back to normal. Then the music teacher vanished. She went to the school on a Wednesday as usual, took a walk in the woods, and was never seen again. A groundskeeper vanished. A few days later a deliveryman went to the police to report that there had been terrible screams coming from the upper floor of the school, and that Louise had acted so crazy that he had been afraid of her. She had started to pull off her clothes, was talking obscenities, crazy.

J.C. Crandle sat up straighter when he neared the end of the story, as if telling it had relieved him of a great burden. "So," he said, "when they got up there, the sisters were both batty. One kid was dead, beaten to death. Two were missing and never did show up. The music teacher never turned up. The other young teacher was found smothered to death. Out of twenty-six kids who had either returned, or hadn't gone away, eleven had locked themselves in one of the upper rooms for three days, the rest were all molested, beaten, tortured, missing, crazy, or dead. That was our trouble, Charlie. And two weeks later when the hotel burned, your guy thought it was funny that no one wanted to talk about *that*!"

"You weren't here then?" Charlie asked.

"No." He took a deep breath. "You'll find out about this, too. Tonight, tomorrow. As soon as I leave, if you're still here in the restaurant. The doctor who went on to Hawaii came home from his vacation and went up to the school and hanged himself. He was my father."

Charlie remained after J.C. left. He drank two cups of coffee and finally went back to the Seaview Motel. He had been able to get a room there, the same motel that Byron Weston would stay at the following night. Postcrisis therapy, he thought, parking at the motel. Postcrisis therapy. He was not ready for bed; it would be hours before he would be ready. He went to his room, placed a call to Constance, and was glad that she was not yet back from dinner. He left a message and went out to walk on the beach in the cold dark night.

□ CHAPTER 6 □

THE NEXT AFTERNOON CHARLIE WALKED TO THE highest reach of the point, the site of the burned-out hotel. He preferred to view the ocean, its vast expanse spread out before him. Actually, there was nothing to see of the hotel. The fire had been thorough in its destruction, and wrecking crews had bulldozed the debris and filled in the cavity that had been a basement and sub-basement. Now saplings were growing in the driveway, in gaps in the brickwork of a former winding path. He stood at the edge of the cliff, leaning on a chest-high stone wall capped with smooth limestone.

The hotel had boasted extensive formal gardens, paths, trails to the beach below—it must have been something in its day, he thought, offering as it had this view of the sun vanishing into what looked like a snowdrift on the horizon. Fog moving in. Dense fog the night it burned, he remembered. The whole point must have glowed like an aurora. And no one had come until it was too late. He scowled at the ocean, which was turning gray now, decorated with ruffles of white foam.

"Mr. Meiklejohn?"

He started, and turned to see an old man at the end of the driveway. At his nod the old man advanced. He wore a baseball cap, a heavy sweater, what looked like sailor pants, and boots. His hair was white and long, hanging out from under the cap, blowing in the wind. His face was deeply seamed and brown.

"Burry Barlow," the man said as he drew near, extending his hand.

His hand was as hard and dry as driftwood, his grasp firm. Charlie leaned against the wall and studied him. Barlow was studying him just as intently.

"Heard you were looking for me most of the day," he said finally and turned to gaze out at the ocean.

"That's right," Charlie said. "I'm investigating the hotel fire. Why'd they let it burn, Mr. Barlow?"

The old man glanced at him, then chuckled. "Don't beat around the bush, do you?"

"Might be the only one in the whole damn county who doesn't," Charlie admitted.

Barlow's chuckle sounded again and he nodded. "We use your little book down at the station, you know. The manual. Pretty good stuff in it. Good training manual."

Charlie waited.

"You talked to J.C.," Barlow said after a moment. "Course, he wasn't here until after his dad hanged himself, so he doesn't know what it was like. Bedlam, Mr. Meiklejohn. It was like Bedlam."

"The hotel didn't burn until a couple of weeks after the trouble," Charlie said bluntly. "No connection."

"Maybe, maybe not. But the trouble hadn't stopped yet, either. Mildred Searles ran her car off the cliff, and Carey Duke went for a walk in the ocean and never came out. That was after the sisters were put away. Maybe we still had trouble, Mr. Meiklejohn."

"Tell me about the night of the fire," Charlie said harshly.

"Right. I was dispatcher, as they must've told you around town. Haven't gone out myself for maybe ten years, but I keep a hand in. Know every road in the county like it was my back yard." He continued to study the ocean as if searching for whales. "Four in the morning got a call from Michael Chubb. Said the school was on fire. That's all. He could see it on his way down to the docks. No one knew if they'd be able to go out fishing—the fog, you know—but they went down to the docks to hang around, see if it lifted when the sun came up." He took a deep breath. "I went out with my glasses and looked over the point here, just a little glow, no more than that, and I thought it was the school, too. We all did. And we wanted it to burn, Mr. Meiklejohn. We surely did want it to burn. In fact, we took it for granted that one of us, someone hurt real bad by all the trouble, put the torch to it. Someone like Joe Eglin, maybe. Poor Mrs. Eglin screamed for three days. You hear about that? She stopped screaming finally and hasn't said a word or made a sound that anyone knows about ever since. If Joe had put the torch to it, there wasn't a one of us who'd blame him. That's how it was."

"When you found out it was the wrong building, you lied about it anyway," Charlie said bitterly. He felt tired, the way he used to feel in New York after prowling through ashes and ruins, even if only for a few minutes. The thought of fire made him weary.

Burry Barlow shrugged and looked over the site of the hotel. "Don't know that it was the wrong building," he said slowly. "The trouble stopped after it burned. Couple of people said they slept for the first time in weeks; we all felt like something heavy and bad had been taken off our backs. Besides, by the time the men got up here, it was too far gone. About all's they could do was watch."

"'Trouble with a hose; electric outage silenced the alarm; you stumbled and were winded for another ten minutes, delaying the calls. . . .' You committed perjury, you know. All of you did. Why are you telling me now?"

"You're one of us, Mr. Meiklejohn, a fire fighter just like us. Didn't seem right, when you knew anyway. But, of course, the record doesn't change, and I'm an old man with a senile mind, memory shot to hell and gone. But you should know."

Charlie grunted; he was one of them, all right. "See any strangers around that night?" Barlow shook his head. "Did you come up for the fire? What was it like when you got here?"

"I came," Barlow said. "It was set, all right, and a good job too. Started up on the second floor, interior room, burned up and down a long time before it reached the outer walls. Funny thing, Mr. Meiklejohn, you know how things sort of lean out with an explosion, point to the center by pointing away is how I think of it."

"An explosion?" Charlie said. "What was in there to explode?"

"Not an explosion," Barlow said meditatively. "I'd say an implosion. A vacuum formed and just sucked stuff into itself. Big beams, things like that pointed all right, leaned in toward the middle." He looked at Charlie shrewdly. "Any explanation for something like that?"

"No. What else? You might as well tell me all of it."

"Yep, there's more." He slouched against the wall, his back to the sea. "I stood right here when it burned. No wind, no rain, just the fog and the fire. Pretty. You know how that is."

Charlie nodded. Fires were the most beautiful things in the world; every fire fighter knew that.

"Yep. Pretty in the fog. Next day, when it cooled off, me and J—me and another guy came up and went in. Found most of two skeletons. Not all, just most."

Charlie felt a chill that could have come from the ocean; a steady wind was now blowing in hard, it was very cold. "Go on," he said harshly.

"Uh-huh. We talked, started to call the sheriff, talked some more, decided to call in the state police instead. Then the other guy got sick and we talked some more and finally we buried them again. They're in there. I said a few words, and that was that. No more trouble, we decided, no more trouble. They were good and dead. For all we could tell they could've been dead for years. So we buried them."

"Males? Females? Children? Who were they?"

"A male, six-footer. A woman, five-five maybe."

"Could anyone have driven up here before the fire?"

"We had to cut the chain across the access road the night of the fire. Rusted together. Well, that's all I know, Mr. Meiklejohn. That's the whole story now. And I'll deny every word of it if it gets out. Thanks for listening." He hunched down against the wind and started to walk away.

"Barlow," Charlie called after him, "thanks."

The old man waved his hand, but did not look back.

□ □ □

In his motel room Charlie poured a drink, turned on the television news, and sat staring at it without seeing or hearing a thing. He had driven past the school on his way to the hotel site and had paid no attention to it; he reconstructed the trip. The school grounds and hotel grounds shared a common fence, the buildings a little over a mile apart. In the fog it probably *had* seemed as if the school were burning, especially to people in town who desperately wanted the school to burn. At least he understood now why the volunteers had been in no rush. He reviewed the various accounts of the "trouble." The music teacher had vanished, and a groundskeeper. The skeletons in the hotel? Why? He drank deeply and put the empty glass down. It was nearly seven and he knew he would get very drunk if he did not eat soon. He wanted to call Constance, but decided she probably had gone to dinner by now. He missed her.

He had left his window open a crack; the wind moaned as it entered. He got up and closed the window. The problem was, he decided, he had let them mix up his fire and their "trouble" in his mind, and he couldn't separate them again. And that was because he was too hungry. Abruptly he left his room for the motel dining room. If Byron got there before he finished, fine; if not, that was also fine. He stopped at the desk to leave a message, and at that moment Constance and Byron Weston entered.

His laughter was as spontaneous and unguarded as a child's when he saw her, ran to hug and kiss her. Ten minutes later the three of them were seated in the dining room.

"I finished by one and we were both ready to leave, so we left. This afternoon and tomorrow the feelies are in control of things," Constance said, holding his hand on the table.

"And touchies and yellers," Byron said gravely.

"And yowlers and pacers and leaders," Constance added, laughing. She and Byron had played a word game describing various therapies during the last hour of the trip. She gave Charlie's hand a squeeze and let go to pick up her menu. "Enough of this levity. I'm starved."

Eventually, they had their food and Charlie was content to listen to Byron talk about his postcrisis therapy.

"Are you treating J.C. Crandle?" Charlie asked.

"You know him?"

"Just met him."

"The answer is no. Actually he wasn't here, you see, until the crisis was over. His father might have been a candidate for our therapy, but not the son. He came home mad as hell, wanting to hit someone. Still does, I bet. But he's not the victim we're out to find and help."

"How about Burry Barlow?"

Byron shook his head. "I don't even know him. What was his connection?"

"Damned if I know. Just wondered." He ate in silence for a moment, then asked, "What about the sisters who went wonko? And poor Mrs. Eglin?"

"You've been getting around, haven't you?" Byron asked. His gaze was a bit less friendly than it had been minutes ago. "Look, our whole purpose is to help those who were affected by the outburst, not those who committed the crimes. They're in a hospital, the state hospital I assume, although I don't know. They probably had electroshock therapy, drug therapy, God knows what all. Not my province, any of that. As for Mrs. Eglin, her condition has nothing to do with any of this affair. She must have been a prime candidate for a schizophrenic break for years. It just happened, the way it does sometimes for no reason that we can ever find. But it is unrelated to the matter we are concerned with."

That was when Charlie began to listen with his public face on, Constance realized. He looked bland—maybe even a little dull—made the right sort of comments at the right times, and was using the greater part of his mind on his own thoughts. And Byron did not suspect a thing, she also realized, with more than a little dismay.

Over coffee Byron asked her to meet with his group the next day, sit in on their discussion of the past month's achievements. She started to turn him down with regrets, when Charlie said, "Why don't you do it, honey? I'm going to be tied up most of the day. Maybe you'll even get an article out of it."

Byron looked flustered for a second. Disingenuously, Charlie asked, "Would you mind if she wrote something about your work here?"

"Not at all," Byron said then. "Of course, you understand that I have written about our work in some detail myself."

"No doubt, but her work does get published in the damnedest places. *Harper's*, *The New Yorker*, places like that." Constance kicked him under the table and he smiled sweetly at her. "Would you like a brandy?"

"Just what was all that about?" she demanded later in their room. "He's not a charlatan, for heaven's sake! The work they're doing is important and worthwhile!"

"I expect it is," he said, taking her into his arms. "I missed you. Your hair smells good. Anyway," he said, when she pushed him away, still glaring at him, "I wanted to let you ask questions, and if he thinks there's a chance of publicity, he'll welcome questions. Publicity is money, right? Grant money, state money, whatever. Otherwise, he might have wanted to steer by himself, the way he did at dinner. I just got out of the way and let him take over, and that's what he did. Right?"

She took a deep breath, then nodded. "Right. He does that."

"So he thinks I'm the dumb cop and you're the brains of the family. And he's right, of course. Get him to show you the records, if you can. Find out who's on his patient list, and what their connection was with the school, and if there was any connection with the hotel at all. Does anyone have nightmares about the hotel, the fire, anything to do with it, that sort of thing. Okay? What made him choose some people and not others for his list? Why not poor Mrs. Eglin or J.C., for example."

She was watching him closely. "Do you think there's a connection between the madness at the school and the hotel fire?"

He shook his head. "No. I don't think anything yet. Too early. I'm just damned curious. And your hair does smell good. Let's go to bed."

□ □ □

Joe Eglin was twenty-eight; his wife Maria was twenty-five. She had not spoken, had not made a sound, had not moved of her own volition in four years. This much Charlie had learned from various people in town that morning. He had driven up into the hills and down a steep road, and had come to the fifteen acres that Joe farmed. It was a pretty setting, with redwoods high on the surrounding hills, pine trees in the valleys, ocher-colored grasses, and a fast-running stream. It appeared that there were millions of chickens and turkeys, geese and ducks, all running loose, most of them on the narrow gravel road. Joe admitted Charlie to his living room with reluctance. The noise of the fowls outside made it impossible to speak and be heard until the men were in the house with the door closed. Charlie had called, had said he wanted to talk about an insurance claim. Apparently that was all Joe Eglin had needed to hear.

"What about insurance?" Joe demanded. He was a little too flabby, too paunchy, and there were dark hollows under his eyes.

"I'd like to see your wife," Charlie said pleasantly. He glanced about the room, spartan in furnishings, very clean. Very dull. The walls were painted light green, a tan rug was in front of a tan sofa, a television and VCR in the middle of the room, two wooden chairs with cushion seats, a coffee table with nothing on it. A venetian blind covered a picture window that was almost the full width of the room.

"She's taking a nap," Joe Eglin said. "What's this all about?"

"I represent the insurance company trying to make sense out of the affair at the Dworkin school," Charlie said easily, as if not very interested in any of this. "We're reviewing claims associated with the Dworkin sisters and their school. We want to get the matter behind us, and you and your wife's names came up. You know, it all sounds insane to me, but I wasn't here. There's a memo with your names, but we can't find a claim. Did you file one?"

Joe Eglin moistened his lips. He nodded toward a chair. "You want a beer, or something?"

"No, thanks."

"We haven't filed yet. I've been waiting to see if she snaps out of it."

Charlie shook his head. "Mr. Eglin, I want to level with you. I heard in town yesterday that your wife is dead, that there isn't any Mrs. Eglin. No one's seen her in four years. You don't let anyone in here. You see where that leaves me? I mean, if I go away and next week you show up at the office with a woman, what does that prove? Did your wife ever have fingerprints made? Of course not. Why would she? I really do want to see her today, Mr. Eglin."

Joe Eglin's fists balled and he took a step toward Charlie, then another. "Get out!"

"Sure," Charlie said. "But, Mr. Eglin, consider. I have the company backing me. If I say in my report that I agree that there is no Mrs. Eglin, where will that leave you if ever you want to collect her life insurance, for example? Five thousand, isn't that it? Not a fortune, but on the other hand, if she does die, you'll need it for the funeral and all." He went to the door and stood with his hand on the knob. "I wonder what it would take to get J.C. Crandle out here poking around. Is there a death certificate anywhere on file?"

"Wait a minute," Joe Eglin said. He was sweating heavily. "Give me a minute. You know about her?"

"I heard something."

"Yeah, I bet. Wait a minute, for Chrissake!" He rubbed his hand over his face. "Okay, she's not right in the head. The doctor would have put her in a hospital and I wouldn't let him. I can take care of her. But now. . . . It's been four years and she doesn't get any better. Did you come out here to offer a settlement? Is that it? How much?"

"I want to see her," Charlie said.

"A lawyer. I need a lawyer. A settlement, that's it, isn't it? I can sue the pants off you and your fucking company!"

Charlie shrugged and turned the knob. "I'll go have a chat with Crandle, let him get a warrant or whatever it takes."

"Wait a minute!" Joe Eglin yelled. "You can see her! She's sleeping. I have to get her up and dressed. Five minutes! Wait five minutes, damn you!"

Charlie waited thirty seconds, then followed him through the living room down a short hall and paused outside a door. He could hear Joe Eglin muttering on the other side. Silently he turned the doorknob and opened the door.

A naked woman was standing in a bedroom, her face toward the door where Charlie stood. Joe was trying to get a robe on her. She was totally without expression, neither resisting her husband nor helping, just standing like a flexible doll. Her hair was unkempt. There was a dark bruise on one side of her face, red marks on her breasts. She was pregnant, six months at least. Her stare was vacant, her face empty. Except for her swollen belly she was desperately thin.

Charlie turned and walked away, no longer trying to be silent. Behind him he heard a hoarse oath, and then choking sobs. He left the house, drove carefully through the chickens and ducks that roamed onto and off the road, to the gate in the high fence, and let himself out.

□ □ □

"Christ!" J.C. Crandle muttered, regarding Charlie with hatred. "Let it rest, why don't you?"

"That girl belongs in a hospital where they can help her, if there's any help for someone like that. She doesn't need what she's got."

"Okay. Okay. When does it stop? When the hell does it all stop?"

Charlie shrugged. They were in Crandle's office. Maria's medical report was on the desk, the police report beside it. Joe and Maria had gone to the school to deliver two turkeys the day the eleven-year-old girl had dived off the cliff. Maria had waited in the car while Joe made the delivery. When he returned, she was holding her head, moaning. At his touch, she started to scream. Dr. Crandle had given her a shot to put her to sleep. He had reassured Joe; she was tense, hysterical, she needed to rest and she'd be fine. When she woke up, she started to scream again. Another shot, and by then the trouble had begun at the school. Maria screamed for three days, when she wasn't heavily sedated. Then she woke up and did not scream. An appointment had been made for the following week; Joe did not keep it. No one at the office had seen Maria again.

Charlie got up and rubbed his eyes. He simply wanted to collect Constance and drive away from here, away from the spiraling madness that seemed without end.

Constance looked alarmed when she saw him. "What happened?" she asked, and took his hand.

"Bad day. Tell you later. What did you come up with?"

"Not enough," she said regretfully. "Look, I told Byron we'd meet him for a drink, but not dinner. Okay with you?"

He kissed her. "My psychic wife."

"And if you'd rather not even have a drink with him, I sort of covered that in advance, too. I said I'd check and either we'd meet him in the bar at six-thirty, or he should not count on seeing us."

Charlie laughed. "What the hell. Let's go have that drink and then duck out for dinner. I'm curious about Wonder Boy and his methods that exclude the really interesting cases."

She looked as though she wanted to comment, then held back. "Okay." She started to go into the bathroom, and at the door she paused and said, "But I have to agree with Byron. I just don't see how any of that mess at the school has anything to do with the fire at the hotel weeks later. It just doesn't make any sense."

That was the problem, he thought grumpily. It made no sense. And yet, he also thought, there was a link. They just hadn't been able to find it. There had to be a link. Someone had taken those bodies to the hotel; they didn't just get up and walk there by themselves. And they had to be the music teacher and the groundskeeper, who was also missing. Old man Barlow thought so, and so did he. There had to be a link. And most important, why had poor Mrs. Eglin screamed? And screamed and screamed.

□ CHAPTER 7 □

THE MOST INTERESTING THING THAT CAME OUT OF the social hour with Byron Weston, Constance decided, was his apology to Charlie. That had been completely unexpected. They had been chatting, the three of them, in the polite way people do when they are mildly antagonistic without obvious cause. Byron had been talking about his training efforts, what his team looked for, how they handled people who wanted to be left alone.

"You have to assume that the ones who need help most are often the last ones to look for it," he said, making rings on the tabletop with his dripping glass. "I thought you were needling me about my two worst failures here," he said, glancing from Charlie back to the intricate patterns he was making. "I'm sorry. I was snappish."

Charlie was surprised and wary. "J.C. Crandle and Maria Eglin?"

Byron nodded. "He's a murderous impulse looking for a place to happen. He gave me the bum's rush when I approached him. And I truly didn't know about Maria Eglin for almost a year. I never even saw her, just her husband." He grimaced and stopped playing with his glass. "I should have known about her. There were hints. He was said to be brutal; she's young, a newcomer to this area, friendless. But in spite of all that, I dismissed her. She just didn't fit the pattern. She didn't know anyone at the school, no friends, no children, no reason to feel guilt over not doing anything. My God, they live miles out in the country. I made a decision that her mental collapse was independent of the other events, a coincidence. Maybe I was wrong. I just don't know. But we have to make those decisions all the time. You draw the boundaries and work within them, or nothing can get done."

"She'd be the first case, in my boundaries," Charlie said.

"But how? She never even got out of the car. He made the delivery, left her in the parked car, and came back in five minutes at the most." Byron shook his head.

"I didn't say I like having her inside instead of outside the boundaries," Charlie protested. "If it's your job to turn over rocks, you probably will find a hell of a lot of things you'd rather not, but you keep turning those rocks."

"But it's not your job anymore. Why are you still turning those rocks?"

"Because I'm the best there is," Charlie said, perhaps too bluntly. "And I learned a long time ago to let the facts determine the outline, not the other way around."

Byron glanced at his watch, finished his drink, and stood up. "I have to go," he said. "I wish I didn't. I assume Constance pumped me and the others today at your request. I hope you find whatever it is you're looking for, Charlie. I really do."

"He's all right," Charlie said after he and Constance were alone again.

"Of course," she said in the tone that meant I told you so.

He laughed. "I know this little dive down the road a piece. Best steamer clams on the coast, good dark beer. How about it, kid?"

□ □ □

While they worked their way through two buckets of clams, she filled him in on the details she had gleaned from Byron and his group. None of the people they were treating connected the fire with the other troubles, or the hotel with the school. "Of course," she admitted, wiping her hands finally, "that isn't as meaningful as it might seem. Patients often follow where the therapist takes them, and if the therapist didn't make such a connection, that path was probably closed. It's all unconscious, on both sides."

He grunted, looked in the bucket, picked up another clam, then put it back with a sigh. "It would sink me," he said. Over coffee he told her about Maria Eglin.

Furiously she cried, "What's the answer? People knew she needed help! They had to know it. They just butted out!"

"There isn't any," he said. "Answer. No complaints, no problems."

When he paid the bill, the waitress in the red pants said, "Hear about J.C.? He went out to Joe Eglin's place with his deputy and beat the daylights out of Joe. Put him in the hospital, so they say."

Charlie thanked her, complimented the food, and wondered: Would that be enough to placate J.C.'s murderous impulse? He doubted it. He took Constance back to the motel. The next day they drove down the coast, stopping here and there, wandering in the rain through the redwoods, beachcombing in drizzle, sunning themselves in Malibu. One week later at breakfast she said, "Let's go home." He was as ready as she.

□ □ □

Constance pushed newspapers to one side of the kitchen table. She propped up her chin in one hand, tapped the fingers of the other on the tabletop, staring off through the glass back door past Charlie, who sat opposite her. They had been home for two weeks. "No good," she said with finality. "Not a mention of the hotels that burned until after the fact. But, my heavens, one cryptic, noninformative story after another about strange happenings—suicides, murders, disappearances, madness, accidents . . . . I keep wondering what the reality of those situations really was." She held up a few of the papers. "In Orick," she said, "the papers were full of the stories of the mad sisters, the insanity at the school, but not a word about Maria Eglin. The doctor's suicide is given a paragraph of non-news reportage; the woman who drove off the cliff is labeled a one-car accident victim; the guy who walked out to sea is called the victim of a freak wave. That's in a place where we know pretty much what was going on. Without more information than in the articles, anyone would take them all at face value. Why not? And there's nothing really strange there, if you take them at face value." Charlie started to speak and she held up her hand. "I know. I know. Thoreson's afraid of a leak if we start asking too many questions. I've been thinking about it, and it might get out if you nose around, but I can do it. There are state statistics, state agencies that keep track of insanity, admissions to hospitals, private doctors' new patients. I'm going to make some phone calls."

"I think we're putting together a pretty comprehensive list of mayhem and altogether weird happenings," he said, leaning back in his own chair across the table from her. But that was part of the problem; they had not been searching for mayhem and weird happenings. They had been looking for something to link the fires. The papers had been arriving for the past ten days; motel records had started a bit later, enough to keep them busy for the next month. But he felt her dissatisfaction. Too long. Too chancy. And worst of all, no paper had printed a line about the hotels until after the fires, but every community had had more than its share of madness and violence. That bothered him most of all.

"Two things are wrong with this method," she said. "First, we don't have a control group. We'd need sister towns, at the very least. Maybe things like these happen all the time everywhere. *Boys Hole Up in School and Set Off Explosives*. Boys have done things like that in a lot of places, when they saw a chance of getting away with it. And this one: *Farmer Kills Neighbor's Cattle*. How many other farmers have killed their neighbor's cattle? We don't know."

"And this one," he said dryly. "*Mother Throws Three Children out of Seventh-floor Window, Leaps after Them*."

"Even that sort of thing happens. Anyway, we need controls. And the other reason is that too many things just won't make it to the newspapers. If the mayor's wife turns into a kleptomaniac, that won't get in the papers. They pay off the bills and quietly take her away for a rest. Or if Mrs. Croesus develops a phobia about dirt and germs and won't eat, you'll never see that in the news. A nice vacation in a beautiful hotel-like setting, that's how they'll take care of that. If a highly regarded man becomes a flasher overnight, or turns his house into a bordello, or does anything short of murder, chances are you'll never know about it. Accidents, disappearances, actual murders, they get reported, not the lesser things. And sometimes the people responsible for the lesser things are just as deranged, just as desperately in need of help, just as likely to commit mayhem eventually if they don't get help."

He shrugged. "You win. What bothers me is that there's no one pattern. People are going nuts in a hundred different ways. Nothing you can pin down, nothing to connect any of that with the hotels."

"No problem about the madness," she said, dismissing it. "That's how insanity works. There are some physical conditions that result in certain syndromes, but functional disorders take too many different forms to look for any one pattern. What I see a lot of in these stories is what my colleagues tend to call paranoid schizophrenia. That's to make sure they cover all bases."

"And you wouldn't call it that?"

"The term is too loose to mean much. Schizophrenia means cut off from reality, and paranoia, you know, feelings of persecution, deeply held feelings, but still. . . . See what I mean? Descriptive, but then what? Not very long ago the good family doctor would say something like, oh yes, you have the grippe, and he would describe the symptoms, what to expect in the days to follow, and everyone was reassured somehow. Descriptive. Now we say things like schizophrenia and use drugs, shock treatments where they're still allowed, and everyone's reassured somehow. It's mostly descriptive, and the treatments are elephant-gun mentality at work. Not many people get cured, although some get better. And no one can say for certain what the cause is. We have ruled out some things—demons, possession by spirits, original sin, an evil nature of the victim. We suspect diet, vitamin deficiencies, hormonal imbalances, a genetic accident. Too many things are suspect. And none of them would fit this pattern, if there is a pattern. Why acute onsets in places so widely separated? It just doesn't make any sense. I'm going to make some phone calls."

Even if there was no pattern in the nut cases, Charlie brooded after she left, there was in the arson fires. One person had started them all; even a rookie could have spotted that much if his attention had been directed to it. Upstairs room, gasoline, forced entrance, between one and three in the morning. One firebug, busy as a little bee.

When Constance returned to the kitchen an hour and a half later, she found Charlie on his hands and knees backing Brutus up into the corner under an antique maple hutch. Charlie was muttering: "John Daniels, Carl Larson, John Lucas, Carlton Johns, John Carolton—" He looked up at her and scowled. "That damn cat snitched my cheese for the last time. I'm going to catch him and rub his nose in the plate and then heave him into the next county. Brutus, you've had it." The gray cat Ashcan had come in to watch; he approached Charlie, sniffing at his hands, and started to lick one. "Out, damn it! This is our final showdown, you asshole!"

Ashcan rolled over and rubbed his cheek against Charlie's arm. Brutus gave a leap, cleared both Charlie's outstretched hands and Ashcan, and sauntered into the living room, flicking his tail disdainfully. Charlie sighed and began to haul himself up from the floor. He scowled harder at Constance, who had started to laugh; she quickly stifled it and turned her back. Her shoulders continued to shake.

"Well?" he snarled, taking the empty plate to the counter.

"I have spies at work. It'll be a couple of days. Who are the men on your roll call?"

"One man," he said. "Bet you five it's one man."

She shook her head. "Betting is against my moral principles. Besides, I always lose. Tell me."

"He's on the motel lists. Always checks in a day or two before the fire, always gone the day after. Drove a '79 black Malibu until last year, when he had an '84, black again. Always has the right state plates on the car, but that's easy enough to arrange. Pays cash for a room. Lists his business as real estate appraiser. People go nuts; he shows up and burns down a hotel. People stop going nuts. Enough?"

She nodded, then asked, "What's a Malibu?"

"Never mind. Just take my word for it—there's a zillion of them out there on the roads. Who's cooking tonight?" His expression had gone innocent suddenly.

"You are. Charlie, assuming you're right, how would he know where to go? That is, if the madness and arson are connected. Not from the newspapers. We can't do it."

"I was wondering that same thing," he said with a touch of smugness. "You have sources, state shrinks, and so on, but you know who else has sources, just as good, or better even? Insurance claims people. Who goes into a hospital without insurance these days? No one, let me tell you. So who pays? You and I every other policy holder on earth. And who keeps the records? Health insurance companies. Sore Thumb thought he had a leak, and so do I. Someone has access to that information, you better believe."

"It would be in their computers," she said, looking past him, thinking.

"Yep. If you know how to go about it, if you have your own little handy-dandy computer at home, if you have a modem, you too can scan the lists, arranged in any order you call up, by area, dollar amounts, diseases, accidents, or illnesses, whatever you want." He went to the pantry and opened the freezer. "You remember those steaks we had over on the coast? Cajun style? Blackened steaks, they called them. Dijon mustard, garlic, and lots of cayenne, wouldn't you say? Anything else?" He came back with a butcher's package. She was walking out of the kitchen. "Hey, where are you going?"

"I'm going to close doors so smoke won't fill the house, and I'll bring the fan from the attic. Open the exhaust before you start this time, will you?"

While the steaks were thawing, he called Phil, who was back from Bermuda. He told Phil he wanted the computer printouts of claims and listened patiently to the many reasons why that was impossible, and then he said he also wanted the list Phil had mentioned of other hotels at risk. He moved the telephone away from his ear and winked at Constance.

When Phil subsided, Charlie said kindly, "And you just take it easy, old buddy, and get well."

"Charlie, about those claims, you know it's probably illegal to give that out. Unethical, for sure; illegal, probably. Sore Thumb will have a coronary. And speaking of Sore Thumb, he's driving me batty. Did you tell him to do something highly immoral and possibly illegal to himself?"

Charlie laughed. "I did, but he won't. One more thing, a list of people at the conference in Dallas when you talked about the hotel fires. A list of attendees."

"For God's sake, Charlie! I can't just snap my fingers and have lists appear! What else do you want? A list of registered voters? List of high school graduates for the years 1950 through 1980? Some other little thing on that order?"

"Now, Phil, don't get testy on me," Charlie said. "Tomorrow? The next day? Send them express mail, will you? Good talking to you, pal. Take care." Gently he hung up. He looked at his package of steaks and started to sing lustily—and not very well—bits and pieces of *The Marriage of Figaro* in no particular order.

□ □ □

Two days later Charlie sat upright at four in the morning. A window, he thought, wide awake, shivering. And gasoline. Constance woke up and said, "What was that?"

"I don't know. Get a robe on." He was already pulling on his robe on his way to the door. He touched the handle, the wood paneling, sniffed, and then opened it. The smell of gas was stronger. No heat, no smoke, no flickering light. Only then did he turn on the hall light and start downstairs. He followed the strong smell of gas to the living room, where a window had been broken. No fire. He went out on the porch and found that the front of the house had been drenched with gasoline. The can was on the porch. Constance was right behind him.

"It's okay," he said, his voice hard and flat. "It'll evaporate fast in this breeze." He picked the can up carefully, using the back of his finger under the handle. It was empty. He carried it inside, through the house to the back porch, where he put it down. Then he inspected the rest of the house, starting at the ground floor, and continuing on to the basement, the garage, upstairs, even the attic. When he finished, Constance handed him a glass nearly full of bourbon. He took a long drink, and stopped shivering.

Constance drew him to the kitchen table where she had a second glass. She pointed to a rock and a piece of crumpled paper. "I tried not to mess up any prints there might be," she said. Her voice sounded strained and unfamiliar. He put his arm around her shoulders and leaned over to read the note without picking it up.

Butt out or the next time I'll light it.

He took a deep breath, raised his glass, and drank again.

Constance had been seized with a fury so intense that it frightened her. Fury and fear, fear of the fury, fear for Charlie. She had flashes of the years in New York, toward the end of his career with the fire department, a few years filled with nightmares, jerking from sleep to wakefulness just like tonight, but without cause. She saw again how he had felt doors before opening them, how his gaze had traveled over a new room, seeking the fire escape, searching for the fire trap, the piled-up clothes behind a door, the flammable curtains, the spilled combustible. She heard again his garble of words as he fought with dream demons who breathed fire, who were creatures of fire. His thrashing about, muttering, moaning, then the sudden jerk into full wakefulness that would remain the rest of the night, whether it was only an hour or two, or six or seven.

Dear God, she breathed, don't let it start again. Please.

The orange cat Candy slunk into the room, complaining bitterly, looking about with wild eyes. Brutus watched through slitted eyes from on top the refrigerator. Ashcan had gone into hiding somewhere. What good were they? she thought sourly. Not a peep out of them, not a clue that the house was under attack. What the hell good were they?

"I'll make some breakfast," she said. "No point in going back to bed now."

"I'll put some cardboard over the window."

"I did it while you were looking around."

"I'll clean up the glass before a cat walks through it."

She started to say no, sit down and try to

relax, but she knew he would not relax again that night. Nor would she.

"He knows we're closing in," Charlie said, as he left the kitchen for the vacuum cleaner. "He's running scared."

And so was she, she admitted silently. So was she.

□ CHAPTER 8 □

IN HIS DREAMS TENEMENTS BURNED, HIGH-RISE condos burned, office buildings burned, factories, single-family houses, schools. He ran here and there futilely as screaming people, ablaze, leaped out of windows. Eventually he was always inside the burning building, running down one hallway after another, feeling doors, watching doorknobs glow red, burst into flames, watching walls start to smoke, char, burst into flames. He ran until he dropped in exhaustion, and the fire raced toward him from different directions. He buried his head in his arms and waited for it, and woke up, sweating, shaking, through with sleep for that night.

The reports came in, the lists arrived,

microfiches, Xeroxes of Xeroxes of newspaper accounts, photocopies of insurance claims, police statements, statements from fire department heads. Thoreson called daily, demanding action; Charlie stopped returning his calls. Phil sent funny postcards but did not call.

Charlie was staring moodily at a photograph of John Loesser, who had left his last apartment without leaving a forwarding address. Outside, a guard dog padded quietly on her patrol of the yard. The cats were in a panic because of the dog, who simply ignored them all. He knew so much, Charlie thought bitterly, and not the important thing: why. Loesser had survived an attack, had quit his job with one of the biggest, most prestigious insurance companies in the world in order to become an independent adjuster who apparently never adjusted anything. Two weeks after his release from the hospital, the first hotel had burned, the one in which he had been attacked. He had access to computer data, knew how to use it, how to interpret it. People began to go mad here and there; Sir Galahad arrived and burned down a hotel; people stopped going mad. Probably he had enough now to make an arrest, Charlie thought; a formal investigation would cinch it, and yet . . . He had no intention of turning over a damn thing until he had a clue about the why. He scowled at the photograph, cursing John Loesser under his breath. You son of a bitch, he thought, why?

Constance entered his study and touched his shoulder. "Charlie, Byron Weston is on the phone. You should talk to him."

Her voice was strange, remote, her face set in the expression she had when she was controlling herself perhaps too much. Charlie moved the photograph of Loesser away from the telephone on his desk, and put it face down. He lifted the extension. "Yeah," he said.

"Charlie, when you were in Orick, you were asking questions about the old hotel. Why? What did that have to do with the epidemic of madness?"

"I don't know," Charlie said softly. "Why do you ask?"

There was a pause; Charlie could hear other voices, then the slamming of a door. Byron returned. "Sorry," he said. "Charlie, did you watch the news tonight, national news?"

"No."

"Okay. There was a story. It'll be a bigger story tomorrow. We have a repeat of the Orick madness, and this time I didn't predetermine the boundaries. I've just been listening."

"Is there a hotel involved?"

"Two of them," Byron said harshly. "No fire, though. Look, you brought up the fact that people in Orick had been infected, affected, something—people I excluded in my study there. Well, this morning a sniper held a trainload of people hostage in a tourist attraction here. Nine people were killed before it ended. My office was called and I flew out and arrived within an hour of the end of the siege. I began to listen to people real early this time, and I let them direct the conversations. They say incidents began over a month ago in the town of Grayling in California, and they link the old hotel to the madness. What can you tell me about it, Charlie? I need help with this!"

"Why will it be a bigger story tomorrow?" Charlie asked easily. Constance, listening, shivered at the sound of his voice now.

"Because some of the survivors are telling reporters that a dead man got up and walked. The press will have a field day with this one."

Charlie talked with Byron for another fifteen minutes; when he was finished, Constance took the phone to make airline reservations for the following morning. She used her name, Constance and Charlie Leidl, she said, spelling it out, and gave her credit card number. Charlie raised an eyebrow, then nodded. She expected Loesser to show up for this one every bit as much as he did.

□ □ □

Flying in to Las Vegas was always a shock, Constance thought, watching the view from her window. Miles and miles of arid wasteland, and then high-rise glitter and neon; barren mountains and straggly sage; and slot machines in the terminal. Then, the silence of the desert and the cacophony of heavy traffic on Interstate 15. Charlie drove, following Byron's directions, to the California border where he left the interstate for a state road to Grayling. An hour out of Las Vegas, Byron had said, but it was only fifty minutes to the small dusty town.

The state road became Main Street where they passed an adobe building, Grayling High School, and then a feed store, a car dealer with half a dozen used cars on display, a few small shops, drugstore, a furniture store, a ten-cent store, a St. Vincent DePaul outlet . . . Everything looked tired, gray, dusty. A scattering of bare trees trembled in a high wind that was very cold. Charlie turned onto Mesquite Street and stopped in front of number 209. Two other cars were already there, one a sleek baby blue Cadillac, Byron Weston's car.

Charlie stopped in the driveway, got out, and went to open the trunk. He hauled out the suitcases, and then stood surveying the dismal scene. The street was not long, eight or ten houses on each side, and then the desert started again. Most of the houses were wooden, paint cracked and peeling on many of them; no more than one or two appeared well maintained, with lawns and some shrubbery. There had been a little activity on Main Street, a few cars in motion, a few people bundled against the wind; here no one was in sight. At the end of the street a dust devil formed and raced away erratically.

"Well," he said, shivering. He regarded the house before them glumly. Peeled paint, gray, a few misshapen sagebrush plants on the sides of the steps. "I don't think," he said, "I'd be tempted to relocate here. Let's do it."

Constance nodded, chilled through and through by the biting wind, just as dismayed and disheartened by the dreary town as he was.

The woman who admitted them to the house was tall, beautifully built, with straight black hair and black eyes. More Indian than Spanish, Constance thought, shaking her hand.

"Beatrice Montoya," the woman said. "I'm Byron's assistant. I'm to show you your room and give you a drink—coffee, whatever you want—and then let you start examining the reports, if you wish."

She led them through the house as she talked. The living room was furnished with heavy black Spanish furniture that looked uncomfortable. Very fine Indian blankets hung on the walls, relieving the darkness and heaviness. They went through the kitchen, sparsely equipped with a stove and ancient refrigerator and scant cabinets, and on the other side of it into a narrow hall painted white. There were several closed doors. Theirs was the last room. Here there was plenty of light, with east windows, white walls, and more of the lovely blankets, one of them on the bed, two on the walls.

"Not the Waldorf," Beatrice was saying, as she motioned them to enter. "But not too bad. Byron said to let you decide. If you'd rather go to the motel, it's only a few blocks away. It's just that it's full of outsiders right now. You know, the curious, a few reporters, ghouls, that sort of thing."

She was too polite, Charlie decided, regarding her thoughtfully when she paused. Too reserved, hardly even trying to pretend she was interested in them. He and Constance were also outsiders, he realized, ghouls, curiosity-seekers. Beatrice started to turn away and he said, "Did you think we'd be better off in the motel?"

She looked startled for a second, then shrugged. "It's up to you. Byron and the others will be back in another half hour or so. I'll let you wash up, or unwrap, whatever, and go put on some coffee."

"I don't know about you," Constance said as soon as the woman closed the door, "but I'm freezing. I intend to change clothes and then we'll see."

When they returned to the kitchen a few minutes later, Beatrice had a tray ready. She picked it up. "This way." She led them into the other side of the house, where they stopped at a comfortable room that probably had been intended as a den. There was a wood-burning stove, some bean bag chairs in a corner, an overstuffed sofa, also pushed out of the way, and two desks and several office chairs. A computer system was on one desk. An assortment of bottles and glasses was on an end table, and computer printouts, maps, rolled-up papers, notebooks, seemed to be everywhere.

A large topographical map had been thumbtacked to one wall. Three red circles made a triangle. Charlie walked to it.

"Here's Grayling," Beatrice said, pointing to one of the circles. "This one is the big resort hotel going up, not quite finished yet, and that one is Old West. That's where . . . where the incident occurred."

Charlie nodded. He had looked up the area at home, but this map was a superb USGS map that showed every rock, every dip and hollow. That's all that was out there, he thought: rises, dips, hollows, chasms, peaks, dry lakes, dry riverbeds, barren rocks, scrub desert brush . . . . Behind him Beatrice was pouring coffee.

"We started at seven this morning," she was saying to Constance, "and by this afternoon, Byron knew we all had to see the location for ourselves. The stories just weren't making any sense, and they vary so much about where things happened. We drew to see who'd go today, who'd wait until tomorrow. So Polly and Mike and Byron went out, oh, an hour ago, maybe. They'll be back any minute now."

□ □ □

Byron wished that Beatrice had come instead of Polly, and knew it was unfair, and even tried to force himself not to see the little byplays that always occurred when Polly and Mike were together. If only Mike weren't such an ass, he thought, and knew that was hopeless too. Mike was an ass, yearning so openly for

Polly's attention that it was embarrassing for everyone around them. And Polly could be a bitch, he also knew, teasing just enough to make Mike even more an ass, but never enough to warrant a dressing down. Mike was twenty-six, Polly a couple of years older and very attractive, with pale hair and blue eyes with incredible lashes. Mike was overweight, a wrestler who would make a damn good psychologist some day, but at the present time was simply a pain in the ass. At the last minute Byron had decided to let Mike drive his Land-Rover in, more to keep him busy than because he feared for his Cadillac. After all, he had thought, the road was used every day by the workers at Old West; it had to be okay. Okay turned out to be an overstatement. It was just passable, with deep ruts and rocky places and precipitous hills. Mike loved driving it. He kept glancing in the rearview mirror to grin at Polly, who was being shaken like a malted milk.

He rounded a sharp curve and Old West came into view. Two buildings, the old hotel and another one halfway down the street, were the original structures, aged, weathered silvery, looking very much at home in the desert. Everything else was new. Dust swirled in the street, settled, swirled.

"See if you can drive all around the place," Byron said when they drew close. The road wound by an area with a portable toilet and a parked trailer, then behind the old hotel, and the new buildings, and finally behind the railroad station, where it ended. The last quarter-mile there was no real road, just a bulldozed surface. It was late enough for the shadows of the buildings to fill the street and made deep pockets of darkness. Wood that had not turned silver gleamed golden in the shafts of sunlight streaking in low between the buildings. As soon as the motor noise stopped, the whistle of the wind rose. The sign hanging over the entrance to the saloon swished as it was lifted, dropped, lifted again. Polly drew her shearling coat tighter, the collar halfway covering her head, and picked up her pad of graph paper. Mike checked his camera and started down the street, and Byron turned his attention to the train station platform.

In his mind he reconstructed the scene of the massacre as he had heard it described over and over that day. The train pulled in on the other side of the platform; people got off and milled about. A broad walkway went down both sides of the street in front of the buildings. Eight feet wide, ten feet, with two steps down here and there, lined with railings, hitching posts, big Mexican pots that were still empty, but would hold greenery one day. People started to move down both sides, looking into the shops, with shopkeepers, customers all in costume, going about life as it had been in 1880. Then the show started.

Byron gazed down the length of the street to the hotel at the far end, half a mile away. On the right from here, halfway down the street, was the saloon. The corral was off to one side of it, not visible from here. The cowboys had come from there, whooping and yelling, shooting blanks into the air. Down a few doors from the saloon, opposite it, was the jail; the sheriff had come out with his gun ready, and at the same time several men had run out from the saloon, also with guns. More shooting, more noise. And then the real shooting had started. Byron turned his attention to the saloon again, to the upper story with a narrow balcony where the madman had held the entire town at bay for three hours.

He scowled at the scene, seeing it the way he had heard it described half a dozen times already. Workers had come from the far end, puzzled by the screams, which had not been in the scenario. They had been shot at too, and several of them had been hit, fatally, according to the stories. The ones who could run away had done so. Some of them had not yet been located.

Someone had tried to drive out in a truck and had been shot. From the balcony the killer could see the entire area, and he had been a good shot. Two men finally had crawled behind the saloon building, out the back way on foot, and they had summoned help. And one of the dead men had got up and walked to the hotel. Byron's scowl deepened as he stared broodingly down the wide street of Old West to the hotel. Obviously the man had not been dead. He had wandered inside, out the back door, out on the desert where he had died, and had not been found. But he had not been dead when he got up and walked. He had not.

Most of the mess had been cleared away, windows boarded up; here and there glass shards gleamed in the golden afternoon sunlight where it streamed in between the buildings. The wind whistled maniacally, and the sign swung up and down with a whooshing, creaking noise. There was nothing else to be gained here, Byron decided, and now looked for Polly. He realized almost absently that he had been noticing Mike for the past several minutes. Mike had stopped snapping pictures, had stopped moving at all, in fact, and was facing away, toward the hotel. Byron had assumed that Mike was waiting for the right light, for a shadow to move or something, in order to get a shot of the hotel. Then Mike dropped his camera. Still he did not move. Polly walked through one of the rays of sunlight, into the next shadow. Slowly, almost ponderously, Mike turned and started to walk toward her. She was concentrating on her feet, avoiding the broken glass. Byron felt his throat go dry when suddenly Mike lunged for Polly.

Byron vaulted the rail of the boardwalk and raced toward them. Polly screamed and tried to run, but Mike caught her and dragged her off the boardwalk, onto the street. She rolled away and struggled to get up, he knocked her down, and this time went for her throat. Byron reached them and grabbed Mike's arm, tried to pull him off. Mike swept him away effortlessly. Byron's hand closed on the heavy camera. He raised it, swung as hard as he could, and hit Mike in the temple. Mike grunted and pitched forward on top of Polly. She was sobbing hysterically.

Byron heaved at Mike's inert body and finally rolled him off Polly and pulled her clear, helped her to her feet. Then he looked at Mike and his stomach churned. Mike's eyes were wide open, unseeing, the stench of death on him.

"Oh, my God!" Byron said, and then again, and found he could not stop saying it. He was half dragging Polly away, toward the station platform, toward the Land-Rover, and she was sobbing and choking, and he was repeating, "Oh, my God!" over and over. She staggered and he held her, then got her moving again, but she looked back and screamed piercingly, and crumpled at his side. He turned to see Mike on his feet, his eyes wide open and blind, coming toward them. He felt frozen, paralyzed. Mike took another step, halting and slow. Byron tugged at Polly; he stooped, keeping his gaze on Mike, who was advancing slowly but steadily. Byron lifted Polly by one arm and slung her over his shoulder and began to back up toward the platform, unable to take his eyes off Mike. He backed up the three steps to the boardwalk, crossed to the other side, and only then turned and ran to the Land-Rover.

Mike had left the keys on the dashboard. He

fumbled with them until he found the right one and turned on the ignition. Mike stopped then, on the boardwalk, twenty feet away; he turned around and started to walk in the opposite direction. Byron killed the engine trying to start it, and saw with horror that Mike had turned his way again. He got the engine going and backed up with a roar, turned, squealing the tires, and raced back over the leveled ground to the road. When he looked one more time, Mike was walking toward the hotel.

□ CHAPTER 9 □

WHEN THEY GOT BACK TO THE HOUSE POLLY WAS conscious. She was shaking and weeping, but able to sit up and, Byron hoped, able to hear him with comprehension.

"We have to call the sheriff," he repeated. "Mike went berserk and attacked you. I hit him and we got out of there, left him behind. Do you understand?"

She nodded.

The sun had gone behind the mountains and now the shadows filled the countryside: inky pools, black pits, unfathomable chasms. The wind had let up marginally, and although it was very cold, Byron knew that neither his nor Polly's shivering was due to the temperature. At the house he brought the Land-Rover to a jerking stop and got out, helped her out, walked with his arm around her shoulder to the door.

Byron was vastly relieved when he saw Charlie and Constance. He told them briefly what had happened and asked Beatrice to call the sheriff. Polly was too shocked to speak yet. Constance took her to the bathroom to examine her injuries, wash the dirt from her face. She was certain the young woman was totally unaware of her.

By the time Sheriff Logan Maschi arrived, Byron had cleaned himself up a bit, and no longer was visibly shaking, but he was pale and had the staring eyes of someone still in shock. Polly was in worse shape, ghastly pale, trembling.

"Holy Christ!" Maschi muttered when Byron finished telling the story. He had condensed it, said no more than that Mike had gone crazy and attacked Polly. Maschi was a heavy man in his sixties, tanned like old mahogany. He wore cowboy clothes: hat, boots, and all, even a silver buckle on his belt.

Charlie watched as the sheriff asked questions, made notes, and got up to leave. Charlie walked out to the porch with him.

"The man on the balcony the other day, did you know him?"

"Yep."

"I take it there was no reason for him to break like that, no medical problems, financial, whatever?"

"Trevor Jackson was the most decentest man I've known," the sheriff said heavily. "Hell, one of the guys he shot dead was his own brother-in-law! And now this." He drew a deep breath. "I just wish to God old man Lorrimer had kept his money in the casinoes over in Vegas. Nothing but trouble since he got that goddamn wild hair up his ass about rebuilding that ghost town. Ghost town! Hah! Tell you this, that town might never get finished. That's for sure. Ain't nobody wanting to go back in, and now this."

"You won't do any searching tonight, will you?"

"Hell no! No point to it. You been out there? Guy with a head injury, falls in a hole, who's to know? Especially by night. We'll look for him tomorrow."

Charlie went back inside; chilled to the bone, he thought gloomily. And the house was not a hell of a lot warmer than out on the porch. He rejoined the others in the den and rubbed his hands together hard.

"Okay," he said. "Several questions. What do you do for heat in this place? What do you do about food? And what happened out there today? First the heat."

Beatrice was staring at him as if he had suggested an orgy. He lifted an eyebrow. "Heat," he said again.

"Sorry. There's a thermostat in the living room. It was so warm early, I didn't think of it." She left.

Charlie turned to Byron. "Food?"

Byron looked blank.

"There's nothing like dinner stuff in the fridge," Charlie said patiently. "I looked. You must have planned on something to eat for dinner. What?"

Byron moistened his lips. "We hoped to get someone to come in and cook, but no luck so far. We've been eating at the restaurant next to the motel. Jodie's. We have breakfast and lunch materials."

"Jodie's," Charlie repeated in satisfaction. He went to the phone, found the telephone book, and riffled through it. Then he dialed, waited a few seconds, and said, "I want to order five steaks, rare to medium rare, baked potatoes, salads for five, all the works. When will it be ready?" He listened, then said, "Of course, to go. When can I pick it up?" He listened again. "Look, you cook, I deliver. When?" He examined the ceiling while he waited, then said, "Gotcha. The name's Leidl." He spelled it. "Okay." He hung up. "Forty-five minutes. Now the last question."

Beatrice had returned. She went to the makeshift bar and poured a drink, then sat down next to Polly on the sofa. Polly was huddled under a blanket, staring at Charlie with wide eyes, very frightened. She shook her head when he glanced at her. He turned to Byron. "What really happened out there?"

This time Byron told it the way he remembered, all of it. Charlie listened intently, and noticed at the same time with interest that the drink Beatrice had poured was really for Polly. She put it in the girl's hands and even helped her get it to her lips. She'd do, he decided.

"You see why I couldn't tell the sheriff?" Byron said helplessly. "Who's going to believe us? And, in fact, I don't believe it myself any longer. I must have just injured him."

"Maybe," Charlie said. He looked at Polly. "You were supposed to be sketching the layout, weren't you? How far down the street did you get? Did you see anything strange, feel anything, hear anything?"

What little color had returned to her face drained away again. Beatrice glared at Charlie. He made his voice harder, flatter. "Polly, I asked you a question."

She drank a little, then said, "I got a headache. I remember that. I was drawing and I felt dizzy for a second or two, and then I had a headache. That's when I decided I had enough in the notebook. That's when I started back. That's when Mike . . ."

"How far had you gone?"

"Past the saloon, not all the way to the end, a few doors from the end maybe."

"And you dropped your sketch pad there, didn't you?"

She looked around guiltily.

"That's all right, but I want you to sketch the place for me now, before you forget the details. Okay? Will you do that?"

She took another sip of her drink and got up,

as if relieved that she could do something. Byron nodded, and Constance felt almost smug about Charlie's handling of the girl. Exactly right, and he had no training whatsoever.

Charlie glanced at Beatrice. "Is there someplace where she can draw and not be disturbed by our voices?"

"Of course. Come on, Polly. Let's go to the kitchen table." They left.

Charlie poured a drink for Constance and another for himself, and sat down near Byron. "Now, fill me in on what the hell's been going on at Old West. Okay? And here at Grayling. I take it that it's involved too."

Byron pulled a notebook from his coat pocket. He remembered and dismissed the memory of how he had dominated the conversation when he had had dinner with Charlie and Constance at Orick, how he had thought then that Charlie was too phlegmatic to be interesting.

"I have a timetable here," he said. "Incomplete, of course, but an indication. The first incident was nearly five weeks ago. Nellie Alvarez had a breakdown and ran out on the desert and vanished. They found her body a week later. That's when I think it all started."

Charlie took the notebook and started to glance through it. Constance asked, "Did you feel anything out there? See anything?"

"No, nothing for me. Polly didn't mention her dizziness before, or the headache, but of course the wind was pretty fierce. That could account for it."

Without looking up from the notebook Charlie asked, "Were all these people at Old West before they went bonkers?"

Byron gave Constance a look of reflexive protest. She rolled her eyes and shrugged.

"I don't know," Byron said.

"Find out, will you?" Charlie said absently, turning a page.

"You tell me something," Byron said then. "What are you investigating? Fire? Or something else? You thought the trouble at Orick was connected with the hotel there, didn't you? And now another old hotel. What's going on? And why aren't you using your own name?"

Charlie had introduced Constance to the sheriff as Dr. Leidl, and himself as her husband without adding another name. He shrugged and stood up. "Wish to hell I knew. Time to go collect dinner. Point us in the direction of the restaurant, okay?"

The town was small enough to criss-cross on foot several times in under half an hour, but the wind was cold enough to make them glad they weren't walking. All the businesses were closed now, Main Street bleak-looking. They went up the two blocks, turned left, and before them the street became state highway again; the black desert, empty and barren, seemed ready to invade the town. Jodie's was a welcoming oasis of flashing neon signs and a crowd of parked cars. Next to it a motel sign said No

Vacancy. The motel was far back from the street, its parking lot also filled.

Charlie drove through both parking lots slowly, scanning the cars, satisfying himself that no late-model black Malibu was among them. Then he stopped near the entrance to the restaurant. "I'm going to bribe the desk clerk while you hunt and gather food. Division of labor, all that." He grinned at her fleetingly and ambled away.

Constance had to wait ten minutes for the order to be completed, and during the delay she talked to the woman behind the cash register. That woman turned out to be Jodie, Lorraine Jodrell, middle-aged, gray-haired, with shrewd dark eyes; she was on a first-name basis with her customers.

"We got wind of the tourist attraction three years ago," she said confidentially. "This place," she indicated the restaurant with a sweeping gesture, "was a pigpen. Beer and hamburgers, that was what it offered, and loud country rock. We borrowed money from Homer's father and bought it, and turned it into a good restaurant. Figured workers deserved decent food, and then, of course, the tourists, when they began to come. Took over a year to get it the way we wanted it." She looked past Constance with troubled eyes. The restaurant was attractive, with many lush green plants in ocher-colored clay pots, a relief from the harsh landscape beyond the windows. "Food's good too," Jodie said.

Constance listened to her, asked a question now and again, and watched the clientele. The restaurant business was good, if quiet. It appeared that every table was filled; the booths that lined the walls were packed. Most of the customers were in Western clothes, local people, with only half a dozen obvious tourists among them. The tourists stood out by the way they were dressed—designer jeans, silk shirts, cashmere sweaters, glossy boots—and the way they stared at the local people. Occasionally someone got up from a table full of people talking in low voices to go join a different table where they were talking in low voices. Many of the tables had only men, and altogether the men outnumbered women two to one. The prevailing emotion was fear, Constance realized. These people were desperately afraid.

". . . be wiped out, of course. Poor Homer, poor old Dad."

"You shouldn't think that," Constance protested. "This will all blow over, the way things do."

"Not this thing. Four, five men vanished, and today rumor has it another one disappeared. People going crazy, doing crazy things. And then the shooting. No one's going back over there. Wait and see. Oh, they'll try to bring in a lot of outsiders to finish up, but when things start to happen to them, they'll take off, too. Wait and see."

"Have you been out there?"

"Once, early on. Took the lay of the land, you see. We send out a lunch truck, hot soup, sandwiches, stuff like that. We have a boy who drives out, sells lunches, and comes back. I went out to see if he could get in and out again. Not sending him any more. That's over with."

They chatted a few more minutes and then the food arrived, packed in a large cardboard carton, and Constance left. It wasn't as if she had learned anything factual, she told Charlie as they drove back to the house. But she had a feeling now for what the people here were going through. They were scared to death.

"They attribute it to everything from an old Indian curse to radiation leaks from the nuclear tests in Nevada. From faulty government nerve gas storage to the work of the devil."

He nodded. "They don't single out the old hotel, far's I could learn. In fact, they're saying they might even go finish the new one, maybe. But it's the old town reconstruction thing as a whole that scares them. Talk's about bad vibes, being blasted with rays from invisible machines, maybe even in orbit somewhere." He sounded morose. Then he said, "You know what time it really is? After ten!"

Constance realized that he sounded so low because he was hungry. They had not eaten since breakfast and that seemed days ago. Something had been served on the airplane that had looked vaguely like fish, but neither of them had tried it. Now good food smells were filling the rented car, and she felt stomach pangs. She patted Charlie's leg, offering sympathy; he covered her hand with his, accepting it.

□ □ □

That night, after they had eaten the excellent steaks and enough accompaniments to feed three additional people, Byron practically forced Polly to take a sleeping pill and go to bed. She acceded only when Beatrice promised to sleep in her room that night, and added that she was a very light sleeper.

"She's afraid Mike will come for her," Beatrice said flatly after the younger woman had gone to sleep. "I think she crosses the line from therapist to patient starting tomorrow."

She looked at Byron levelly but did not add the rest of the statement that hung in the air. He did not refute or acknowledge the implication that perhaps tomorrow he also would change roles.

"Let's see what tomorrow brings," Charlie said in the lengthening silence. "And tonight I'll level with you both about my own investigation. Afterward you tell me if you want to opt out, or to cooperate. Okay?"

He summarized the incidences of fires that had spread out over a period of six years and ranged from coast to coast. "In each case where we've been able to dig out details, the events are the same generally. People start going mad, terrible things happen, then the hotels burn and it all stops. That was the pattern at Orick, and so far it's the same here."

Byron looked blank. "That's all you have?"

"That's it," Charlie said almost cheerfully. "The way I see it, you two, and anyone else you bring in as part of your team, have the perfect chance to ask questions that the police won't be bothering with. They wouldn't know what to do with answers anyway. First, we need to know just who was in that hotel, or even near it at any given time. Some went mad and some didn't. Why? The people from town here who went crazy over the last few weeks, what was their connection? Who vanished? The story is that four or five men have disappeared, but what does that mean? It's one thing if a settled family man doesn't show up again, and something else if a transient moves on. Presumably the sheriff's men, or state troopers, or *someone* searched the entire reconstructed town for the men who vanished the day of the shooting. Why weren't any of *them* affected? You see what I mean? You can ask questions of that sort and get answers that no one else is in a position to get. I sure as hell couldn't."

Beatrice looked disbelieving. She shook her head. "It doesn't make any sense. Why the hotel? Why not the town as a whole? Why now? They've been working on the place for two years. People have been in and out of every building there hundreds of times without seeing anything out of the ordinary."

Charlie nodded approvingly at her. She'd do,

he told himself again. "All good points. Points I have no answers for. But in every case I've mentioned there is an old hotel that's been closed for many years. And in every case troubles ended when it burned. Sorry, that's all I have to go on, but that's how it is." He turned to Byron whose eyes were narrowed in concentration, all traces of shock gone now. "Is there electricity over there?"

"No. That's one of the things they argued about in the beginning. They decided to keep it the way it was back in 1880 hereabouts. There's a generator unit in a truck for power equipment they're using for construction."

"Another similarity. None of the places was wired, or else the electricity was turned off and had been off for years." He grinned at Beatrice. "You can see how I'm clutching at any straws I can find. You want to think about it awhile?"

She looked at Byron and stiffened at the expression on his face, the intense look of concentration that furrowed his forehead, tightened his mouth. "We can't turn our work into an investigation for an insurance company!" she said sharply.

Byron started and opened his mouth to respond, but Charlie stood up and beckoned Constance. "Let's go for a walk," he said. "Cold or not, there's a bright moon, and they say the desert in moonlight is a rare treat. Game?"

She nodded, as troubled now as Beatrice was. They got into warm coats and started to leave. At the door they were stopped by Byron's voice.

"If we don't help, what then? What will you do?"

"Oh," Charlie said, "talk to the sheriff, the state police, whoever's in charge. See if they'll have a go at it. I think they might."

"That's despicable," Beatrice said. "You don't know what shape those people are in. They need help, not harassment."

Charlie shrugged. "Maybe I know, maybe not. I do know there'll be more just like them if we don't get to the bottom of it. See you in a little bit."

□ □ □

They walked on a dirt road that led away from town. The wind was light now, and the air was fragrant with strange smells, not of leaf mold, but more primitive odors of exposed earth and rocks and the most primeval of plants. Behind them a dog howled, another barked sharply, and in the distance a creature answered, or taunted—a fox or a coyote. The desert glowed in the moonlight. The shadows were the black of the abyss and the light was silver, cold, and alien.

"You're upset with me," Charlie said after they had walked several minutes in silence.

"A little. She's right, you know. Therapist-patient—that's a relationship that should not be subverted for any reason. But you're right too. That's the dilemma."

He grunted, his hand on her arm warm and full of strength.

"As soon as you catch the arsonist, you're through with the job you were hired to do."

This time he didn't bother to grunt. He knew.

"And what difference will it make just to confirm what you already suspect, or even know? That the hotel has something in it that does that to people? An invisible, untraceable, portable something that makes people crazy? I mean, you already have accepted that much."

"Yep. But why not everyone? Why just some people?" His hand tightened on her arm, but his voice was light and easy when he continued. "You haven't said the other thing. I'm out of my depth here. I have to go to the police eventually—why not now?"

She was relieved that he had brought it up. And it was true, that was the other thing that had to be discussed. "Charlie, what if it's a gas? You can't sample it or analyze it. What if it's a ray of some sort? What if it's a mad scientist's escaped discovery? People have searched those buildings and found nothing. What can you do alone?"

"Don't know," he admitted. "But picture the scene. I go into the police station and say: by the way, there's something weird in that hotel. And the kind captain says, I've been over every inch of it, pal. So have the FBI, or the ATF people. Nothing's there. I say, yeah, but look at how those poor people go nuts. And he says, you look at my statistics, pal. Thousands of people go nuts every month. And I take my hat in hand and go home."

"You were convinced," she pointed out.

"I know. But I don't have to state my case to a police captain, or a commissioner, or a mayor, or anyone in a position to tell me I need a rest leave. That helps. Talking to people in Orick, reading all those papers, seeing Polly, it all helps. But, honey, I've had over a month to think about it. Unless and until I get John Loesser with the gas can all I've got is a theory that I don't even believe in yet. So I'm playing it alone for now. But you're right. Eventually we get help. Eventually."

They had been walking downhill for several minutes, a gentle slope that was hardly apparent, but suddenly they both realized that the lights of town had been eclipsed by rocks. Now there was only the silver moonlight, and an uncanny silence. Constance shivered.

"Right," Charlie said briskly. "Back to the house, hot coffee, people."

It was amazing how fast that had happened, he thought with gloom. He had wanted to investigate, see if his idea had any possibility of success. He now doubted that it did, doubted that he could catch his guy with the gas can out on the desert on the way to the hotel. The damn land was just too treacherous.

"You know what makes it so hard, why you'll have trouble convincing anyone else?" Constance said. "Fear. You're touching on two such basic fears. First, fear of insanity. Everyone's afraid of it even if they don't admit it. And fear of the walking dead. Our myths and nightmares, our horror movies are full of that one. Accepting that such a terrible thing could happen shatters every belief system we hang onto. If that's possible, anything is, and that's too frightening to deal with."

The lights of the town returned to view. A dog howled, another barked, and from a vast distance a more primitive creature answered. Its voice sounded mocking.

□ CHAPTER 10 □

THINGS WERE HAPPENING, CHARLIE THOUGHT the next afternoon, just not the right things. A helicopter flew in circles for a time, searching for the missing people; officially four in all, he had learned, including Mike. None of them had been found. A parade of automobiles, jeeps, trucks wound out onto the desert, into Old West, and wound out again. The sheriff returned to ask Byron questions, the same questions, eliciting the same answers, and they were of no help. Byron and Beatrice went to Doctor Sagimore's office, where they were interviewing people. Polly begged off. The sun came out and the day was too warm. The dogs did not bark.

Constance had started listening to the tapes made over the past two days by Byron and his team. In real time, she said with an eloquent shrug. Beatrice returned for lunch, glanced at Polly, and insisted on taking her to Las Vegas, where she put her on a plane headed for home. Polly had become a patient overnight; she had wept in her room all morning.

Most of the day Charlie wandered around the town talking, listening, asking a few questions. He drove over to the new hotel nearing completion—an opulent high rise that looked incongruous on the desert just across the Nevada state line. It was luxurious, with gaming rooms on the first floor, a mammoth swimming pool, playground. Welcome to Nevada, he thought, surveying it. He wandered out back and saw where the train loaded passengers, climbed aboard and walked the length of the train, as richly finished as the hotel, with red plush seats, and gleaming brass fixtures. He chatted with some of the men who had returned to work here. No one was working down at Old West. And finally he returned to the house where Constance was at the kitchen table, still listening to tapes and making notes now and then.

"Package from Hoagley," she said, pointing to a manila envelope. She rubbed her ears.

He had ordered a complete rundown on John Loesser, and here it was. His school days through college, the death of his wife in an airplane accident, the attack that put Loesser in the hospital and evidently killed the Danvers family. Charlie sat down heavily as he read.

"I've got the son of bitch," he muttered after a moment. He stared past Constance. "Today, tomorrow, he'll show up. Soon now."

After another second or two, she said, "Charlie, it's time to bring in the local authorities. You've done your job."

He looked up. His eyes were just like the little pieces of obsidian she had seen for sale at the airport. Apache tears, they were called. He grinned, but it was meaningless; he wasn't even seeing her, she knew.

Constance caught his arm. "Listen," she said quietly. "All day I've been hearing these people talk about the horror down at that place." She picked up a tape and put it down again hard. "Charlie, there are degrees of madness, different manifestations, varying levels of homicidal impulses, or suicidal impulses. The ones affected by whatever is down there are extreme examples. It's as if every repressed murderous thought is activated, set loose. Do you understand what I'm saying?"

They heard the front door open and close; Byron and Beatrice walked into the kitchen. He looked haggard, very pale; even his elegant beard had started to look unkempt. Beatrice was shaking.

"We just heard," Byron said. "One of the sheriff's men who was in the search party today went home and beat his wife senseless. She was five months pregnant, lost the baby. She'll recover, probably. Neighbors subdued the guy, and he curled up and started to cry and hasn't stopped."

"When will it end?" Beatrice cried.

"When the hotel burns," Charlie said.

"For God's sake! Let's tell the sheriff what you know and let them burn the thing down!"

"And then it will just start up somewhere else," Charlie said wearily. "Next month, in three months, next year, sometime."

Beatrice ran to the telephone near the back door. "I'm calling the sheriff. We have to warn people to stay out of there even if we don't do anything else."

Charlie shrugged. "I say we sit tight until we have the firebug and then decide."

"I don't give a damn about the fires and the insurance!"

"Neither do I," Charlie said in a low voice. "But this firebug has something we need. Two things. Information, and immunity. Apparently he can walk in there and set his fire and walk out again unscathed, or else he's so crazy he can't be driven any further. I say we need him before we do anything else. If the sheriff or his men close in on him, there's going to be shooting. Chances he'll survive are practically nil considering the state of everyone's nerves around here."

She stood with her hand on the telephone, meeting his gaze unblinkingly. Then she drew a deep breath and turned away. "One more day," she said. "Tomorrow at this time I won't let you talk me out of telling everything you've told us."

Byron went to make them all drinks and returned to the kitchen with a tray of glasses, which he handed out. "Charlie, have you considered that your man might register in a motel over in Vegas? It's just an hour away. You'd need an army to keep track of who goes in and out at night over there."

Charlie sipped bourbon hardly diluted at all with ice and water. Just right. "He's a city man," he said then. "Same as I am. I've been all over the area today, just trying to get a feel for it, where you can drive in it, how fast. He'll need to do much the same. That's his pattern; it never has varied. He goes in and scouts the area a day ahead of time, then lights his fire and vamooses. I don't think he'll change this time." If Loesser did change this time, lit his fire, made his getaway, it could be years before they got this close again. If Byron hadn't called, he wouldn't have known about Old West until too late, after it became another arson statistic.

Beatrice and Byron left for dinner in Las Vegas soon after this. "I want to get away from here for a few hours," he had said. "And I want to get you away with me."

Constance and Charlie walked to Jodie's. He dropped in at the motel for a chat with the desk clerk, came back, and shook his head. Nothing yet.

The restaurant was filled again, and more subdued than the night before. The conversations were lower, the expressions on the faces of the customers darker. Constance and Charlie sat in a booth near the rear of the restaurant, where he had a good view of the place. They would shoot first, he thought again glumly, and he knew he couldn't blame them a damn bit.

"Well, we might as well talk about it," Constance said after they had sat silently for several minutes. "You or me?"

He grinned, and this time meant it. "You."

"Right. The people on the tapes are all locals, construction workers, or people who were hired to run the shops. You know, the dry goods store, the saloon, all those people. They were out there one other time for an orientation, but it was noisy and filled with the construction crews that day, the saws going, and so on. Again and again they say it was very different on the day of the shooting. Apparently the generator makes a lot of noise, and when it was turned off that day, the quiet was eerie; the town seemed haunted. Many people mentioned that period of stillness, how strange it was. Something frightened them during that short time. Most of it you have to discount as after-the-fact rationalizing, but not all. At least four people complained of dizziness and headaches. The dizziness passed, but the headaches lasted for most of the time, at least until they were all so frightened that they simply forgot about them."

She took a deep breath, considering, remembering the terrified voices, the shrillness and incoherencies and babble. "Anyway, the train blew its whistle on the butte before it was actually in sight, and they turned off the generator, and the few construction people ducked back behind the hotel. They moved the truck that housed the generator so it wouldn't be in view and spoil the effects. That's when, they say, there was the eerie silence, when Trevor Jackson must have got his rifles from his truck. They all seem to have at least two rifles in their trucks."

She shook her head in wonder, then went on. "No one mentioned seeing him do it, but they don't know when else he could have done it. He went inside the saloon through the back door. The train pulled in making a lot of noise, blowing the whistle, and people began to spill out, all laughing, having a good time. The plan was for a few speeches, a welcoming ceremony or something like that. The guests were all shareholders and friends who had gathered in Las Vegas, had a party the night before, and were going to wrap it all up at Old West. Then Trevor began to shoot."

Charlie had listened intently. He relaxed a bit now. "Pretty much the same story I kept hearing from various people who aren't patients. Also, what I got is that the guests on the train have all scattered back to their various homes. If any of them are nuts the family probably won't mention it."

She looked pained at the expression, but she did not protest. "Charlie, there are other implications here. In some cases the insanity and violence seem to come on together, but Trevor had time to get his weapons and ammunition. He must have looked normal to anyone who noticed him. And the sheriff's deputy who went home and beat his wife, he must have appeared normal. They aren't all like Mike, who reacted with instant violence. You don't know what to expect from John Loesser. He may appear to be as rational as . . . as an insurance agent, and be as homicidal as Mike."

"You think Loesser's crazy?"

"Well, of course. I mean, making a career of setting fires, giving up his profession, his entire life apparently in order to do it. Why? You don't?"

"You're the expert," he said with a slight grin. Actually he thought John Loesser was behaving in a totally reasonable way: he searched for and found a nest of vipers and burned them out, then searched again, and again.

They had eaten their meal and were ready for coffee when a waiter dropped a tray with several glasses. Instantly half a dozen men were on their feet, their hands under their coats, or in pockets, in a way that made Charlie hold his breath until someone laughed and they all resumed their seats. The laughter was not picked up, and it had sounded artificial, more a sob than mirth. The waiter had frozen in place. Carefully he moved away from the mess at his feet when a busboy appeared and started to clean it up.

"Let's go home for coffee," Charlie said in a voice that had gone flat and tired.

□ □ □

The next morning Byron called from the doctor's office immediately on his arrival there. "Charlie, I thought you'd better know this. Some forensic people are coming in this morning to take air and dirt samples from Old West. The sheriff's escorting them out around nine."

Charlie felt relief mixed with regret. If Loesser turned up today, this might make him take off again, go to Vegas and wait out the official types, or leave the area altogether. On the other hand, if there was something that could be analyzed and countered, Loesser could wait. They'd find him. He gnawed his lip, frowning at the wall map of the triangle that was made out of the points Old West, Grayling, and the new hotel.

Slowly he narrowed his eyes and moved in closer to the map. He traced a ranch road that wound around rocks, up and down steep inclines, meandered on south. But it was within a mile of Old West at one place, accessible from a dirt road that left the state road there. Another four or five miles. It was possible, he thought.

"Let's go watch," he said to Constance.

She was startled. "I don't think that's a good idea at all."

"Not with them, over here." He pointed to the spot he had picked out, more than a hundred feet higher than Old West, separated from the site by a deep ravine. There was no way to reach the town from that road, he had decided, but that was fine with him. He had no desire to get close to the hotel yet. Not yet. Maybe never.

She studied the map and nodded with some reluctance. Was a mile far enough away? She hoped so. "I'll get the binoculars. We should take the Land-Rover, don't you think?"

He followed her to the bedroom and opened the suitcase, brought out his old Police Special, and loaded it. Then they were ready.

The first part of the drive was fast, on the state road. The next section was six miles long and it took nearly an hour. "It's not even a road," Constance cried out once when the Land-Rover tilted precariously as the left wheels rode up and over a boulder. The land was gray; the sage was gray-green; the sparse grasses were gray. Boulders, dirt, vegetation were all camouflaged the same color, hiding from what? Rimrock was black here and there, and in a sheltered spot or two where winter runoff nourished more growth, straggly trees huddled close together. They were gray also.

The track curved sharply around outcrops, dived down slopes, climbed other slopes at a steep angle, turned back on itself around a deep gouge in the dirt. There were cacti here, dwarfed and thick, with wicked-looking needles. Finally Charlie stopped the car, shaking his head at the next turning place. It was pointless to pretend he could maneuver it. A goat track, maybe, he thought. He visualized the map again. That was supposed to be the road that would take them to the edge of the ravine where they could hide behind rocks and have a clear view of the Old West scene.

"How far do you suppose it is?" Constance asked.

"Maybe a mile. Walk?"

She nodded. "I sure don't want to drive on that."

They walked the last stretch, and came around a turn to see the tourist attraction off to the left. Through the clear air, the buildings were sharp, the railing on the boardwalk visible even without the binoculars. They looked around for a good spot to wait and observe. In the sun, they were too likely to be seen from over there, Charlie decided, but in the shade it was cold. Finally they walked around a boulder to sunlight where they would wait until there was something to see.

"At least it's too cold for snakes," Constance said after they were settled.

Charlie shuddered. Snake country. Scorpions. Black widows. What else had he read about it? Gila monsters? He thought so. In the summer it could reach well over a hundred degrees by this time in the morning, so arid you could dehydrate and die within a couple of hours. And yet, he marveled, it also had a beauty of its own. The air was so clear, the shadows had such sharp edges, were so deep and black, the sky so distant and blue, it was like being in country not yet used, not corrupted somehow.

Now that he was no longer moving, he could see that the gray was not uniform. The rocks had touches of color, streaks of green, flecks of a flashing mineral. Gold? Silver? Quartz? He tried to think of other minerals that would gleam in the sun like that, but he kept coming back to gold, and decided arbitrarily that what he was gazing at was gold. A contrail appeared, two parallel lines as sharp as a geometry problem. Two parallel lines didn't meet when he was in high school, but now they did, he mused. He watched the plane draw the perfect lines, and then stiffened, as he felt Constance draw a deep breath and hold it. A second later he heard it too, the sound of automobile engines.

They moved to the front of the boulder, keeping in shadows now, and watched three cars come into sight one by one on the dirt road behind the old hotel. That road was nearly as bad as the one they had driven, from all appearances; the caution the drivers were showing was apparent. The lead car stopped by the generator truck and a man got out and climbed into the truck, as the car moved out of sight behind the hotel. The other two followed. Suddenly a blast of roiling smoke shot up from the truck, and its roar carried the mile to Constance and Charlie. She felt that she could almost smell the fumes.

"They'll need light in the basement of the hotel," Charlie murmured. "Maybe in the interiors of some of the buildings." The cars had reappeared at the end of the railroad station, and they stopped there; men got out. There were seven in all. Charlie recognized the sheriff, but none of the others, who went to work at once. He and Constance took turns with the binoculars, although there was little worth watching. They took scrapings of paint, samples of dust, parings of wood. They put the samples in vials or plastic bags, labeled everything, then moved on down the street to repeat the action at regular intervals. At the far end several of them walked into view with an orange extension cord and a box. Other wires were plugged into the box, and the men separated, carrying light with them into the hotel and the first building by it. All the work was methodical and precise and slow. None of the conversations carried this far, only the noise of the generator truck; no smoke was showing now.

When he had the binoculars again, Charlie swept the entire town, then continued off to the corral, where the desert started again, up a steep hill that ended in a rimrock. He continued to study the surrounding terrain, back to the town, the railway station. He followed the tracks until they vanished behind a rocky hill, picked them up again only to lose them on another curve. Then he stopped moving. A man was standing in a deep shadow, hands in pockets, Western hat hiding his face; he was also watching the scene in Old West, from that side of the ravine. "Loesser," Charlie said under his breath. "I'll be damned!"

□ CHAPTER 11 □

CHARLIE WATCHED THE MAN HE WAS CERTAIN WAS John Loesser, and Constance continued to watch the activity in Old West. The men had split up into groups; pairs on each side of the street were making systematic searches of the buildings and shops, vanishing into shadows, emerging, padlocking each in turn. In the center of the street, midway between the hotel and train station, three men stood in a tight cluster, talking; one of them was the sheriff, who gesticulated now and then, pointed this way and that, indicated the train tracks, the saloon, with wide-arm motions. The other men were collecting samples of everything that could be scraped up, scooped up, or dug out of wood. Now and then the searchers carried the electric line into the buildings. They moved down the street slowly. Beside her, Constance heard Charlie mutter. He lowered the binoculars and squinted.

"He went behind those rocks," he said. At the same time two of the men approached the hotel, paused on the wide porch, then entered, carrying a light with them.

Constance did not realize she was holding her breath until her chest started to ache and she felt lightheaded. She exhaled softly and felt Charlie's hand on her arm in a firm grip. He was still intent on the rocky slope where the other man had vanished.

Below, the collectors and scientists had finished their chores and were walking back toward the cars. The searchers finished the last building before the hotel and stood as if uncertain that they should enter. One started to walk toward the sheriff, who now left the other two men he had been talking with; they turned to go to the cars also. The sheriff spoke with the two who had finished their side, and they all looked toward the hotel. One must have called out, but his voice did not carry to where Constance was watching. He strode toward the hotel, then turned and went around the side of it to where the generator truck was parked. The two who had gone inside the old building appeared on the porch, one of them winding the electric cable as he walked, dangling the bulb protected by a wire cage. They had all dispersed by now, some of them possibly to the cars, hidden by the train station, when suddenly the man winding the cable dropped everything and fell to his knees, clutching his head. The sheriff ran toward him as another man ran from around the hotel; he threw himself at the sheriff and they rolled in the street. A car revved loud enough that Constance could hear; it plunged from behind the train station and roared across the desert picking up speed as it raced over rocks, over cactus and sagebrush, until it went out of control in a shallow dip and rolled over and over down a slight hill. It came to rest in a cloud of dust that only gradually settled over it. The sheriff had got his gun out by now and he swung it and hit his attacker in the head. Now all the men were running; dust clouds made it impossible to tell exactly what was happening. Men were dragging the injured, half carrying each other, stumbling until they were all out of sight around the saloon. A car sped away, behind the hotel, behind the workers' area, and back up the dirt road, the other car close behind it.

It had all happened so fast, so unexpectedly, that Constance had hardly been able to follow it. She felt drained, exhausted suddenly, and now she let out a long shuddering breath. Beside her Charlie had grabbed her arm hard. "Jesus Christ!" he breathed. "Jesus!"

Neither moved for several minutes. The dust settled down below, but in the street the electric cable looked like a snake, and out on the desert a short distance, the car was unmoving, on its back. No one had emerged from it.

"Let's get the hell out of here," Charlie said. Fear made his voice thick and almost unrecognizable. They backed away from the ridge, watching the old town until they were well away from the rim, and then he hurried her back the way they had come, to where they had left the Land-Rover. His face was set in such rigid lines with a faint sheen of sweat that it looked metallic. And that was the worst of all, Constance thought, terrified. For Charlie to be afraid was the worst of all.

□ □ □

Charlie drove to the motel before returning to their house. Nothing yet. No John Loesser, no late-model black Malibu. But the son of a bitch was in the area, he knew. At the house, he eyed the phone grimly, then looked up the sheriff's number and dialed. His face was still set in rigid lines, his eyes hard and flat-looking.

"Charles Meiklejohn," he said to the phone. "Tell Sheriff Maschi I have to speak to him before he sends anyone in to Old West to collect that body. I'm staying at Dr. Weston's house in Grayling." He hung up.

Constance busied herself making coffee, anything to keep moving, she thought, anything to stop the scene from playing like a tape loop in her head. "How much are you going to tell him?"

Charlie was pacing in quick jerky strides. He did not stop. "I don't know yet. I hope the bastard hasn't already sent a bunch in there. God, I . . ." The phone rang and he snatched it up. "Meiklejohn," he said in a clipped voice. "I called, Sheriff," he said, "to give you some advice. Have you already sent people to Old West to collect the guy in the car that smashed?" He closed his eyes, then said, "Get on the radio, Sheriff, and tell them to keep the engine running all the time they're in there. Whatever it is won't go near them if a motor's running. Can you get the message to them?" He listened, then cut in sharply. "If you don't want some more homicidal maniacs on your hands, get through to them and warn them! I'll be here!" He slammed the receiver down.

Constance had stopped slicing bread, and now resumed. "Sandwiches," she said, "and coffee. Nourishment to see you through when they haul you off to the pokey. I'll visit every day, of course."

He came to her and put his arms around her, rested his cheek against her hair with his eyes closed. "What you'll do is go home and see if the damn cats are starving to death. Okay?"

"Not okay. Then who'll bring you cake and files and such?"

He backed off a bit and held her shoulders, looked directly at her. "I'm not giving them Loesser yet. He's mine."

"I know. Liverwurst and onions, or ham and cheese?"

"You know damn well that's not even a choice!"

"For me it is," she said. The phone rang and he left her to answer again, expecting the sheriff.

He listened, and very softly said thanks and faced her once more. "That was my tame desk clerk. Loesser just checked in." His voice was silky smooth.

□ □ □

Grayling was filled with more outsiders than it had been since their arrival, Charlie noted. More news specials? Probably. He was surprised that Loesser had been able to get a room. He was calling himself Jerry Lawes this time; sticking to his pattern. Charlie nodded when he drove through the motel parking lot and found a year-old black Malibu. Another part of the pattern. The desk clerk had given him the room number—147, first floor rear. The drapes were drawn over the window. Charlie pulled in at an empty slot and got out of the car. Constance came around to get in behind the wheel, and he walked away. At the black Malibu he paused briefly at the driver's side, slipped a flattened wire down the window opening, jiggled it, and opened the door. He pulled on the lights, then closed the door again. He went to room 147 and tapped on the door. When it opened on the chain, he said, "You left your lights on, mister."

The door closed; the drape moved a little, then fell back into place, and the door opened. The man came out and started for the Malibu. Charlie walked by his side and said pleasantly, "We'll take my car instead. But first we'll turn off the lights, just so no one will ask any questions." The man froze, then jerked around to look at Charlie, and Charlie had one more shock. This was not the man in the picture; he was not John Loesser.

"Who are you? What do you want? Get away from me!"

"Mr. Lawes, don't make a scene. Just go on to your car and turn off the lights. Then we'll go someplace and have a talk." Maybe he wasn't John Loesser, Charlie thought darkly, but he was the man he had seen out on the desert watching the mayhem at Old West. The man did not move for another second, and Charlie said even more softly, "I have a revolver in my pocket, Mr. Lawes, and if I shoot you now and say you were out there today when people were going mad and trying to kill each other, why, I think I'd be a hero." Lawes blanched, and they began to walk.

They went to the Malibu, where Lawes turned off the lights; they walked side by side to the car, where Constance was waiting, and they drove back to the house in silence. Charlie thought he could almost hear the machinery at work as Lawes stared ahead: gears shifting, toggles on, toggles off, switches thrown, everything erased to start over. Constance led the way into the house and waited until they were inside to close and lock the door. Charlie studied the man then. About six feet tall, slender, fair complexion, blond hair—all that fitted Loesser's description, but this man did not look like the picture Charlie had memorized. He was not Loesser.

"Who are you?" Lawes demanded.

"Uh-uh," Charlie murmured. "My question. We were just about to have a sandwich. Let's do it now."

□ □ □

Constance began to reassemble the sandwich material and Charlie pulled a chair away from the table. "Please empty your pockets, and then sit down," he said.

Lawes looked from him to Constance and back again. "You're both mad. This is kidnapping! I'm leaving!"

Charlie took his hand from his pocket, bringing out the .38; Lawes stared at it wide-eyed. "At this particular place and time," Charlie said soberly, hefting the gun, then pointing it at Lawes, "it's a little hard to say who is mad and who isn't. I believe most people around here would understand anyone who shot without proof right now. Your pockets."

Lawes continued to stare at the gun as he pulled things from his pockets, moving carefully. There was not much: car keys, motel key, change, cash in bills, a matchbook. No wallet.

No identification. Charlie watched dispassionately. He shook his head when Lawes stopped. "Most people have ID, driver's license, registration. You just have cash. Strange."

Charlie made him turn around and put his hands on the wall and then patted him down; there wasn't anything else. He picked up the roll of bills, five or six hundred dollars, and put it back on the table.

"Take your stuff," he said, moving back a step. "And now let's all sit down and have lunch."

Constance came around the counter with a platter of sandwiches, smiled at Lawes, and went back for the coffee. He stuffed his belongings back inside his pockets. They all froze when the doorbell rang.

Charlie had put his gun away. He motioned to Lawes to move ahead of him. "Do you mind, honey?" he asked Constance. "I'll show our guest the Indian art in our room."

She waited until they had gone into the bedroom at the end of the hall, and then went to see who was at the door. Sheriff Maschi stood there glowering, his face dark red and angry. "I'm looking for Meiklejohn," he said.

"Oh, come in, Sheriff. He's around here somewhere. I'll go find him. Do you want a sandwich?"

He followed her to the kitchen and she hurried ahead to the hall to the bedrooms. The sheriff stopped to wait.

"Sheriff Maschi," she announced inside the

bedroom. Lawes looked desperate. His eyes were examining the room as if seeking an exit.

Charlie glanced from him to Constance. "Mind waiting here until I get rid of him?"

He forced back a grin at the look that swiftly crossed Lawes's face. Constance shook her head, and Charlie walked out, closed the door. At the kitchen he reached for the platter of sandwiches. "Sheriff Maschi, you're just in time for lunch. Let's go to the den." There was a thump from the bedroom. Charlie picked up the platter.

"What was that?" the sheriff demanded, looking past him.

"Just Constance exercising. Come along." He led the way to the den.

□ □ □

Carson Danvers had not believed his luck when Charlie Meiklejohn left him with this woman. He had not even given her the gun, and a glance proved that she did not have pockets capable of hiding a weapon. He waited a few seconds, then moved to the bedroom window. No screen, of course. He unlocked the latch, and she came to his side.

"Charlie really wants to talk to you," she said politely. "Let's sit down and wait for him."

"Another time," Danvers said and shoved the window up all the way. He felt her hand on his arm and shrugged it away, and then found himself sitting on the floor. It happened so fast he wasn't even sure she had done something. She didn't look as if she had done anything. She pulled the window down partway and smiled at him. Gingerly he got to his feet.

"Let's wait for Charlie," she said in her nice low voice. Her smile was as pleasant as it had been earlier. Not a hair was ruffled. "A long time ago," she said easily, "Charlie decided that women should learn to defend themselves if they have to. I wasn't happy about it at first, but then I got pretty good. Our daughter practices, too. Sometimes we put on mother-daughter demonstrations, but I always feel self-conscious when we do. Please sit down. You take the chair; I'll sit on the bed here."

He eyed her silently and she stopped smiling.

"I don't want us to be enemies," she said softly, "but neither do I want you to try to leave. At worst, I'll call the sheriff and I think he'd shoot you, just as Charlie thinks. They are so very afraid right now."

He slumped down on the straight chair. "You don't know what you're getting mixed up in."

"Not as much as you do, I expect. What's down there? What's in the hotel?"

"The devil," he said. "It gets to people and turns them into monsters. And it laughs and looks for the next one to invade. They won't find it with their samples of dirt and paint. It hides until they're unprotected. It's pure evil down there, that's what's in the hotel. Pure evil."

The image of Father Patrick flashed before

her eyes, his face grave and troubled; she heard his warning again. She blinked the memory away and shook her head. "Madness isn't evil. That's medieval superstition. Those people need help, not condemnation."

"You can't help them!" he cried. "They're tools of the devil, past help. All you can do is burn out the evil in the old building and wait for it to show up somewhere else and burn it out there." He hung his hands between his knees and bowed his head, as if exhausted. The scar on his cheekbone had turned bright red. "Once the devil claims them, they're his to do his bidding. You can't help them."

"That's what it means to be insane," Constance said. "It means being irrational, doing things that defy explanation. Turning on people without warning. Many of them simply withdraw, become empty, catatonic. They aren't evil. They're just very ill."

"You don't know," he said miserably. "I've seen them. One minute happy, loving, giving, trusting, then demonic. In a flash they're possessed and get the gun and shoot his mother and father. In the face. He shot her in the face, I saw him, possessed, demonic . . ."

He talked in an undertone, not looking at Constance. She had been as bewildered about who he was as Charlie. Not Loesser. She had studied that photograph, and he was not Loesser. As he talked, she remembered the report the police had filed about the attack on Loesser, the deaths of the Danvers family, their disappearance. She felt a stab of pity for this man.

"Mr. Danvers," she said gently, "the boy loved his parents, both of them. Everyone said so. Something affected his brain. He couldn't help himself; he didn't know what he was doing. He became extremely ill, not possessed, not invaded by evil. He was to be pitied, Mr. Danvers."

He raised his face, haggard and pale and very tired. "You know?"

She nodded. "We know."

He began to sob and somehow she got him to the side of the bed where she put her arms around him and held him as he wept.

□ □ □

"Why'd you lie about who you are?" the sheriff demanded as soon as Charlie led him into the den.

"Now, Sheriff, I didn't, if you'll recall. I introduced Constance and said I was her husband. God's truth. You want a liverwurst with onions?" He poked at the sandwich with a look of distaste. "*She* thinks organs are edible, God help her."

"I don't want no sandwich. Look, Meiklejohn, I want some answers. What are you doing here? Who hired you? To do what? How did you know about the motors down at the old town?"

He stood with his hands low on his hips, like

a gunslinger, Charlie thought with interest. He wondered if they still practiced quick draws. He looked at the sheriff with candor and said, "I'm here for the ride. Constance is a psychologist, reviewing the records of the various problems here. I came along because I didn't have anything better to do. And I figured it out about the engines from reading the reports. Every single instance of madness came about only when things were all turned off over there. It seemed to add up. Worth a shot, anyway." He picked up a ham and cheese sandwich.

Sheriff Maschi drew in a deep breath and reached past him for a liverwurst. "We got our guy out of there without any more trouble. How'd you know about him?"

"No secrets hereabouts," Charlie said, chewing. "If I were you, I'd sure have some barricades put on every road going over there."

"Yeah, yeah. We are. And a guard on each one."

Charlie stopped chewing. "How far away from the town?"

"Far enough." He reached for another sandwich. "Goddamnit! I've been over everything down there half a dozen times! Nothing's in there!"

Charlie nodded with genuine sympathy.

"You really retired? Pretty young to be retired."

"From the New York Police Department? Never too young to retire."

"Yeah, I guess. I've been sheriff for twenty-nine years. Feuds, fights, brawls, shoot-outs, vandalism, survivalists and environmentalists mixing it up, you name it, we've had it here. But this! Last year it was wetbacks and airloads of dope being dropped. Bad news. I'd take back all of it in exchange for what we've got now. All of it, doubled. Wish to hell I was retired, reared back on my porch watching the paint peel on my house."

"You thought about calling in the Feds?"

"Yeah, more and more. Maybe I'll do that. After the reports come in, maybe I'll do that." He finished the last bite of his sandwich and nodded at the platter. "Good. Thanks. Look, Meiklejohn, you get any more ideas, give me a call. Right?"

Charlie walked out to the porch with the sheriff and watched him out of sight, then turned grimly back to the house. Now, he thought, he wanted some damn answers of his own. No more games, Lawes, or whoever the hell you are, he muttered to himself as he strode down the hall to the bedroom. He hoped Constance hadn't hurt him too much, not enough to keep him from talking anyway. He pushed the door open and stopped, completely nonplussed and helpless. The man who had splashed gas on their house, the man he wanted to sock was sitting on the bed in his wife's arms, crying like a baby.

Constance glanced up at him and raised an eyebrow. "We'll be out in a minute or two."

□ CHAPTER 12 □

CHARLIE STALKED TO THE KITCHEN, TO THE DEN, the living room, back to the kitchen. Constance finally appeared.

"He's in the bathroom, be right out."

"He'd better." She passed him, poured coffee and sipped it. When the man entered the kitchen, Charlie stood with his hand clenched.

"Charlie," Constance said from across the room, "this is Carson Danvers. My husband, Charles Meiklejohn."

Carson turned bewildered eyes toward her. "I thought you said you knew."

And Charlie found himself speechless. After a moment he muttered, "I'll be damned!" His anger flared again. "You son of a bitch, why'd you douse my place with gas? I'm going to beat the crap out of you for that!"

Carson Danvers spread his hands helplessly. "I don't know you, anything about you. She said you knew who I am, and even that's a lie. What's going on?"

Charlie turned to regard Constance with suspicion. She tilted her head and sent the message: he's telling the truth, and he felt his hands relax, his shoulders sag a little. "I wish to hell I knew," he snarled.

"You'll have to be John Loesser," Charlie decided two hours later; they had sat in the den talking all that time. Danvers, Loesser, whatever he chose to call himself, was still pale and red-eyed, but he was calm. He had been able to talk about that first attack, what he had done, what he had seen. He had not been able to eat anything. "We have to call you something," Charlie added aggrievedly.

The other man nodded. "I have identification in the glove compartment of my car. John Loesser."

"Okay. So I hired you to assist me in this investigation. That's covered. But damned if I know what you'll do, or what I'll do either, as far as that goes." Something about Loesser nagged at him, and suddenly he realized what it was: he had the glinty eyes of a fanatic. Religious fanatics, political fanatics, sports fanatics, they all seemed to share that one common trait; their eyes glittered. John Loesser's eyes glittered. And Charlie knew precisely what John Loesser would do as soon as he had the chance. The glittery eyes, the scar on his cheek that flamed now and then, even his gauntness added up to a picture of a man driven by forces he could not resist. He wondered if Loesser ate or slept when he knew the thing was loose in a hotel again.

John Loesser drank coffee and put the cup down. "The same pattern will hold as before. They'll look for radiation, chemicals, gas, anything. And they won't find a thing. Eventually they'll go away. I go in and burn the building down and everything stops. Pretty soon people don't remember much about it."

"To start somewhere else," Charlie muttered.

"Next week. A month. Three or four months. It starts again somewhere else." He shook his head. "I've tried to help them. Two different times I sent letters, made calls, told them everything I could think of, and it was the same. They go in and get samples, or look around. If they turn off the lights, or engines, whatever, they go mad—many of them go mad—and they hurt each other. They go back with others, and try to find something again, more men, armed men, same thing. Over and over. I tell them to keep motors running, and if they do, they don't find anything. If they don't they go mad. Same over and over." He grinned a crooked grimace. "One of *them* burned the hotel once. Beat me to it. They knew, and called it unsolved, another arson fire."

Constance had been writing. Now she looked up from the table. "Were all the buildings wooden—frame buildings?"

"Yes."

She made another note and frowned at the paper before her. "Why just here? Why not in Asia, Africa, Europe?"

"We don't know that it isn't happening in other places," John said. "No one but the three of us knows there's cause to link the incidents in this country."

"Well, we have to tell them that," she said almost absently, gazing again at the notes she had written. She did not see the way John Loesser's jaw became rigid, how the scar flared, the way his hands clenched. Charlie did and became more wary than before. "What I have," Constance said in her practical manner, "is a list of similarities. One, the hotels are always isolated, at least a mile from other buildings where there are activities going on. Two, they all were wooden. Three, they don't have electricity, or it isn't working. Four, not everyone is susceptible to whatever happens. Five, the madness has no particular pattern. Six, people who are affected seem to have a compulsion to return to the hotel. Seven, neither time, distance, nor treatment seems to alleviate the psychological condition. I'll have to look into that one to make sure," she murmured, and wrote.

"You forget a couple of things," John said savagely. "The dead people get up and walk through the doorway to hell. Their bones turn up later."

Constance turned her pencil over and over and shook her head. "We don't know that."

"You're just like the others," he said with great bitterness. "There's a line you can't cross, isn't there?"

Constance studied him and finally nodded. "Yes. Of course. That's true of everyone, including you. How hard did you try to get help? Did you go in person to the police? Of course not. You sent anonymous letters, made anonymous phone calls. You knew as well as I that you would be ignored; you would be free to carry on your own private vendetta, and when they did look into the situation, without the links between all the hotels, without your personal testimony, they would be stymied. You dealt with your own guilt by ignoring the implications, hiding behind superstition about the thing you burned out again and again. What drove you to that, Mr. Danvers? Fear? Afraid of crossing the line to examine what might really be in those hotels? This is much bigger than a personal vendetta, and you know it. It's going to break wide open, possibly right here in Old West, in Grayling, and then how will you manage your fear and guilt?"

He looked as if he were ready to leap from his chair and start running, perhaps never stop. Before he could move, Charlie murmured,

"That's a funny thing about it always being a hotel. Why? Why not abandoned farmhouses, or barns, or warehouses, or anything else you can name? In this country most of them are made of wood, if that's the deciding factor."

John leaned back in his chair. "I couldn't find a reason."

"Me neither, not yet anyway. Let's brainstorm. What do hotels have in common besides many rooms?"

"Lobbies," Constance said.

"Long halls," John added after a moment.

"Did they all have more than one floor?" Charlie asked. John nodded. "More than two?"

John Loesser frowned, remembering. "The ones I had anything to do with all had at least three. Two of them had four floors."

Constance wrote: *three or more stories*.

"Why did you always start your fires on the second floor, near the center of the building?" Charlie asked.

"I wanted to get as near the door as I could."

"The door. You've mentioned it before, but why those particular doors, not just any door?"

"*His* door," John Loesser said. Constance snorted, and he went on almost desperately, "The door the devil comes through."

Charlie remembered one of the rumors he had heard, that some footprints had gone to a door that connected two rooms and stopped there. "You said it was like a shadow that filled the doorway."

"Not really. Like a void. Emptiness. I turned

my flashlight on it and the light just stopped there, not like shining a light into the dark of a room."

"Did you ever try to go through it?"

John looked as if Charlie had gone mad. "I tossed a rock in once. It just vanished. I went to the other side, out through the hall into the next room. No rock. Just the blackness, the void. All the way to the top, side to side, down to the floor. No doorway, just the void, the entrance to hell."

"How high are those doors in the old hotels? A standard door is six-eight."

"Higher. Eight feet, three and a half feet wide. Over my head a good bit. At least eight feet."

"Another similarity," Charlie muttered, wishing he knew what to do with the similar items.

Soon after that Byron and Beatrice came back. They were both showing the strain of interviewing shocked survivors all day. Beatrice looked near tears when she sat down with a large drink.

"The same thing over and over. How could it happen to Mary, or Ralph, or Tommy? What's wrong with Susan? Why did so and so turn on me that way? I loved him, her, whoever." She held up her glass in a mock salute. "Cheers."

"What do you tell them?" John asked, watching her.

She and Byron had accepted him as Charlie's assistant without question. Beatrice shrugged and said wearily, "There's not a lot to say, now is there?"

Byron tossed a couple of tapes to the table. "We're mostly trying to keep them talking for now," he said. "We're encouraging people to say everything that comes to mind dealing with this . . . phenomenon, so that it won't sink below consciousness and return to cripple them at a future date. The therapy is a bit difficult." He was as tired as Beatrice, as frustrated and helpless as Charlie. He looked at John Loesser, then at Constance and Charlie. "We don't know what the hell we're doing, that's the problem. We don't know why those people went mad, why Carlos turned on Luisa, why Mike tried to kill Polly, why . . ." He stopped abruptly as his voice started to get shrill. "Sorry," he said and went to the bar to pour himself bourbon.

Constance had been listening distantly, thinking of the list of similarities she had jotted down. That was part of it, she thought, but all along they had been ignoring the other part, the people who actually went mad. "Byron," she said, "we need to look into those cases. Maria Eglin, the Dworkin sisters, the others. Who was it, Carlos? As many as we can."

"Not my field," he said.

"Mine neither, but we have to. Look, if there are lesions, physical damage of any sort from chemicals, from anything, that's one thing, but if the primary maladaptive functions are endogenic in nature without any immediate activating agent, it's a different avenue of approach. Have there been autopsies yet of any of the affected people? I want to know if there have been lesions found. Not in the cortex, or neocortex, obviously, but perhaps the hypothalamus? Who would know?"

Byron's look had changed from impatience to interest. "A hallucinogenic? Something like that? It could be. A chromosomal examination . . ."

Charlie turned to John Loesser. "Didn't you say you could cook? It's that or Jodie's restaurant, or my scrambled eggs. There they go." He watched Constance, Byron, and Beatrice seat themselves at the kitchen table and start to make sketches, diagrams, God alone knew what, he thought. "Let's go shopping."

John Loesser was watching Constance with near fascination. She was too many people, he decided, too complex to comprehend. He found his gaze moving on to Beatrice, so dark against the fairness of Constance, and for the first time in over six years, regarding this young woman who looked like an Indian, he felt the pangs of longing for a woman other than Elinor. When Charlie touched his arm, he was startled from a great distance away. "I'd like to cook," he said.

"We'll need to know if they've done CAT scans, EEG's, what drugs they've tried, what effects . . ."

Charlie and John left without drawing the attention of anyone at the table. And that was Constance in her working persona, Charlie thought happily. He admired her more than he could express.

□ □ □

Outside, Charlie said, "If I had a can of gas in my trunk, I'd be scared to death the sun on it would set it off. Gets cold as any pole here at night, but that old sun heats up real fast real early."

John Loesser stood without motion for a few seconds. "I won't bolt," he said. "Why didn't you turn me in when the sheriff was here?"

"I didn't think you would," Charlie said. "Let's walk. It's only a couple of blocks to the store they call a supermarket. Only a couple of blocks to the motel, too."

"Let's get my car then." He laughed shortly. "I'll move my spare gas into the shade somewhere. You didn't answer. Why didn't you turn me in?"

"You're the only person I know who can walk into that place and walk out again. Seemed a shame to lock you away somewhere."

John Loesser stopped again. His voice was strained now when he spoke. "I told you what I know. It's the devil in there. They won't find anything, and your wife won't." She would want to reason with it, he thought with bitterness. Devise tests for it, find out what made it work, how it operated, why. But no reasoning was possible with evil. It was its own excuse, and Constance did not, maybe could not, understand that one basic truth about it. "I'm going to torch it, Charlie. I have to."

"Maybe you will and maybe you won't. Maybe I'll help you when the time comes. I know a few tricks you haven't thought of. Let's get your car and shop before the store closes."

Jodie's parking lot was jammed full; two California state police cars were there, and an ABC television van. Charlie steered John across the street, and approached the motel from the opposite direction. When they drew near the small lobby, they could see a nattily dressed woman and a man in jeans with a camera slung over his shoulder, talking to the desk clerk.

"You want to move in with us?" Charlie asked.

"Yes. The damn fools will get into the hotel somehow. The new thrill of the week in thirty seconds, after this little message."

"Right. Let's get your gear and your car and beat it before someone spots us and wants an eyewitness account of the strange happenings in that sleepy little town on the edge of the great California desert. Come on."

□ □ □

Carson Danvers had been a master chef; taking an alias did not change that. He had bought an ordinary piece of pork, Charlie knew, and common things like tarragon and cream and wine, potatoes, carrots, and salad makings. Yet he transformed them into a gourmet meal, and in under an hour. It just wasn't fair, Charlie thought, that he verged on gauntness.

Over coffee, Beatrice asked, "Have you been a detective very long, Mr. Loesser?"

He had flushed over the praise, and now he said very gravely, "I'm not really a detective. I'm more an authority on old buildings." And that was the truth, he added silently. He probably knew more about old abandoned hotels in the United States than any other living person.

"Isn't there a television around here somewhere?" Charlie asked. "I think Grayling's made the big time with the news."

Beatrice remembered where it was and John went with her to get it from one of the bedrooms. They all watched the news at ten. As Charlie had said, the sleepy little town had made the big time.

"How do you account for those happenings?" a pert young woman asked a bearded man. Beatrice and Byron had groaned together when he was introduced.

"Mass hysteria, more likely than not. It has happened again and again through the ages, you see. One adolescent girl faints and sets off a pattern of fainting, that sort of thing. As soon as the focus swings away from the people caught up in a movement such as that, the occurrences stop. A year later no one wants to talk about it. Ashamed, you know; they feel foolish and can't account for their own behavior."

Byron switched channels twice. Grayling took thirty seconds on one newscast, an entire minute on another, and was not mentioned at all on a third.

In their room later, Constance asked Charlie, "Can we trust John Loesser to stay put?"

He grinned and held up car keys. "I picked his pocket. There was another key in a magnetic contraption under the fender. I found it too."

"That poor man," she said then with great compassion.

He nodded. "You know the best thing about this damn cold house?"

"What?"

"Bed. A warm bed, cold room, hot woman."

She groaned and bit his neck.

□ □ □

Late the next morning Constance hung up the telephone and went searching for Charlie. He and John Loesser were going over every case step by step. John knew about all of them that Charlie knew, and several others. Constance watched them from the doorway to the den for several seconds as she thought out her plan. Better to drive to Las Vegas and fly to Los Angeles, or just drive the two hundred miles and be done with it?

"Charlie," she said then, "you remember Jan Chulsky?"

He looked blank. "Nope."

"Of course you do. She came to our wedding.

We exchange cards and even talk now and then, at least several times over the years. We went to school together."

A patient expression settled on his face as he waited.

"She's treated some of those people up in the state hospital, and she'll be in Los Angeles for the next few days. She commutes."

Charlie nodded and turned to say to John, "Now we'll see the old boy network swing into operation."

"The question is," Constance said, ignoring the comment, "do I want to drive to Las Vegas and fly, or just drive over. I'd have to land at the L.A. airport. Ugh. I'll drive."

"And this is known as thinking on your feet," Charlie added to John. "Want me to tag along?" he asked Constance.

This time she looked blank. "What for?"

He followed her to the bedroom where she packed enough for overnight. "Jan's going to have the records printed out for me by the time I get there. And I'll spend the night in her apartment and drive back tomorrow. I'll call and tell you when. Oh, her number." She made a note of it for him. "And you'll keep away from that place, won't you?"

He embraced and kissed her. "There's no place on earth I want to visit less than Old West at this particular time. Be careful out on the desert."

Charlie and John continued to compile data until shortly after four, when Charlie stretched and yawned. Strange how empty the house felt, he thought for the third or fourth time. As soon as Constance was gone, a house felt like a simple building; when she was inside with him, her presence seemed to fill it. He was aware of her at all times then, moving about the kitchen, in her study, in the bedroom, out digging or planting in the garden—even that counted. But this house felt bleak and empty and cold. The coldest damn house he'd ever spent any real time in. It leaked air at every joint, every window, around the doors. Must be a bitch in the summer when the air leaking in would be superheated.

John leaned his head forward into his hands, propped up on the table. "We have to tell the police," he said dully, surprising himself with the realization.

"Yeah. I'm afraid so." So far they had amassed information that said forty-two people had died; an unknown number was in various mental institutions around the country; and a further unknown number was suffering the after-effects of the attacks. Twelve people had vanished. And, as Constance had warned early on, they just knew about the ones who made it into the records. How many more were being treated privately? Unanswerable.

"Okay," John said. He was benumbed by the totality of the figures. He had managed not to think about the victims. That had not been his job, he had decided long ago; there was nothing he could do about any of them. His job was to track down the devil and burn it out when he found it. And it wasn't working. It just appeared somewhere else and started over again.

"They'll arrest me," he said, and found he did not care. That never had been a real consideration. Freedom had meant only that he could find it again and burn it again, and try to make it up to Elinor and Gary, the two people he had loved beyond expression, the two people he had failed.

"What for?" Charlie asked, and they both thought of Constance asking just that, with just that inflection a few hours ago, when he had asked if she wanted him to go with her. Charlie grinned. "They say that people who live together begin to look alike after a while. Not us, no sir. We just talk alike. But it's a valid question. You're a respectable independent public insurance adjuster, dragged into this because I needed your expertise since you've been following these arson fires for the past several years. It'll fly."

"There hasn't been any arson here."

"Right. I made the connection between the fires and the cases of people losing their marbles, unprovable at this point, but worth investigating. I called on you to help." He shrugged. "And besides, do you give a shit if they believe me? What can they do, thumbscrews?" He grinned again, this time enjoying the thought. "Sore Thumb will have a fit when he finds out I've blabbed his little secret."

Charlie had to leave a message for the sheriff

again. He called back within a few minutes. "It's out of my hands, Charlie," Sheriff Maschi said with evident relief. "The governor turned the whole damn mess over to the state police. They're sending in their team first thing in the morning."

"That won't quite do," Charlie said. "It's bigger than the state police, I'm afraid."

There was a long pause, then the sheriff said, "You at the house still? Might drop in for a sandwich, cup of coffee, something."

"Bourbon?"

"Sounds good to me. Five minutes."

"What the hell," he said in less than five minutes when Charlie put a glass of bourbon, hardly touched by ice or water, into his hand. "It's after five, and I ain't got any duties to speak of right now."

Charlie introduced John Loesser, the insurance adjuster, and the sheriff didn't ask him a single question. He leaned back on the couch in the den, put his feet on the coffee table laden with papers, and savored his drink.

Charlie straddled one of the wooden chairs, just as relaxed as the sheriff, and started to talk. Only John couldn't be still. He moved around the room, touching this, straightening that, studying the map on the wall, and finally interrupted. "I'm going to make something to eat. You want some dinner, Sheriff?"

The old man nodded, keeping his steady gaze on Charlie, his face as unreadable as a piece of the desert. Beatrice and Byron arrived home;

Beatrice went out to help John; Byron joined Charlie and the sheriff. Every day he and Beatrice looked more exhausted, more helpless.

Charlie did not reveal John Loesser's identity, or that he had set the arson fires; he told the rest of it. When he finished, the sheriff handed him his empty glass. Charlie got up and refilled it, refilled his own, and waited.

"You know it don't make a bit of sense," the sheriff said finally. "Why didn't you tell me yesterday?"

"Tell what? Like you said, it don't make a bit of sense."

"And there ain't been no fire here, neither. What brought you to this place if you're investigating fires?"

Charlie shrugged. "It's exactly like Orick, except for the fire. And Camden, and Longview, and Moscow, Idaho, and all the others, except for the fire. Guess I thought that would come, too."

"I called him about Old West," Byron said tiredly. He looked ten years older than he had appeared in San Francisco in October. "We were up at Orick at the same time; I knew he was looking into something that might have a bearing on my work. So I called him."

Sheriff Maschi was frowning at nothing in particular now. "Dick Delgado is taking charge," he said finally. "Young, forty maybe, ambitious. Lorrimer, the owner of Old West and the new hotel, is upset. He wants this all straightened out right now, wants his men back on the job over there, wants any shadow removed, superstitions put to rest, wants his grand opening. So he puts a bug in the governor's ear and the governor brings in the state investigators and they tell me to herd my cattle and let them get on with the business of clearing up a non-mystery. Suits me. Four months I'll have my thirty years, and I'll be sixty-five. Both together. Four months. Hate to think I could blow it, and I know damn well that if I tangle with Dick Delgado, I blow it real good. They want that attraction to open for the Christmas trade, you know. Jesus Christ, Charlie, I wish you'd stayed home."

"So do I, Logan," Charlie said softly.

The sheriff looked at his drink and set it down. He got to his feet and went to the wall map. He reached up and pointed to the wall above it. "Up there's Death Valley. And over here is the Devil's Playground." He touched the map in an area only a dozen miles or so from Grayling. "Devil's Playground," he repeated. "Only seems to me the devil ain't playing games. Seems he's playing for keeps."

"Sheriff," Byron asked then, "if you can accept this, why don't you think this other man will? Delgado? We can tell him exactly what Charlie's told you."

Sheriff Maschi waved his hand, as if waving away gnats. "Not what Charlie told me so much as what I saw for myself. I saw those men go crazy. Dick Delgado ain't seen anything like that yet. He'll have to see it for himself. And I figure he will tomorrow. He will."

"What do you mean?" Charlie asked, but he already knew the answer.

"He's getting a crew together in the morning, and they aim to go in there and prove there ain't nothing in there and never has been. First thing in the morning."

□ CHAPTER 13 □

"SHERIFF," JOHN LOESSER SAID, "THEY WON'T listen to you. That captain won't believe he can't just walk in and take charge and put an end to it. That's what they always think. Would it help if you could get some outsiders to tell them what happened in other places? I mean cops, even army officers."

"You got names like that?" Sheriff Maschi regarded him with more interest than he had shown before.

"I'll give you some names," John said, and sat down on the couch, started to write. His hand was shaking so much his script looked like that of an old man.

Charlie watched him also for a moment. John's scar was vivid, his face pale; a line of sweat was on his upper lip. "Our resident expert," he said to the sheriff in a light tone. "He's been watching this thing happen for several years." The sheriff made a noncommittal sound.

There were five names on the list John handed over after a minute or two. Names and towns, no phone numbers. "They shouldn't be too hard to reach. The towns are pretty small, like Grayling."

The first name was Foster Lee Murphy. John remembered him quite well. He had marched eight men into a plantation mansion that had been turned into an inn and finally abandoned altogether. He remembered the live oak trees shrouded with pale Spanish moss, the wraith-like fog that drifted head-high and was warm. He never had felt warm fog before that night. He had watched from behind an oak tree that spread its arms out over a hundred feet, arms as thick as an average tree trunk, also warm. Earth, trees, fog, all warm that night. It had been a noisy night, with insects, a whippoorwill, tree frogs in full voice. And then the shooting. Screams. Foster Lee Murphy had taken eight men in; six ran and stumbled out. At three in the morning of the next day, John had gone in.

He had heard nothing of what the sheriff said on the telephone, but when Maschi hung up, his face was bleak. "Noxious swamp gas," he said. "Murphy says the official report lists toxic fumes from an upwelling of swamp gas as the cause of the illness there." He put his finger on the next name. "Luke Hanrahan."

The hotel had been on a bluff overlooking the Mississippi River. One man had walked over the edge; one had vanished. John had watched from across the river the fumbling attempts to find the evil by surrounding it first and advancing in a solid line. A great tugboat pushing a long river train of cargo had saved the men. John had felt precisely when *it* turned off, when it turned on again after everyone had left, but first one man had walked off the bluff; one had gone into the hotel and had not returned, ever.

Maschi said without inflection, "One guy went AWOL; one tripped and fell off a cliff while under the influence of alcohol. Case closed." He tried one more name, and this time was told that a few men on an investigation of drug dealers had got hold of and tried some bad dope.

Silently John went to him and took the piece of paper from his hands, tore it in half, and let the pieces fall to the floor. "Forget it," he said. He walked from the room.

Sheriff Maschi made a few more calls, an FBI agent he knew in the area, a captain in the state investigation office, others. Tomorrow, they all said; they would look into the matter tomorrow. He put in a call to Delgado; it would be returned, the answering sergeant said. He put in a call to the lieutenant governor; that one also would be returned. He tried to call the local representative in Congress and got an answering machine. Finally he walked away from the telephone, his face expressionless.

"You mean no one will listen?" Beatrice asked incredulously. "That's insane!"

"Not really," Sheriff Maschi said. "It's the chain of command. Probably the lines are hot with calls going in for Delgado. And probably he's telling them all there's nothing to be worried about, the sheriff's a senile fool who got kicked off a case and is expressing his discontent."

In spite of the distractions, John had prepared another superb dinner. He was incapable of cooking anything but excellent food. He ate very little of it, and no one talked during dinner except for comments on the meal. Shortly after that Sheriff Maschi took Charlie's arm and they went back to the den.

"I'll be watching in the morning," the sheriff said. "Want a ride?"

"To where?"

The sheriff went to the map and put his finger on a spot. "I figure about here, about a mile away, safe distance, I'd say."

"No road," Charlie murmured, looking at the spot.

The sheriff snorted. "People's been traveling that desert a good many years without worrying overmuch about roads. Around seven?"

Charlie nodded and soon after that the sheriff left. Charlie returned to the map and studied the terrain carefully. He was startled by John's voice at his side.

"Forty-two dead. How many more tomorrow morning? I'm going in, Charlie. Tonight."

Beatrice and Byron were at the kitchen table talking in low voices. Charlie glanced at his watch. Twenty minutes before nine. The supermarket closed at nine.

"Let's take a walk," he said.

John couldn't do it alone, he was thinking as they walked in the clear, cold air. That was the problem, the only problem. Men were staked out on the road leading into Old West, and that meant he would have to go cross-country, and that meant not alone. The sheriff might be able to do it, but not John Loesser, not Charlie, at least not at night. He visualized some of the crevices he had steered around carefully, some of the boulders that had almost upended the Land-Rover, and that was in broad daylight. And the Land-Rover was high; it could clear rocks that John's car would not clear. The sheriff's deputy had come to collect all of Mike's belongings, including his car; they would have to use John's Malibu. Charlie grinned bleakly at the thought. This was what he had set out to do: find the son of a bitch and his black Malibu. And he had. He had.

In the grocery he bought a quart of orange juice in a waxed carton, a box of cereal, a package of waxed paper, a gallon jug of milk, and a package of candles. There were six twelve-inch tapers in the box. John watched, mystified. He had expected them to buy lighter fluid, or kerosene, or something flammable.

"It's a multipart problem," Charlie said as they walked back to the house. "We can't get closer than half a mile, maybe more like a mile, with the car. And the men staked out will be looking down there from time to time. As soon as they see a blaze, they'll be down there, and they will have trucks or cars. Two, three minutes at the most, not enough time to get out before they get in. You've had a clear shot at it before, but not this time. So we prepare our little time bombs and get the hell out before there's a blaze to see. If we do it right, the building will go up like a torch, no problem there, and we'll be well away from it."

"You can't go in there, Charlie. Not half a mile, not even a mile. My God, you should know that by now."

"I don't intend to," Charlie agreed. "I stay with the car, with the motor running, the getaway car, as we call it in the trade."

At the house Charlie paused to gaze at the moon rising over the rocky hills. It was large, not quite full. Good news and bad news, he thought. They would be more visible in moonlight, but without it he doubted they could find their way in at all. He had counted on the moon, and at the same time knew it could add shadows and distort sage, turn it into lurking monsters or boulders. Well, he thought, you do what you can. No more, no less. He turned to enter the house.

"I know why I'm doing this," John said then in a low voice. "But why are you? You could sit back like the sheriff and just let it happen."

Charlie shrugged. "Damned if I know," he said lightly. "Keep thinking we need time, need real plans, need deliberation. We don't need to charge in and hope for the best. We're buying time, that's all." But it was more than that. He thought of the snappily dressed young woman he had glimpsed in the motel lobby, and her cameraman; thought of the bright young men in the state police force, the other reporters in the area, the innocent, ignorant bystanders. All hell would break loose, he knew, if they didn't do this tonight. Delgado and his men, armed men, going mad, others rushing in for the story, the thrill—all going mad. He thought of Maria Eglin, standing like a stony-faced doll, mad. And Polly, who had witnessed the madness at first hand, and might not be good for anything for a long time because of it. He shrugged again. "You play cards? Got any cards?" John shook his head, and it was just as well.

Actually Charlie had his own deck of cards that he always traveled with. He did not offer to play with anyone, but started laying out solitaire. He lost and gathered them up, shuffled, and started over. Beatrice and John talked in the den. Byron read through reports until nearly eleven and went to bed. Beatrice went to bed soon after that. Without looking up from his cards, Charlie said, "Why don't you rest? I'll call you."

John hesitated, then went to his room and lay on his bed, staring at the ceiling. He knew he would not sleep. He never slept before he faced the devil again.

Charlie dealt the cards over and over for the next hour, then he put them away and retrieved his bag of groceries, which he had left on the porch. He retrieved John's can of gasoline from the side of the house and took it in. He poured the milk out in the sink, rinsed the jug and set it to drain. He started to pour out the juice, but filled two glasses first, and emptied the rest. As he worked, he sipped the orange juice. He emptied the cereal into the garbage, prodded it down out of sight and covered it with crumpled newspaper. Then he got out the candles and measured one against the cereal box, trimmed it to size, and put it down, and repeated this with the juice carton, cutting a second candle to fit inside with about an inch and a half to spare. He trimmed the wick ends of the candles to expose nearly an inch, and dropped all the shavings and the extra pieces into the cereal box. He pushed the waxed-paper lining down the sides of the box, and began to tear more waxed paper from the supply he had bought. He crumpled each piece and pushed it down in the box until the mass was several inches high; then he worked one of the candles down through it so that it was upright, supported by the paper nest he had made. He added more paper until the box was two-thirds filled. He cut through the juice carton, making a hinged lid, and wiped out the interior, and then made a second paper nest for a second candle. He surveyed them both and nodded. He closed the carton and the cereal box and put them both on the table; they looked perfect, he decided. Now he went to the bedroom and looked at the Indian blanket on the bed, but found he did not want to destroy that. It was too beautiful. He removed it and took the second blanket instead, an old brown one that looked like Army issue. He started back to the den, paused at the bathroom and added two towels to his bundle, and continued. John came from his room and followed him silently. Charlie put his finger to his lips and took his supplies to the den, returned to the kitchen and got the bottle of salad oil and took it back to the den. He closed the door this time. Moving without haste he spread the blanket on the floor, laid the two towels on it, and then sprinkled them with the oil. It pooled and puddled, as he had known it would. He left it to soak in and went out to pour gasoline into the gallon milk jug. Finally he cut a strip from the edge of the blanket, put it aside, and then began to assemble his package. He folded the blanket in at both sides to cover the towels, then folded the entire package lengthwise and put the jug of gasoline and the cereal box and orange juice carton in a row on it. He wrapped them all neatly, used the strip he had cut to bind the whole thing, and had enough left over to form two loops. He stood up, lifted the bundle, and slipped his arms through the loops; it looked like an ungainly bedroll. It was ten after one.

At the same time Constance lifted her foot from the accelerator with a jerk. Automatically she glanced at the rearview mirror. She had hit eighty-five again, she realized, clutching the steering wheel in a death grip. She did the arithmetic again; she was about ninety miles from Grayling, eighty miles of which was Interstate 15 and the remaining ten miles state road. Less than two hours. And Charlie was probably asleep, sprawled on the bed, his arm flung out on her side, as if searching in his sleep for her.

At eleven she had realized that she would not sleep in her friend Jan's apartment that night. For several minutes she had resisted her impulse to leave, had got a drink of milk, nibbled on a cracker and cheese, settled down once more to read through the various reports Jan had gathered for her. Finally she had tossed her few things back in the overnight bag and left, taking the papers with her. Nothing had come with the feeling, only the intense need to go back, to make certain Charlie was all right. Go back, go back. It had come down to just that: Go back!

The first hundred miles had taken more than two hours. She had had to find a gas station, fill up, get out of the Los Angeles traffic, head north in the maze of freeways. The next ninety miles would take an hour and a half at the most, closer to an hour. On both sides of the interstate the land had yielded to desert, wrapped in the surreal light of the oversized moon. The landscape was grotesque with elaborate shadows that seemed to have nothing to do with the objects that cast them. The land was silver and black under the luminous sky, and on the highway eyes appeared behind her, came close enough to blind her, then turned into glaring devil eyes that dwindled and disappeared. Monstrous trucks with thousands of red eyes rushed on her, swerved, vanished, and the roar existed in her ears without the substance. Her car shuddered.

□ □ □

At two Charlie and John left the house quietly. Charlie drove the Malibu. He had memorized the map, knew exactly where he had to leave the state road, head out across the desert. He did not hum under his breath, although if John had not been with him, he would have.

They drove southwest, skirting a rocky hill north of the road. Charlie slowed at four and six-tenths miles, and turned off the highway shortly after that. They would follow the base of the hill to its northern extremity, then turn and zig-zag up a slope until they were on the ridge overlooking Old West. On a road map it would seem a snap, but the topographical map had shown the route to be treacherous and deceptive. Old rivers had gouged the land here; there was a dry lake bed, with areas of quicksand remaining where the poison alkaline waters had gathered below the surface, trapped by hardpan, or an impenetrable rock ledge. The rocky hills had been shaken by earthquakes more times than history could record. Rocks had slipped and slid, piled up precariously only to be dislodged days or even minutes after the cartographers had gone, changing the topography, sometimes beyond recognition.

But Sheriff Maschi said he intended to drive in and would watch from that ridge, Charlie told himself firmly. That meant it was accessible. Period. As soon as he left the highway, he turned off his lights, and he and John sat silently waiting for their eyes to adjust.

Finally Charlie began to drive. Within two hundred yards, the car lurched and came to a grinding stop at an angle. Neither man spoke for several moments. "Not a shadow," Charlie said then. Carefully he opened his door and looked out over a drop-off on his side; five or six feet only, but enough to roll them. More carefully he backed up a few yards and stopped again. "Okay," he said. "One of us has to walk it first, guide the other one in. Take turns. You want to go first?"

John had not made a sound during this. Now he swallowed hard and nodded. "Sure."

It was excruciatingly slow. John walked in a back-and-forth pattern, making certain there was room for the car to move in. Once he and

Charlie had to roll a boulder out of the way to avoid backing up hundreds of feet. The dry lake gleamed smooth and deadly off to the left. All around them the desert seemed frozen: no animal stirred, no night bird flew or rustled; everything was holding its breath, waiting for them to pass. Then Charlie was the guide, walking back and forth, beckoning as he went. They turned at the edge of the hill and started the last part of the trip. It was three in the morning. The shadows had shrunken, hugged the sage and rocks, creating small black caves at the bases. Charlie was guiding when the Old West town came into view. He stopped and gazed at it in the moonlight. It was less than a mile away, two hundred feet below them. The buildings were shadows looming above the land; the two old buildings with silvered wood caught the moonlight and reflected it eerily. The hotel looked bigger than Charlie remembered; he knew that was a trick of the light, nothing more. He moved on, waving to John to follow. This was not a good place to stop. They needed an area where they could turn the car, have it pointing out when the job was done. They would drive back around the hill, stop and wait for the fire to rout the thing in the hotel, and then return to watch it burn. By then there would be enough morning light to allow them to drive out faster than they had come in. By then the state police would have their hands full down there, not be watching for strays on the desert, they hoped. The only real danger in all this, Charlie told himself again, was in showing a light in the darkness. That would be visible for miles. He found a spot where John could turn the car around with half a dozen forward and backward maneuvers. Then they both stood and regarded the scene below. Less than a mile, Charlie thought with some uneasiness, but the car's engine noise was behind him, signaling safety.

Charlie returned to the car and pulled out the pack he had assembled, slipped his arms through the loops.

"I'm going down," John Loesser said at his elbow.

"Nope. There may be a guard down here. And he could be crazy as a bedbug, or sleeping, or listening to a radio. Point is we don't know. But John, keep the motor running, right?"

His voice was low and easy, revealing nothing of the fear he felt. John Loesser hesitated a moment, then nodded. They shook hands, and Charlie started down the slope cautiously. Fifteen minutes to get down there, he was thinking, checking his slide. Not a good time to start tumbling, take it easy, no rush. Fifteen minutes to get there, five to arrange things, ten to get back. Not bad, not bad. He dug in his heels and grabbed a boulder when loose dirt shifted beneath his feet. After a moment he started again. Half an hour.

□ □ □

Constance was aware that headlights had appeared behind her, but she ignored them as she sped through Grayling to the house. She ran inside, to the bedroom where the bed had been torn apart, and stood there for a second. She looked inside John's room, hurried back to the other one, and searched the bureau drawer for Charlie's gun. It was there, and it was loaded. She slipped it in her pocket, turned, and ran from the house. Sheriff Maschi caught her on the porch, and her hand tightened on the gun in her pocket. That was what it was for, to keep anyone from stopping her, she realized.

"That damn fool gone?" Sheriff Maschi demanded.

"Let me go," she said. "I have to leave."

"You can't get near that place," he said, holding her shoulders. "That goddamn fool." He shook her with anger. "They'll hold you until morning, then escort you back to the house. Come on. Come on. I know where that damn fool went." He nearly pushed her to the police car.

He slowed down at the spot where Charlie had turned off the highway, sweeping the area with his searchlight, then drove on to leave the road half a mile farther down. He drove with his lights on, bumping and jouncing, but making good time, swerving now and then, cursing steadily.

Constance did not speak; she stared ahead fixedly and now and then relaxed her grip on the gun, but she did not take her hand away from it.

□ □ □

The moonlight was tricky, Charlie thought, crouched behind the corral fence, examining the hotel and the street of Old West. Moonlight flattened everything, erased depth. No radio noise, no motor noise now, but he hoped that was simply because he had gone out of range. Nothing moved. He edged around the fence and onto the porch of the old silvery hotel. The boards creaked alarmingly, but there was no help for that. He stepped in closer to the building, hoping the boards would be tighter there. Twice he had seen a light on the ridge opposite where John Loesser was stationed; the state police, no doubt, on patrol, out of range. The fact that he had been able to see their light meant that he had to be careful with his, he knew, and did not use his small-beam flashlight yet. A tarp was over the double doors at the front entrance, the way the construction men had left it when they decided not to come back. The heavy plastic-coated material had been nailed down loosely. He pulled it away from the door frame enough to permit him to enter; inside, the blackness was deep and hollow-sounding. He waited for his eyes and ears to adjust before he moved again.

No one had been out back, on the porch, or anywhere else in sight, and he was certain no one was in this building with him. Not yet. He flicked on his flashlight and looked around swiftly. He knew the renovation of the hotel had been started, just not how far it had gone. There were two-by-fours stacked up, other lumber here and there, but the floor and the outside walls were intact as far as he could tell. As soon as he was away from the tarp-covered door, he turned on his light again, and this time kept it on and began to move fast.

In the upper hallway he removed his pack and began to arrange his materials. First the blanket, then, at both ends of it, the nests he had made for the candles. He poured the gasoline on the blanket carefully and let it soak in for a moment or two as he opened the bath towels he had soaked in cooking oil back at the house. He covered the blanket with them. He did not want fumes to ignite prematurely; and when they did ignite, he wanted an explosive reaction. He folded the sides of the blanket in over the edges of the towels and examined it all with his flashlight. Finally he went to the candles and lighted first one, then the other. He closed the top of the juice carton, then the cereal box top, counted to five, examined his candles again, and grunted with satisfaction. He left the hotel quickly. He was tempted to open a can or two of paint, but the heat would do it for him. Don't be greedy, he told himself, swiftly scanning the street, the other buildings. Then he was in the corral, out the other side, and on his way up the slope to where John Loesser was waiting. It had taken less than five minutes.

John Loesser's relief left him feeling weak when Charlie reappeared. Not a flicker had betrayed him, not a sound. Experience counts, he thought dryly. Charlie started up the slope.

□ □ □

Mike Dorrance and Larry Womack had pulled the dumb assignment, they both agreed. Sit on a barren ridge and guard a ghost town. They had grumbled at first, and then had frightened each other with stories of cougars and Sasquatch and flying saucers; they had shared a couple of joints, and for two hours had alternately dozed and jerked awake. "Guard it from what, for Christ's sake?" Womack had exclaimed when they first arrived in the jeep at midnight. The old town looked like a movie set down there. Delgado had not said from what. He had drawn a line on a map and said don't get any closer than that, and don't let anything or anyone in. That was all.

There were only three possible ways to get in: by the road on the other side of the valley that had been barricaded, over the narrow-guage railroad tracks, or through the open desert and over the damn ridge they were to patrol. Now and then one of them left the jeep to walk a dozen or so feet and look around, but there wasn't anything to see. Womack emptied his thermos of coffee, stretched and yawned, and went to have a look around this time. It was getting colder; a chill breeze had started to blow in. He went the ten feet or so that they had decided was their patrol, and then he stopped and shook his head. Lights, for God's sake! Who the fuck would be wanting in at this hour? Delgado? A relief car? He hoped so.

He called Mike Dorrance and they watched the lights wobble over the rough ground. Then Mike heard another engine. He turned his head, listening hard. "Hear that?"

It took a bit longer for Womack to make out the noise. He nodded, more frightened than he had been at the talk of cougars. He reached into the back of the jeep and pulled out a semi-automatic rifle. The approaching lights went out. Nervously they waited. The car must have gone around rocks, behind a hill, something. Very slowly they accepted that it was coming the rest of the way without any lights, or that it had stopped and whoever was in it was coming on foot. Mike Dorrance drew his .45.

"You cover the guy coming in," Dorrance said. "I'll find the other one."

They separated, moving cautiously, very nervous.

"Two cars," Sheriff Maschi muttered at the spot where the tracks he had been following suddenly became tracks of two separate vehicles, one set going off to the right, one to the left. The air was pungent with the fragrance of newly crushed sage, and that was as much a trail as the car tracks. He made his decision and turned to the right. He had his lights off, just in case someone was on the ridge opposite Old West; he had not considered that Delgado would have a patrol on this side. But that was what it looked like to him now.

He inched forward again, then stopped. "Hell and damnation," he muttered. "If that's Delgado's patrol, they'll blow us off the desert if we sneak up on them. I'm going to scout ahead. Can't be much farther, ain't much farther you can get."

"You keep the motor going," Constance said, opening her door. "I'll look."

"Stick close to the rocks there," he said. "It's got to be just on the other side of that outcrop."

She slipped out, did not let the door close all the way, and vanished into the shadows of the outcropping. A second or two later, Maschi heard, very close to his side of the car, "Old man, turn off that engine and toss the keys out! Pronto! Or I'll blow your head off!"

He jerked around to see a man with a rifle pointed at his face. "I'm Sheriff Maschi," he said. "Who are you?"

"I don't care if you're the king of Siam," the man said. Maschi heard the tremulous note of fear, the soft undercurrent of nervous excitement, and he knew this man would shoot him.

"I'm here on official business," he said, and pushed his door open. "Delgado knows I'm up here, goddamn it!" He swung his legs out the door and with every second he expected to hear the report, feel the impact. The man was moving in; suddenly he sprang and grabbed Maschi and twisted him around, slammed him face first onto the back door. He reached inside the car, yanked the keys out, and put them in his pocket while Maschi gasped, trying to get his breath.

Constance edged around the outcropping; there was the black Malibu. She let out a breath. The engine was running. Then she stopped again. A man had appeared; he reached into the car and pulled the keys out, and at the same time John Loesser stood up. She had not seen him until then. He had been squatting at the top of the hill, looking down, she realized. The man who had taken the keys yelled, "Freeze! Police!" John froze.

She realized suddenly that the other engine had been turned off, and she pushed away from the rocks, shouted, and then felt disoriented, dizzy, out of control. She reached for the rocks to keep from falling; a stab of pain in her head made her close her eyes. When she could open them again, the dizziness fading, she saw the officer with the gun moving almost in slow motion in her direction, the gun raised. His face was blank; the moonlight intensified the mask of madness over it. Behind her someone was yelling. The madman turned from her and went that way, walking like a zombie. At that moment, Charlie appeared over the edge of the hill; when he saw her his expression became incredulous. And then he changed. He stopped advancing. He stood without moving. A strangely hurt look passed over his face; his eyes flickered but did not close.

Constance found the gun was in her hand; she did not know when she had taken it from her pocket. She raised it, aimed at Charlie, and fired.

□ CHAPTER 14 □

CONSTANCE HEARD JOHN LOESSER YELLING, heard other gunshots, and paid no attention. Charlie was sprawled on the rocky ground, not moving. She raced to him, pulled his jacket open, and located the wound, high on his right arm.

"Start the engine!" she screamed at John Loesser and began to search through Charlie's pocket for his knife. She found it and cut the jacket away from his arm, cut his shirt away, and rolled up the sleeve to make a pressure bandage. Another light came on, shining on Charlie; the sheriff stood over her cursing.

"How bad is he?"

"It isn't too bad. We need a hospital, a doctor. . . ." She looked up finally and he was shocked at the lack of color in her face. "He . . ."

"Yeah, I know. I'll get the other fellow to help carry him to my car. Just hold that bandage in place another minute or two."

John Loesser sat in the Malibu revving the motor, staring at Constance. Sheriff Maschi had to shake his arm before he was heard. "I need help," he said again. "Listen to me," he ordered when Loesser got out of the car. "Delgado's man killed his partner, tried like hell to kill me, and he shot Charlie. You understand?" Loesser stared without comprehension. Maschi repeated it roughly, and finally he nodded. Together they returned to Charlie near the top of the ridge. The hotel suddenly became a torch; flames exploded from half a dozen upper windows all at once. The light breeze scattered sparks and a second building erupted.

Sheriff Maschi and John Loesser got Charlie into the back seat of the sheriff's car, with Constance holding the pressure bandage. Her face looked like ivory, even her lips. Delgado's men would come collect the body of the officer, the sheriff said to John Loesser.

He looked at the man closely. "You okay? If you're not, sit tight. Delgado's going to be up here in no time." He glanced at Charlie and shifted gears. "We'll be at the clinic in Grayling." The glow from the fire was like a false sunrise, he thought distantly. Before he drove away, he added, "You know that if anyone went down that slope, there'll be a trail. People out here put stock in things like trails. Lots of loose boulders around, though, might've rolled down when they were disturbed. Never can tell." He left, driving fast.

John Loesser went back to the edge of the ridge and watched the fire that was leaping from the saloon to the dry goods store. Then he started to roll boulders over the edge of the hill. He did not stop until cars and trucks appeared on the road going to Old West on the other side of the valley.

□ □ □

"Mrs. Meiklejohn," Sheriff Maschi said, glancing over his shoulder at her. She wasn't going to faint, not yet anyway. "Listen a minute. Delgado's man went crazy, just like we all expected someone would. He shot Charlie, and then his partner. Case closed. Got that, ma'am?"

"Yes."

Thank God she didn't argue. He went on: "Now, listen, Constance. You mind if I call you that?" He didn't wait for her response. "We have to tell the doc what you think might have happened to Charlie. We can't let him be fixing up your husband when he wakes up, and not be prepared, just in case."

"Yes," she whispered. "I know."

When had she told him anything, she wondered. "John Loesser saw. He knows."

"Way I figure it, he knows more than he ought, considering how he just got here, but anyway, we agreed that Delgado's guy did it. I took you up there to meet Charlie and his associate. We all wanted to see the show when it started, and then Delgado's man started shooting. Delgado's not going to like it, but what the hell can he do?"

He was talking to fill in the black spot of doubt that was in the car with him. He had counted the shots, he knew when the shot had come in from the edge of the hill, and by the time he had got there, Loesser had been inside the car racing the motor, and she had been on the ground taking care of Charlie. That had been plain enough. And he knew the only thing that could have made her shoot Charlie was the awareness that *it*, whatever the hell it was, had tried to take him.

It was all Delgado's fault, sending two guys out without telling them anything. Two more men gone: one dead, one raving out on the desert. Charlie maybe infected, whatever the hell that meant. And if he was crazy, then Constance. . . . He cursed under his breath. Goddamn Delgado, let him take the rap for it all, including Charlie.

□ □ □

John Loesser/Carson Danvers watched in awe as the whole town blazed. Abruptly he turned and left. "The whole damn town," he muttered. Had Charlie planned that? He knew better, but the police probably would assume it. And this time they might look harder for the arsonist. He wondered how much insurance would be involved this time, and he did not want to hang around long enough to find out. He knew, with regret, that it was time to kill off John Loesser.

He drove to the clinic to check on Charlie. He was sleeping, his arm bandaged up to his shoulder, restraints on his legs, on his good wrist. John hesitated in the doorway to the small makeshift hospital room.

"I'm leaving," he said softly to Constance, who was sitting by the bed. She still looked ghostly pale.

She started, then relaxed and stood up. "They'll want to ask you questions," she said. "They'll take fingerprints maybe, find out . . ."

"I'm leaving," he said again, and this time she nodded. "I don't know yet where I'll be, or when." He looked past her at Charlie. "I'd like to know . . ."

Almost in a whisper she said, "There's a place in New York. Father Patrick Morley. It's a home for boys, on Houston Street. Tell him . . ." She shook her head. "I don't know what you should tell him. I'll call him as soon as we know." Why was Charlie still unconscious, she wanted to ask, demand of him, of anyone who might know something about *it* and how it worked on people. She reached out, her hand was on his arm, but she withdrew it and shook her head. She didn't dare ask; the question implied her fear about Charlie, and she was desperately trying to refuse even the possibility that he had been affected.

The doctor came in to examine Charlie again; John Loesser was gone when he was finished. Constance sat in the chair by the bed once more, waiting.

At two-thirty in the afternoon, Charlie stirred, grunted when he tried to roll over, and finally opened his eyes. Constance pressed the call button, as she had promised to do, and watched Charlie. The doctor entered, holding a syringe. If Charlie woke up insane and violent, the restraints might not hold, he had warned Constance.

Charlie blinked at the ceiling and tried to lift his arm, then his torso. He turned his head and saw Constance. She watched the puzzlement, the pain, and finally anger that he could not move, and when he looked at her, she found that she was holding her breath.

"Charlie," she whispered in a long exhalation. The terror she had been holding back, the tears, the guilt, the uncertainty, all exploded together and she lowered her face onto his chest and wept.

□ □ □

They decided that Charlie would be as comfortable at the rented house as in the clinic, and Constance took him home just before dark.

Sheriff Maschi had dropped by to help.

"No more dope," Charlie said firmly in the den, his feet up on the coffee table, his arm supported on the sofa arm. "A double bourbon, kissed by an ice cube, and forget the water." While Constance made drinks, he looked at the sheriff. "What's going on?"

Logan Maschi shrugged. "Too much. Your pal is gone, the insurance guy, John Loesser. Caught a plane out of Vegas to L.A., left his car in the lot. That whole town's burned to the ground, lock, stock, and barrel. Delgado's man is still out there wandering around on the desert, far's anyone knows. His partner's dead, of course. Thanks," he said to Constance and took a glass.

Charlie took his own and drank, less deeply than he had intended. He still had too much dope in him, he knew. Nothing that the sheriff had said so far seemed very important. The important thing was that Constance had shot him and saved his life. He watched her move about the den, watched Maschi watch her also, and knew that Maschi was aware that she had shot him. He was gazing at her with near reverence.

Sheriff Maschi drained his glass and stood up. "I'm going home. Charlie, Constance, take it easy tonight. Tomorrow you'll have Dick Delgado to deal with, and he's madder'n hell, but there's not a hell of a lot he can do, far's I can see."

"One question," Charlie murmured. "Why pin it on Delgado's guy? Not that I object, but why?"

Maschi shrugged. "Delgado's going to be looking for a way to get you, get me, all of us. Be careful with him. Like I said, he's mad. No point in having him put Constance through a lot of grief, though. No point at all. See you."

Charlie grinned at Constance after they were alone again. "Thanks, by the way."

"Think nothing of it," she said, just as airily. "Will that story hold?"

"Should. Who's going to refute it?" He yawned. "Christ, let's sleep. You haven't closed your eyes at all yet. Come on."

□ □ □

Delgado was as angry as Sheriff Maschi had said he would be. His face had been flushed, his eyes black and dangerous-looking, and he had been helpless. He had asked questions and left again. Now Byron leaned forward and regarded Charlie with a steady gaze.

"Look, you're the only one we know who was attacked and recovered. And you, Constance, you saw what was happening, recognized what was going on, and you were in the zone of its influence. This may be the breakthrough we've needed from the start. Charlie, can you remember how it felt, what you thought, anything?"

Charlie opened his good hand and flexed his

fingers, then started to close them as if around an object. "Like that," he said, watching his hand. "Being squeezed, like a soft snowball that is going to crumble any second. Only not with anything physical. Pressure, not electrical actually, but not physical either. That's as close as I can come."

"Was it painful? Hot? Cold? Steady? Intermittent?"

"Painful," Charlie said, sipping bourbon between words. "Steady."

Byron turned to Constance. "What did you feel and see?"

She described it exactly as she had lived through it, the disorientation, the blinding pain, dizziness. She looked startled, then added, "But I kept feeling something afterward. Like a charged area, like under a high-tension tower." She shook her head in quick denial. "Not like that, not really. I don't know what it was like. All around me."

Byron was making notes as they talked; now he put his notebook aside and picked up his drink, scowling darkly at it. "You're both sure it wasn't directional? Like a beam of energy, rays, something like that?"

"Already thought of that," Charlie said. "Just wasn't the way it was."

Constance was equally certain. Whatever she had felt had been all around her, not coming from any one direction. She described the state policeman and his look of madness, and then said, "I knew that whatever had hit me was attacking Charlie, only the effects were different. I was doubled over with a stabbing pain in my head, but he looked hurt, erased somehow, blank."

"Can you put it in a time frame?" Byron asked. "Apparently the policeman was attacked at the same time, and you couldn't watch what happened to him. How long did it go on with Charlie before the shot?" He believed the mad deputy had shot Charlie, as everyone else did.

She reconstructed it in her mind, her distance from Charlie, taking the few steps she had taken, raising the gun, firing. Finally she said, "Ten seconds, fifteen at the most." She looked at Charlie and said softly, "I saw the moment it attacked you. One moment you were looking at me and I could read you, and then you were blank, hurt. I saw it happen."

And the shot had set off a rush of adrenaline, an electrochemical shock reaction in his brain that must have been explosive to the thing, whatever it was. As much as any motor was, any electrical activity. By then John Loesser had got the Malibu engine running again, and the danger was past. But if she had not shot him, if she had stopped to think, to take better aim, to do anything, he would be dead, he was certain. Dead at the hands of the sheriff, or Delgado, or the other madman, his own hands, hers. And if not dead, then brain dead, living dead, maybe for twenty or thirty years or longer. He shuddered.

"When I get back to L.A. I'm going to see if I

can't get some people from the physics department to investigate all this," Byron said, but he sounded doubtful.

"The problem," Charlie said, "is that there's nothing to investigate until it pops up again somewhere else. If you hear, let me know, will you?"

"And you, too."

□ □ □

Delgado returned once more to demand information about John Loesser. "We just met the man for the first time right here," Constance said calmly. "He's an independent adjuster."

Charlie shrugged, then winced.

"We'll find him," Delgado said. "And when we do, we get him for arson, and that, Meiklejohn, means we'll have you as accessory."

"Then arrest me already," Charlie said. "Because if you don't, I'm going home tomorrow. You know damn well your men were scrambling because of gunfire a long time before the blaze started. I was busy getting shot at personally, and John Loesser was busy trying to keep the car motor running. Shit or get off the pot, Delgado."

He left in a white fury.

"He's right," Constance said. "No jury will believe we all just happened to go up there to see the show. Not at three in the morning. Charlie, can they do something to you? As accessory?"

"I'm not a damn accessory," he grumbled.

She looked startled, then whispered, "Dear God."

□ Chapter 15 □

Two weeks later Charlie and Constance were in Phil Stern's office with Phil, Thoreson, Sid Levy of the Bureau of Alcohol, Tobacco and Firearms, Arson Department, and Fredrick Foley of the FBI.

"Charlie," Sid Levy said, "this is a fairy tale, right? Look, we've known each other what, twenty years? Enough. With fires, we never played games before. Why now, Charlie? Why?" Sid's cheeks were pink, his hair white; over the years he had become heavy through the middle. It would take very little makeup for him to be a good Santa Claus. Charlie had often said he was the second best arson snoop in the country.

Charlie looked slightly bored. "I've given you

a champion arsonist, Sid. He's a real pro. That's hardly a game, old buddy."

"So? You give us a name. Where's the man? Dropped off the face of the earth, that's where. And you tell us a ghost story. What should we do with the ghost story, Charlie?"

"Set up a team, bring in scientists, people with equipment to deal with it, and the next time this thing shows up, be ready to finish it off for good."

Sid shook his head sadly. "Not my department."

Charlie turned to Fredrick Foley. Put him in a tux and stand him on a wedding cake, Charlie had once said of him. He'd look right at home there. He was a dapper man, almost delicate-looking, which was deceptive because he was a runner who entered marathons and usually finished very early, though never a winner, never attracting attention that way. Everything about him was meticulous—his stylish dark hair, his manicured nails, his custom-made suits. When he talked he revealed his origins, the Bronx. "Well?" Charlie asked mildly, watching him.

"How I read it is that this man, Loesser, turned the corner when he was first attacked by the kid. Did something to his head, and he's seeing the same thing happening everywhere he looks now. Happens, so I hear. So he lights a fire and moves on. I've read the reports, Charlie, all of them, and there's just nothing to latch onto. Nothing."

"Okay," Charlie said, and stood up. "I tried. I've given you all the dope. Do what you want with it."

"Look, Charlie," Foley said, "you admit no one knows where it might start up again, or when, or even if. What do you expect? Station someone at every abandoned hotel in the country? Wait for it to show? And this equipment you think we should dream up, for what? You don't even know what we should look for. Charlie, you really think they'd blast something like this, if they believed in it at all? Don't kid yourself, pal. They'd take it home to play with. But they won't because there's nothing to go on. Bring us something solid, Charlie, okay? Something we can get our teeth into."

"More than forty dead people. Not solid enough? Couple dozen nuts in institutions. Not solid? What would it take, Fred?"

"I don't know. But I'd know it if I saw it."

Constance had been watching silently throughout the meeting. Phil Stern was satisfied; he was not connected with any company that would be hit with a massive claim as soon as the legalities were settled. Thoreson was thinner-lipped than ever, furious with Charlie for letting the arsonist set the fire under his nose. His company had been the major insurer of Old West. He had said with unconcealed bitterness, even hatred, that he regretted making that drive out to engage Charlie in the first place. At least no entire town had burned previously. Sid was unconvinced of anything more than the arson fires. But Fred Foley, Constance thought, would take a few steps, would probe a little. She had risen when Charlie did, and they moved together toward the door. She glanced at Phil, then the others, and said, "If anyone does hear about madness in connection with an abandoned building, I hope you remember to keep a motor running, or set up some kind of electrical field. Come out to visit, Phil. Good evening," she said generally to the others.

Charlie picked up his coat from a chair. A paper bag was under it. "Almost forgot," he said, putting the coat on. He picked up the bag containing a large object and crossed the office, handed it to Thoreson. "You left it at our place," he said.

Thoreson's thin lips seemed to vanish; he glanced inside the bag and turned livid.

"Thought you might have a use for it," Charlie said. He went to Constance and took her arm as they left. In the hall outside the office they stopped and he said, "Pay up."

She dug a five-dollar bill from her pocket. The gas can was Sore Thumb's. "See why I don't bet ever?" she murmured, and they went to the elevator. She had disbelieved very briefly. Not a real threat, Charlie had said. Sore Thumb had just wanted action, pretty damn quick.

"Well, you tried," she said in the elevator.

"And we both knew where it would get us. Okay, dinner with Father Morley, prepared by his newest miracle chef." But he was troubled by what Foley had said, and he cursed himself for being a naive idiot. Obviously the FBI would want to study it if they got involved at all.

□ □ □

Constance did not think this arrangement was what she had been thinking of when she gave John Loesser Father Patrick Morley's name. She had meant for him to get in touch with Patrick, who could relay news about Charlie's condition. At least, she told herself once more, that was what she had told herself she meant back then. Now John Loesser was cooking for the boys' home. He had dinner with her, Charlie, and Patrick that night. The dinner, pork with rosemary, sauteed apples, potatoes Chantilly, green beans in vinaigrette . . . . She sighed her satisfaction over coffee. John Loesser knew how to make coffee, too. She remembered the awful brew that Patrick had given her in October when she delivered apples. Another lifetime.

While two of the teenage boys cleared the table, John told about the son of a friend. "He went through the course right up to cakes and pastries, did really well on everything. Then they spent a week making tiered cakes, decorated them all beautifully, and had them all on display for the parents' day ceremonies. When the time came, the teacher and judges went down the tables, sampling icing, rubbing it between their fingers testing for graininess. They tasted it, and went to the next test. They cut the cakes. When they got to Bill's, he burst into tears. The following week he dropped out of chef's school and enrolled as an architecture student."

One of the boys giggled and, shushing each other, the two hurried from the room. John watched them with a slight smile. "I'm starting cooking lessons here. They're both enrolled."

Patrick brought out a bottle of brandy and they leaned back savoring it and the very good coffee. "You know how the police track down people who try to hide?" Charlie said, watching the film of alcohol climb the inside surface of his glass. "Old habits. A stamp collector just can't resist a philately show. Readers haunt libraries and bookstores. Football fans, model airplanes, whatever the old pleasure, it still pleases, and the fugitive thinks, I'll go this time. There'll be so many others, no one will notice me. That's the first thing. Then there's the name. It's really funny about names, how attached to them we all become. The guy runs and hides and changes his name from Timothy Wells to Tommy Will. Or Ralph Warren to Robert Williams. They seem to go for the same initials every time, or the same sound, something to hold onto from the past. Sometimes they even mix up their own names with their mother's maiden name, or their wife's maiden name, but it's the same effect as soon as you know the variations available." He swirled his brandy and finally tasted it, then sighed. "All right!"

Patrick and John had both been listening intently. Now John nodded. He was calling himself Carl Lambert these days. He glanced at the door, and said in a low voice, "I told Patrick everything, Charlie. I thought it wasn't fair any other way."

"I tossed John Loesser to the wolves," Charlie said bluntly. "I hoped it would be enough to make them want some of the action. It wasn't. They think Loesser went nuts years ago and sees other nuts every place he looks."

John shrugged. "Did you really expect anything else?"

"Damned if I know," Charlie admitted. "I wanted something else, but can't say I expected it. Foley, the FBI agent, probably will look into it, but without much enthusiasm or money. Only because he's thorough. You have your computer set up here?"

John Loesser nodded. "Charlie, I'm a simple cook now. With classes to teach. I'm out of that game."

"Right. And if you get wind of a new series of incidents, let me know real fast, okay? If I can get Foley involved alone when there's something to see, he'll make a good ally. But he's got to be persuaded that there is something first."

John was shaking his head with regret.

"Listen to me, pal," Charlie said, leaning across the table, closing the space between them. "If you go in alone and get yourself killed, we've lost our best shot at it. You have more experience than all the rest of us combined, and I want you alive and well. I'm going to get the son of a bitch, John, Carson, Carl, whatever you call yourself. With your help or alone, I'm going to get the son of a bitch."

"You don't dare get near it," John said. "You may be more susceptible than ever after your encounter."

Charlie nodded grimly. "With your help or without."

They left the private dining room, returned to Patrick's study, and agreed to keep in touch, tried to formulate a plan that had a chance of working. Constance listened, joining in only when asked a direct question. She felt her gaze resting on Charlie again and again, and tried to force herself not to look at him, not to study him, examine his features for a change, for a sign that something had happened and was still happening with him.

She had told Charlie about the brain damage the insane people had suffered. Their brains looked as if they had been riddled with tiny pellets, or perforated with acid, or electric wires had burned their way through. No salvation was possible after such massive destruction of brain tissue. It varied from brain to brain of those who had been autopsied, but in every case the damage had been irreversible. Whatever had done that to those other people had also attacked Charlie, forced its way into his brain enough to make him stop his movements, to freeze, to look hurt and blank. She watched him with fear that became terror now and again.

By nine Patrick was too tired to play host any longer, and they got up to leave. No one knew what to do about the thing, Constance thought wearily. She had gone over it with Charlie, with Byron, with herself, and there seemed to be no answers to the question it posed.

Driving home Charlie outlined his thoughts about it. "It's not directional, not like microwaves. It's not intelligent. It's inoperative in any sort of electric field, or where there are motors running. It needs space for its portal, if what John saw was a portal. But damn it, people have to go somewhere when they vanish. They have to come from somewhere when their bodies turn up again. We'll call it a portal, a black hole that fills a doorway, that takes time to start and turn off, that needs more space than ordinary doors have these days. I'm assuming the size is important, and the isolation, and the lack of anything mechanical in the area—peace and quiet."

"Charlie," she said when he paused, "if it's like the signal from a television transmitter, it doesn't matter where it comes out, only where it originates. You could keep blowing up television sets for the rest of your life."

"Even if Foley could get anyone interested," Charlie said, as if she had not spoken, "what would be the point? They would try to communicate with it, like an ant nest trying to communicate with the foot as it descends. How long have we had things like microwaves, radar, lasers?"

"I don't know."

"Me neither, but not very long. A hundred years ago we couldn't have traced a microwave to its source, no matter how hard we tried. Who knew about radon in houses fifty years ago, much less how to measure it?"

Constance drew in a deep breath, strangely reassured now. He had been so quiet for so many days, so distant, she had thought with rising fear. This was Charlie back, angry, arguing out loud, talking it through for his own benefit as much as hers.

"Why not intelligent?" she asked during the next pause.

They had left the city now, were on Highway 17, heading north. Snow was expected that night and it was very cold; the road had little traffic. About half an hour farther on they would stop at a roadhouse where she would have coffee and Charlie a double bourbon; after that she would drive, another hour and a half at the most, if she dawdled.

Although she hated driving in the city, and usually chose to go by train, she had offered to drive both ways this trip, to spare Charlie's arm, but he had wanted to drive. He never had minded the traffic, had grown up with it, and sometimes complained it was too eerily silent in the country. She let the thoughts flow through without trying to stop any of them, patiently waiting for Charlie to answer her question.

"What are they after?" he said finally. "Those autopsies didn't show any damage except to the brain. Right? The liver, heart, lungs, all intact, and the brain riddled with holes. They're after the contents of the brain. They're doing brain scans on living tissue and killing it!" His voice grew harsher as he spoke, and suddenly the car swerved. He caught it and held it steady, both hands hard on the wheel.

"Charlie? What's wrong?"

"Don't know." He began to tap the brake, shifted down, and came to a stop on the side of the road. "Don't know," he said again in a strange remote voice. He leaned his forehead on the steering wheel.

"Charlie!" She heard the panic in her voice that could no longer be suppressed.

"It's okay," he said, in his usual voice. "It's okay. You'd better drive."

They got out and changed places and strapped themselves in. She touched his forehead, cool. He caught her hand and kissed her palm, but he looked frightened, as frightened as she was.

Without prompting, he began to talk about it. "I had a feeling of being in a small, dark place, pressed in. It was suffocating, no doors or windows, too tight." He had seen it, felt it, had been there, and at the same time had been driving, watching the road, talking to her. The two sets of sensations, of memories, occupied the same time, the same place. He shook his head.

"Has it happened before?" Constance asked, very calm now. Perhaps too calm, Charlie thought.

"A couple of times, less intense than this one, not as real or as long."

"What about the onset? What starts it?"

He reached over and rested his hand on her thigh, the way she did with him when he drove. She covered his hand with hers for a moment, returned it to the steering wheel. She rarely drove with one hand on the wheel; he did most of the time. His hand on her leg now told her he did not want her to speak in her professional voice, not to him. She swallowed hard and glanced at him.

"Charlie, can you talk about it? How it starts, how it ends, anything?"

He patted her leg, but kept his hand there. "You've known," he said slowly. "I've caught you watching me."

"I knew something was wrong," she admitted. She was speeding and made herself slow down. The roadhouse was ahead, but she had no intention now of stopping anywhere. Home, she kept thinking, go home.

"Yeah, you knew. Okay. I'm doing something, it doesn't seem to matter what, like driving just now, talking. Then there's another feeling of being somewhere else, cramped, in a dark space. Both feelings are there together. One doesn't interfere with the other one. It just happens all at once. Nothing goes with the feeling. No need to do anything about it, go anywhere. It's almost like a memory of being there, wherever it is. Then it's gone. Again, no warning, no fading away, just not there."

He was facing straight ahead, no longer looking frightened, and that was right, Constance thought, because she had taken all the fear into herself. It lay coiled over her heart, squeezing.

She drove them home too fast, now and then remembering not to speed, then finding herself edging back up to seventy-five, eighty. It started to snow lightly during the last half hour, a fine dry snow that could accumulate to a depth of several inches before morning. She parked in the garage and they went inside their house, where Charlie went to the kitchen and mixed hot buttered rum. The cats stalked around him indignantly, as if to demand a stop to the nonsense, coming and going at all hours, making it snow. Charlie muttered as he danced around them to make drinks.

"When I come back, I want to be a cat," he said, pushing Brutus out of the way with his foot. Candy cuffed Ashcan on her way to weave infinity patterns around his feet. He pushed her away too, and she walked stiffly out of the room, grumbling. "Tomorrow," he went on, "they'll sit in the window and watch me shovel snow, use the snow blower, freeze my ass while they complain about not enough yeast on their food, or not enough chicken liver. What a life!"

"Well, I'll sit inside and let you play with snow, too," Constance said. "You know I want to hire one of the Mitchum boys to take care of it."

"Nope. My job. You don't complain about not enough chicken liver or yeast on your food, and that, my darling, makes all the difference."

"Charlie," she started, but he caught her in a tight embrace, buried his mouth and nose in her hair and drew in a breath.

"We'll talk about it," he said into her hair. "Tomorrow. Tonight we'll have our nice hot drinks and go to bed. Okay?"

She pulled back and shook her head vigorously. "Not tomorrow. We'll talk about it now. Charlie, you are not going mad. You have nothing to worry about as far as brain damage is concerned. You wouldn't function if you had the kind of brain injury the others showed."

"Good," he said. "So let's have our drinks and go to bed."

"Charlie, look at me! Stop this!"

His face was set in hard ridges and lines. She trailed her finger across his cheek, down his chin. "Charlie, please. I don't know what's happening to you, but it isn't like the others. You know it isn't."

His facial muscles relaxed a bit and he nodded. "I know."

□ □ □

Over the next two weeks they both pored over the accounts of insanity, the terrible effects the thing had had on others. Constance made her special Christmas cookies, and they both shopped, bought and decorated a tree, and welcomed their daughter home for a week during the holidays. And they waited. Charlie had another attack, no worse than before.

There was the damn cramped space, darkness, a feeling of being hemmed in, and during it he was perfectly aware of his actual surroundings.

He called John Loesser, invited him out.

"Can you come to dinner? Any time. Or we can meet you in the city."

John would come out by train, he decided. Patrick was ill, probably would be admitted to the hospital again for treatmcnt. New people were due at the home, to relieve Patrick of his duties. It was time to move on, but first he would visit.

It snowed again the day John was due. The yard was like a postcard scene, with snow piled high on sweeping branches of the blue spruces, and banked against the front of the house up to the windowsills. Constance tended her bird feeders and looked at the lovely world with troubled eyes. Cardinals and chickadees waited for her to move on so they could eat; the cats watched them broodingly, too lazy and warm inside the house to be a serious threat, but wistful. Constance shivered and hugged her parka closer around her. It was her fault, she thought suddenly, remembering the day they had picked apples, remembering that Charlie had taken the arson case only because she had been so busy, going here and there, speaking, publishing. She shook her head and hurried back inside, denying the thought as hard as she could. She and Charlie both went to pick up John. Charlie did not do any driving now.

Her dinner was not up to John's standards, but he was too polite to mention that, and, in fact, was very complimentary. They had coffee and Cognac in the living room before the fire, each of them with a cat. Ashcan had been stuck with the stranger and for several seconds had hesitated, sniffing his shoes, then his trousers, finally a hand, before he eased himself onto John's lap where he curled up and started to purr.

"Tell me about those doors," Charlie said then without preamble. No mention had been made until now of the strange happenings or fires.

John nodded. "Right. A blackness that filled the doorway. I walked around it in one of the buildings, looked at it from the other side, two connecting rooms with that . . . that void in between, exactly the same on both sides; just a void, an absence of light."

"Did you toss something in besides the rock you mentioned? Especially at Orick?"

Now John looked startled. "Yeah. Twice. Once was at Orick. The first time was at Moscow, Idaho. I made a Molotov cocktail—I thought that was appropriate—and threw it into the blackness. The fire burst out all around and I ran out. Period. I couldn't tell if it went all the way through, or got stuck, or bounced back into the room. So I tried again at Orick. This time I made a time bomb, sort of. Not as well as you would have done, I guess, but I tried. I rigged up a cardboard box, propped it up with newspapers, and put a wine bottle on top of it. I found one of those corks with a hole through it, the kind that wine makers use, and I put a cotton cord through it into the bottle, filled it with gas, and used the twine as a wick. When the fire reached the paper holding the box up, it was supposed to burn it, let the bottle roll down into the void, the blackness, taking the burning wick with it, and soon the whole thing should have caught. I didn't hang around to see if it worked."

"Something worked," Charlie murmured. "One of the firemen out there said there was an implosion. He was pretty sure of the word he used."

John shrugged. "It didn't work enough to slow them down."

"Maybe it didn't go in far enough," Charlie said absently. "Or it wasn't a big enough charge for the job. Or something else."

Charlie always knew when Constance was signaling him. It wasn't anything that he could demonstrate or prove; usually neither of them would even talk about it, but there was something. When he was feeling jovial about it, he said she scratched him between his shoulder blades with invisible fingers; when he was bothered by it, he said she turned her witch eye on him. Whatever it was, he knew. And she was signaling now. He glanced at her.

"You can't go near it again," she said. "Charlie, you know you can't go near it again."

He did know, but he also knew that it had touched him, that something was in him that had not been there last month. He regarded her soberly and did not agree, but did not dispute her either; in fact, he did not acknowledge her in any way. For a moment she looked foreign, alien, unknowable. He shook his head and turned back to John Loesser.

"Several people have gone through the doorway, haven't they? And returned? Some of the people who disappeared. Very thorough searches were made of the hotels, and yet their remains turned up in the ashes. Probably two in Orick."

"They turned up dead," John said bluntly. "No one's gone through and come back to talk about it."

"Let's hope that pattern is not invariable," Charlie said after a moment, and then he smiled, his usual warm, somewhat skeptical grin that took many years off his age and made him look vulnerable.

◻ CHAPTER 16 ◻

THE FIRE BURNED LOW WHILE THEY TALKED; THE wind had started to howl outside, and now and then a gust blasted its way into the chimney, swirled the blaze strangely, and blew smoke into the room. More snow, Charlie thought with resignation. A real storm was due this time; John would be a house guest for a couple of days at least.

John was explaining his problems to Constance now; until he had a new identity established, it would be difficult to get a car, a new driver's license, any ID at all.

Charlie grimaced and made a note on a scratch pad, handed the paper to John. "If you've got cash, you can get a car here, license, whatever you need. No questions will be asked. Any idea where you'll go?"

John shook his head. "Thanks for this. It didn't occur to me that you'd know." He leaned forward, upsetting Ashcan who protested and stalked away. "Charlie, I think the FBI is interested, after all. I've talked to Beatrice a couple of times; she said they're asking questions. Some scientists from JPL are interested, too."

Charlie shrugged, but the thought of the scientists from the Jet Propulsion Lab getting involved made him distinctly uneasy. "I thought they'd ask around. Byron's keeping me posted with what they're up to. So far about all he can report is that there's no periodicity in the events, assuming, that is, that they have enough information to work with." He stared at the quiet flames, thinking fire was the prime example of how good and evil can coexist in the same place, same time. He said, "The people Byron's been in touch with are saying there can't be anything to it, but if there is, it's the find of the century. They've turned the big computers on to the problem of source, periodicity, probabilities of its happening again and where." He laughed without humor. "They have a new puzzle to solve, a new game to play along with their Star Wars problems."

"Christ," John muttered. "They'll be like all the others. No one believes until he sees what it can do, and then it's too late." He shook his head. "Maybe it's best. They can be in position within hours, no doubt, as soon as the reports start coming in about madness anywhere near one of the hotels. Let them do whatever they want. God knows, I don't want this to be my personal war any longer."

"What will they do?" Charlie asked, turning to Constance. She and Byron had discussed this part, he knew.

"First, they'll seal the area, we think," she said. "They probably will set up equipment to measure radiation, radio signals, whatever they can think of that they know how to measure."

John snorted. "The very instruments they use will stop whatever it is they want to find."

"Maybe. But they don't know it, or believe it if anyone tells them. They'll want the scientific data. They probably will use animals for experimentation in the beginning. Birds in cages, cats in cages, dogs, maybe even chimps. And then sacrifice them to examine their brains." Both men were gazing at her with unconcealed looks of distaste. She rolled her eyes. "I'm not making the rules, guys, just telling you the procedure if you want a scientific study. Eventually, if the thing is still contained, they'll have to use people, of course. The dilemma is that if you protect the people, there's nothing to find; eventually they'll decide volunteers are in order."

Charlie exhaled a long breath and turned his brooding gaze back to the fire. "There's a story I came across years ago," he said. "It's about this missionary in Africa back around the turn of the century. He'd been out for months before any mail caught up with him, and then he had a newspaper, the first he had seen since his arrival. He read it, then read it again, over and over until he had memorized it. Finally, he put it aside and his natives snatched it up and carried it away. Such powerful magic, they thought. It had to be powerful magic, or why would he have bathed his eyes with it for so many hours?"

Constance nodded. "Think of the implications of a newspaper," she said to John, who was looking confused. "Language, education, manufacture of paper and ink, invention of the printing press, delivery systems, systems of gathering news. . . . It might well be considered magic."

"I always wondered what the natives actually did with the paper," Charlie said. "Stared at it? Rubbed it on themselves? The ink would have come off, of course; magic ink? Rubbed their eyes with it? Could put an eye out like that, I'd guess. What will our people do with the thing in the hotel?"

□ □ □

That night eight inches of snow fell, and during the next day six more inches. The next afternoon Constance watched Charlie and John Loesser drawing hotel plans at the kitchen table.

"Okay, this is the hall, the one up in Camden. And you think the door with the shadow must have been about here. Right?"

"I don't know. I wasn't looking for it then," he said. "I was acting from instinct, copying more or less the first layout. Later I began looking for it, not then. But if it was like the others, then yes, it probably was about there. I simply glanced in rooms and noticed that there were open doors that night."

Charlie shuffled through the pages of graph paper, then withdrew one. "This is the Moscow, Idaho, hotel. This is where you tried to toss a Molotov cocktail through?"

John moistened his lips. That was the first one he had actually tried to examine. He had groped his way through the echoing building, aware of rot and crumbling flooring, aware of the moan of the wind through cracks around every window that had long since been replaced by boards that had worked loose, hung crookedly. Talking about it now had brought back that night with chilling vividness. The corridor had stretched out before him, doors closed on both sides of it, like the entrance to a mine. The beam from his flashlight had been lost in the darkness. He remembered the webs, real cobwebs that had become burdened with dust, and the other webs that were not real, but were like an electrical charge that would not be brushed away, no matter how often he tried.

He became aware of Charlie's quiet patience.

He moistened his lips again. "I went up the stairs and began trying doors, first one side of the hall, then the other. About midway I found it. Connecting doors, the door missing, and the abyss in its place."

He opened the door cautiously and the wind moaned as it forced its way through cracks in the boards at the windows, brushed him on its way to the corridor behind him. He swept his light from left to right, examining a wall, the windows, another wall, and then stopped. Where the beam of light landed on a wall, the surface appeared with faded wallpaper hanging off in long curling streamers, then the unpainted boards, the window frames with peeling paint, and then nothing. The light stopped when it touched the abyss. It reflected nothing.

"So you went out to the hall and into the next room?" Charlie prompted after a few seconds.

"Same thing. It filled the doorway, top to bottom, and it simply swallowed the light. I threw the rock from the second room and went back to the other one, but it wasn't there."

Constance rubbed her arms briskly; goose bumps gradually subsided.

Charlie found the plan of the Moscow, Idaho, hotel grounds, which showed the county road that wound up a hill to it and a fishing camp less than a mile away. He already had drawn a circle with the circumference of about a mile. Six people had wandered into the danger area and had gone mad; ten people had died before the hotel had burned down. Why there? Why for God's sake there?

Suddenly he said, "That's the wrong damn question!" Constance and John looked startled. "Why not there? That's the question. Look, there are a number of things we know, or can assume. It likes wooden buildings. It doesn't like electricity or mechanical things. It likes big doorways to set up shop in. It doesn't give a damn exactly where it is as long as the place meets those criteria."

"That's crazy," John said.

Charlie shook his head. "Remember the moon lander we sent up? I recall that there was a good bit of unhappiness about where it landed, not the best place for studying the lunar surface, not where the scientists wanted it, but a place where its chances of landing safely were best. And the Martian probe? Again, not exactly where they wanted to have a look around, but a place that met other criteria. Sort of like that old one about the guy on his hands and knees under the streetlight. A cop comes along and asks what's up. Lost my watch, the guy says. And the cop asks where. Over there, he says pointing down the street. Then why the hell are you looking here? The light's better, he says."

"You don't think our people are doing this," Constance said in a low voice, her goose bumps back again.

"No. Think about the Martian probe, honey. We land a gizmo that is programmed to do certain things. It doesn't do anything else, just what it was told a long time ago. Let's pretend. Here's the probe." He pushed his coffee cup to the middle of the table and cleared an area around it. "First thing is turn on the light." He drew a large circle around the cup. "Next, you start collecting and analyzing everything within reach. Now here are some poor little blind Martians; they can't see the light, but they can feel something funny about the air, maybe it gives them a headache. If they wander too close, they get analyzed." He pushed a few crumbs into the area, then scooped them up and dropped them into the cup. "Poof, gone. Never knew what hit them."

"In time," John said bitterly, "they'll figure it out, but how many crumbs have to go first?" He held a roll over the cup and crumbled it.

"What scares me," Charlie said then, "is the possibility that they'll learn about that damn door and try to move it to a safe place where they can explore it at leisure. I wonder what kind of programming it has to protect itself from such an eventuality. Would we lead the savage headhunters home? Why assume they might?"

"It might not even be programmed," John said. "Maybe there's an intelligence guiding its every move."

"Don't think so," Charlie murmured.

"Seems it would have caught on by now that you're hot on its tail with a gas can and changed its *modus operandi.*"

Constance looked from one of them to the other as they spoke. The goose bumps had gone, but the chill had settled inside her, squeezing her hard and tight. "Stop it!" she cried in an unfamiliar voice, her speaking-to-an-asinine-bureaucrat voice. "You're both acting like children," she went on, dripping ice water with each word. "You make assumptions and then act as if each one is undisputed truth."

"You're absolutely right," Charlie said then in the same tone, with the same inflection she used when he was being unreasonable. She clenched her fists and drew in a deep breath. Charlie glanced at John and said judiciously, "She likes lists. We should make a list of possibilities. You want to go first?" he asked her, gazing at her with a blandness that made her want to hit him.

"Our own government could be testing something. A scientist could have a runaway experiment. A foreign government might be doing it. Mass hysteria might have magnified a simple effect. There could be gases in those buildings. We didn't know about radon twenty years ago. Who can predict what will be discovered next year? Mass hypnosis. Like the Indian rope trick." Charlie was not writing. He was regarding her with great warmth and sympathy, she realized, and she stopped talking. The silence held for several seconds. She said, "Charlie, what's wrong with you? Do you know?"

Her voice was almost inaudible, but he heard the question, knew what she meant, knew the reason for the pallor that had spread over her face, knew about the ice that had invaded her. It was within him too.

"I just have assumptions," he said gently. She opened her lips; when no sound emerged, she nodded. "Something sends a gateway, a doorway to a building where chances are good that it will not be disturbed. Maybe it could operate just as well out in the open, but we don't know that. Maybe it simply takes time to get things ready; we don't know that either. When it is operational, there is an area that it can influence, a field, a pattern of some sort of radiation, something. We don't know what it is, just that it seems to extend out for roughly a mile in all directions. Up? We don't know. Down, into the ground? We don't know. Some people seem to be unaffected by it, like John. About one out of four people who experience the effects of this field, radiation, whatever it is, go mad. They become murderous, or suicidal, or completely withdrawn—catatonic—or show other symptoms that we generally associate with insanity. They are incurable; their brains are destroyed by the radiation, or force. Let's suppose they are invaded by something that riddles the brains, then departs. But whatever it is, it can also activate the various systems that make people move. It can make dead people get up and walk. It forces them through the doorway, the portal to wherever the sending mechanism is, possibly. Maybe there is more elaborate testing equipment there. We don't know that, either. Until the building housing the doorway is destroyed, it continues to exert its influence on those it has invaded. They go back to it if they can. Dead people get up and go to it. Later, after the fires, their bones turn up in the ashes sometimes. Not always. Not all of them."

Constance started to speak and he regarded her with a gaze that was distant and strange. "We know it's true," he said. "That damn building in Old West was searched from top to bottom, and after the fire the remains of two men were found in the ashes. One of them was Weston's assistant, Mike, and he was dead before he went in. Probably the other one was too, but we don't know. They went through the portal and came back out. They went somewhere, stayed there for days, and then showed up again. The rock John threw in, the Molotov cocktail, they went somewhere, too."

"Why didn't the burning gasoline destroy that 'somewhere'?" she demanded. "You're guessing, just guessing about all this."

He shrugged. "All we can do is guess. Maybe there wasn't enough air to sustain a fire. Maybe there are protective devices. Maybe there's an interim space before you get to the actual source of the thing itself. Maybe it admits only people, not objects. But it admits people and everything they are wearing or carrying on their persons. Sheriff Maschi said one of the corpses in Old West was holding a wrench. That guy took it in and brought it back out."

He rushed on before she could speak again. "When the doorway senses a motor, electrical activity above a certain level, it turns off, just like that, and then turns on again as soon as quiet returns. The thing isn't gone during that period; it's just not working. The activity doesn't force it out, is what I'm saying. Nothing has forced it out of anywhere yet, except fire. And that doesn't seem to have any effect at all on the sender, the source, whatever it is. Maybe it doesn't even know a receiver, a doorway and its field have been destroyed. Maybe its programming doesn't allow for that. Maybe there is a time limit involved. After so long, it stops, the sending mechanism scans for a new location and sets up a new field there. We don't know. Maybe it can just attach itself to a carbon-based material, wood, and when the wood burns it collapses."

Constance had not moved as he talked, almost too fast to follow. Suddenly he stood up and went to the counter, brought back the coffee carafe and poured for them all. He looked inside his cup, took it to the sink and put it down, and brought out a clean one from the cabinet. Outside, the silent snow continued to accumulate; birds streaked to the sheltered feeder, away again in flashes of red and black.

She thought of a show she had seen, people talking about organic methods of pest control. "If you put these granules down," a bearded man had said, sprinkling tiny pellets on a table, spreading them with a pencil point, "the ants find them irresistible, don't you see. We have a film." She had watched the ants struggling with the grains that had assumed gigantic proportions among them. "They get them inside the colony and with the humidity and warmth, the pellets emit fungus spores," the bearded man had gone on. "Deadly to the ants, of course." Time bombs, she had thought, and switched channels. Time bombs. Would the doorways be like that? Time bombs? In her mind she could see men struggling to cut away a door frame from the surrounding walls and floor, without warping it, without touching the opening at all. They could do it, she realized. They could haul it away and set it up in a laboratory somewhere, and when the laboratory power was turned off, it would go to work with its diameter of madness reaching out for a mile all around. Or would sensors tell it to increase its power? Or not to function at all? Or do something altogether different? What it had done to Charlie was different; no one else had exhibited his symptoms. Maybe it would emit fungus spores, deadly, of course. She knew she was on the verge of insane laughter, and forced herself to lift her cup, to sip the steaming coffee, to stop seeing ants and bearded men talking about death too nonchalantly.

She kept her gaze on her cup then, and said, "You didn't answer my question. What's wrong with you? Do you know?"

He shrugged and said almost lazily, "Nothing much. I think we've got a tiger by the tail, the biggest damn tiger in the world, and it's taking us here and there as it wants."

She knew he was evading her again, and he knew she was well aware that he had not yet answered her, and by now she must know that he would not. Could not, he corrected. There had been few secrets over the twenty-five years of their marriage, but now and then there was a secret. Now there was a secret, he corrected again. The others had not lasted very long.

The snow was letting up slightly; the sky was lightening. When it stopped he would get out the snow blower and start working on the driveway, the walks around the house. He groused about clearing snow, but in fact there were times when he enjoyed the labor, enjoyed the still cold air and the pure beauty of a world under wraps. He would enjoy it that afternoon. The unanswered question hung over them heavily, silencing John who did not know their many varied ways of communicating but seemed to understand that no new business should be raised right now. Constance continued to watch the cardinals at the feeder, but her gaze did not shift to follow their flight, to focus on newcomers. Charlie looked at the snow but he saw the cramped black space, smelled strange air, felt pressure against his head that grew and grew until he wanted to swipe at his hair, knock it away. And he saw the doorway that John had described with loathing and terror. But to Charlie it was not a thing to fear. It was velvety blackness that would be welcoming, that yearned for him even as he yearned for it. During the past few weeks he had dreamed of that doorway several times. In his dreams he walked toward it at first, then ran, and then, miraculously, the way it can happen in dreams, he flew unencumbered by his awkward body, and, flying, had gone to it joyously, only to come awake in a sweat.

He knew he would not get near an area where it operated. He knew he would resist the temptation to approach, to see it for himself. He knew it was insane to think anything else about it. And yet, he thought bleakly, he felt like a bee so loaded with pollen it could hardly fly, and was unable not to launch itself and return to the hive. Programmed to take home pollen, it could do nothing else. Something had invaded his head, he thought clearly, and it wanted to follow its programming and go home. Knowing this made all the other things he knew about the doorway and his need to stay away from it inoperable.

▫ CHAPTER 17 ▫

WE FEAR OTHERS, CONSTANCE THOUGHT THAT afternoon at the front window, watching Charlie clear the driveway, because we don't understand their values. And even more because we suspect they have no regard for ours. John Loesser came into view with a shovel to attack the front walk and steps. Sometimes his scar from the plastic surgery seemed a bright red line of warning; other times it was invisible altogether. She wondered if he saw it every time he shaved, if he touched it now and then, remembering. And she wondered if he realized that she was immune also, if he had thought through what it meant for those who had had the wrenching headache, the assault of pain, and then looked up uninvaded. Polly had come away like that. And she had also.

It was inhuman; there was no defense, and she was deathly afraid of it, whatever it was. John was immune, she was, but Charlie had been affected. She no longer saw his red jacket, the snow plume, the emerging black driveway. Charlie had been affected, she said again, hearing the words in her head. How? She did not know and if he knew he would not say. But she accepted that the only way he would be safe was if they found and destroyed whatever it was that operated the doorways and the fields of insanity that surrounded them. How many times had countless humans come to that same awareness? There is the foreigner, the alien, the enemy that must be killed.

She thought of the presentation she had prepared for the meeting of psychologists and psychiatrists in San Francisco, how vehemently she had denied that xenophobia was innate, how rigorous had been her arguments proving it was a learned response. In theory she might still take that position, but in practice, now that every cell in her body seemed sensitized to a threat, when she could see how Charlie had changed because of contact with the alien presence, now she knew that something more primitive than her reasonable mind was motivating her, dictating her every thought. And that more primitive part knew the strange other had to be destroyed.

Abruptly she turned from the window to go

to the kitchen to make apple pie for dessert. Hot apple pie and cheese. John was a better cook than she was and he would make dinner, but she would make the pie. She almost wished she had a gingham dress and a starched apron with apples and strawberries appliquéd on it; she would be certain to rub flour on one cheek, have the house fragrant with spices—cinnamon and cloves—and the men coming in from their chores in the frozen wasteland would realize the American dream. She stifled a giggle that threatened to turn into a moan and went about her own chore of making pie.

□ □ □

"I hardly ever use the electric stove in the winter," she said later to John, who was studying the wood range with interest. "Even for pie," she added. "Of course, in the summer it's a different matter."

"It's a no-win situation," Charlie said, tired but feeling good from his exertions with the snow. His face was ruddy, his eyes bright. He and Constance were at the table, leaving the cooking area to John, who had never cooked on a wood stove. "I cut the wood for exercise, and she makes things like pies."

"Use the electric stove," Constance said. "That one takes getting used to—" The phone rang and she reached behind her and picked it up. "Yes?" She listened for moment, then said to Charlie, "It's Byron, for you."

Everything changed. They had been at ease, and now the air was thick with tension. Charlie's voice was charged, probably not noticeably to anyone but Constance, but she knew. He sounded more relaxed than ever, sleepy, but his eyes had lost their shine and now looked blank, blind even. He listened, then said, "How do you know that?" Listened again. "Can't," he said then. "In case you haven't heard, we're snowed in. Be a couple of days before anything moves around here." This time he listened longer and then drawled, "How are things, Fred?"

Foley, Constance thought, Fred Foley, the FBI agent. Now they made a tableau, John unmoving at the stove, Charlie looking asleep with the phone at his ear, she frozen at the table. The cat Brutus stalked into the room and glared at them, turned, and left again.

Finally Charlie said, "Sure, Fred. Sure. If I see him I'll tell him." Very gently he hung up. "They want you," he said, glancing at John. "I said I'd tell you if I see you."

"They know I'm here?"

"They seem to think you're in New York somewhere, in the city. Byron said Beatrice told them."

John shook his head. "I didn't tell her where I was. She couldn't have told them."

"They really want you," Charlie said kindly. "If they think they can find you through her, well . . . Anyway, Byron and Foley will be in the city tomorrow, if they can get a flight in, or the next day. They said to tell you they'll wipe the slate clean, whatever you've done in the past, all forgiven, understandable."

"Dear God," Constance whispered. "It's started again, hasn't it?"

"Well, they didn't say that in just so many words," Charlie said. "But if they're looking for John to run point for them, I'd assume it has started again." He crossed the kitchen to stand at the wood stove with John. "Now, you tell me what kind of heat you want, and I'll tell you which wood will provide it. Quick and hot, the little sticks of applewood. Medium and sustained, the oak."

"They must have clamped down on information going into the mainframe," John said, looking past Charlie. "There wasn't anything yesterday."

"I suspect that's right," Charlie said. "And they do have resources, you know."

"I should go."

"Snowed in, remember? Snowplows hit our road out front after the interstates are clear, and the federal highways, and the state roads. We're way down on the list. Let's build up the fire now."

He built the fire while John started chopping onions and carrots. He admired the way a master chef handled the knife and food he dealt with, seeming to pay no attention at all to what he was doing, but instead to be thinking out loud.

"Beatrice must have mentioned to Byron

Weston that she had talked to me," John said, at the counter. "They're tapping her phone, the bastards. Flying in to New York. Must be within driving distance then. Probably have it sealed off already, if they can get to it. Might be snowed in. No leaks this time. No way to find out where it is." The knife stopped in midair, then resumed. The carrots had been reduced to the size of rice, the onions almost to a mush. He pushed everything to one side and started on garlic. The knife blade flashed with precision. "They don't need me if they just want to burn it out. They want to study it, have someone who can go in and out for them."

He stopped cutting and turned to look at Constance. "What do you want?" she asked.

"I want it utterly destroyed. To hell with their studies."

He resumed chopping.

Charlie stood out of the way, listening, watching, his arms crossed. So far he had found no fault with anything John said. Strange, he thought then, he had tried to interest Foley, Sid Levy, anyone, had told them everything—nearly everything, anyway. And now that they were involved he just wanted them all out again. He had wanted them to use their vast powers of destruction, and now. . . . If you call on the gods to hurl thunderbolts, you'd better be pretty damn nimble. Byron Weston had been excited, unable to conceal his excitement over the phone. Chance of a lifetime, Charlie thought soberly, the find of the century, of the millenium. A bunch of kids playing with dynamite caps.

"I could get in touch with them," John said, cutting parsley now. "Find out where the damn thing is, then split."

Charlie snorted and turned to the table where Constance sat, very watchful, very still. "Martinis," he said. "We are asking this guest to cook without a martini at hand."

She set the table while he mixed drinks, and then they turned on the radio for news: it was all about the storm and road problems and school closings. When it became obvious that no one was listening, Charlie turned it off again.

"Sid Levy," he said suddenly. John Loesser was stuffing chicken breasts with the vegetables he had sautéed. He glanced at Charlie with no understanding, and continued his work, frowning in abstraction. Charlie looked at Constance. "Sid might know where the thing is supposed to be."

He left the kitchen and returned in a moment with his telephone directory, already open, his finger on one of the names. He made the call from the kitchen.

Neither Constance nor John spoke or moved as Charlie performed on the telephone. He had an index card that he shook before the mouthpiece; he scraped the phone with his finger; he blew long whistling breaths across it, all the time complaining that he could not hear, please speak up, slower, louder, they were having a blizzard, for God's sake! "I told you," he said, although he had not told Sid this before, "I can't hear you any more than I could hear Fred Foley. Where? Say it again! Where?" He crumpled the card and blew across the mouthpiece and listened intently. "I'll call you back tomorrow, or the next day. Are you there, Sid? Can you hear me? I'll call back when the lines are in order again."

He hung up. "Lake Pike, New Jersey," he said softly. "We're to meet at a hotel in Lake Pike and go on from there." Constance had already gone for the atlas. They pored over it together and located the small village at the edge of Kittatinny Mountain. "Deceptive," he murmured then, studying the surrounding countryside. "Summer houses, boys' camps, fishing camps on the lake, and the river, what, five miles from town? Skiing nearby. Deceptive. It looks empty and is probably crawling with people."

It was rugged, mountainous country, probably not plowed out all winter, and humming with traffic all summer. Their atlas did not show the topographic features of the area, but Charlie could remember it generally from past trips—steep hills, rotten-slate hills, fast mountain brooks dammed here and there to make brilliant blue lakes that came complete with A-frames and trailers, retreats for religious groups, boy scout and girl scout camps, and hunting and fishing resorts. Two hours from

New York, when the roads were passable. Two hours from home, when the roads were passable. And now with the snow storm in the area, it might as well be on the moon as far as accessibility was concerned. Of course, he thought then, the army had snowplows, too. National Guard plows? Foley would find a way to get in; there would be personnel to see to it if he had any priority at all.

□ □ □

They were at dinner when they heard the snowplow on the road in front of the house. Charlie had not completely finished the driveway. He had learned not to dig it all the way out until after the plow had gone by. Otherwise he had to do it twice. An hour of work, he thought distantly. Tomorrow, after one hour of work, he would be mobile again. Heading toward New Jersey.

"This is wonderful," Constance was saying to John. "Not quite chicken Kiev; better, I think. I'd like to keep you." She spoke to John Loesser, but her gaze was on Charlie, had returned to him again and again; she felt almost that she could follow his thoughts about the snow, the driveway. "Sit still, John," she said lightly, "I'll clear and bring coffee and pie. Charlie, ice cream or cheese?"

He nodded, caught himself, and said cheese. The cheese was pale sharp New York cheddar;

the pie was spicy and fragrant and warm; the coffee excellent dark Colombian. Charlie brought in Cognac. So very civilized, Constance thought. So very civilized.

"You know," Charlie said then, "only three percent of arson fire cases are solved annually?" John shook his head in amazement. "Fact. We know who did it most of the time, but proof is hard. Very hard. The evidence goes up in smoke, you see. So this guy has a big insurance policy on his warehouse, say, and it burns while he's at dinner with a dozen other people. We know it's arson, and we know who is responsible, but so what? He collects and that's that." He sipped his coffee, touched the Cognac to his lips, and sighed in contentment. "Sometimes when we go in there's still a wall standing, maybe a lot of walls standing, and we know they won't stand very long, so we set a charge and tumble them ourselves. With proper precautions, of course. Lots of ways to tumble those walls, depending on what else is in the building. Chemicals, that's one thing; natural gas, something else. Wooden frame, concrete, lots of steel beams—they're all different, take different approaches."

"What are we going to do, Charlie?" Constance asked then in a low, steady voice.

He shook his head.

"It's us, or no one," she said. "Not you alone. Not you and John. Us."

"I should have finished the job years ago,"

John said. "I didn't know how. My little Molotov cocktail! Tell me what to do, Charlie. How to do it. That's all I want to know. How."

"Can you ski?" Constance asked him.

"Afraid not."

Constance said, "Look at the map." She got up and brought it to the dining room table. "Here's Lake Pike. Let's say what we're looking for is within a ten-mile radius." She consulted the scale and then measured off about an inch from the village, traced a rough circle with that diameter. "What we want is somewhere in there. Hills, mountains, brooks, the lake. And all snowed in, I bet. They'll plow the road, maybe even the driveway to the hotel we're after, but they'll also have people there to keep out intruders. We're intruders. So, if we go in at all, it has to be off the road, off the driveways, through woods, through snow that may be hip-deep, deeper even. Skis or snowshoes. Can you manage snowshoes?"

"I'm from Virginia, Constance. Not too much chance to learn skiing or snowshoes. If you can get in, so can I, if I have to wade through it up to my chin."

She brushed that aside. "Tomorrow morning while Charlie is finishing the driveway, I'll give you a lesson. You can practice when we go to town to get the charge. MacPeters will have the stuff you need, won't he?" she asked Charlie in the same breath. MacPeters was with the volunteer fire department.

He nodded, watching her with amusement as she turned back to John Loesser, whose look was not at all amused.

"Cross-country skiing isn't a thing like downhill," she said. "If you can balance at all, you can do it. And you don't go very fast or anything like that. It's rather like walking with funny shoes. You'll see in the morning." She added, generously, Charlie thought, "Don't worry about it. Maybe there won't be enough snow over there to worry about. More coffee?"

"I'll do it," Charlie said, waving her down. He left with the pot to make more.

"So we have a charge," John was saying as Charlie went out. "And you teach me to ski in a hour or so in the morning, and the roads are clear enough to drive over to New Jersey, and we manage to avoid Byron and Foley and their group—"

Abruptly Constance stood up and walked from the room. In the kitchen Charlie was at the sink unmoving, both hands clutching the edge of the counter. She hurried to him and took his arm. It was rigid. After a moment he shuddered, then looked at her. Again, she thought. She was certain she had known each and every time he had gone away like that. That was how she thought of it: he went away for a few moments, a minute or longer. Then he came back. And when he came back he did not at first recognize her, or anything else. His eyes were blank, his face expressionless. That changed and his expression was of fear, then he was Charlie again. Neither spoke. She squeezed his arm slightly, kissed him, and picked up the coffee pot.

"I'll do it. Do we need more logs inside tonight?"

Candy came in complaining about strangers cooking in their kitchen, and Ashcan followed, darting suspicious glances here and there. Charlie danced around them both, cursed them, and went to check on the fire, on the supply of logs, and now Constance stopped her coffee-making motions and shut her eyes hard for a moment. "You can't have him!" she said under her breath. "Leave him alone!" Her words were addressed to the thing behind the black door, the thing that lived in the abyss, the thing that had touched Charlie with evil. "We'll blow it to hell and gone," she added, still not moving, answering John's unfinished question. When they had the charge and did whatever they had to do to get it to the right place, inside the black doorway, they would blow the evil back to the hell it had come from.

She made the coffee and they all went to the living room before the fire that hissed and crackled now and then, but was mostly quiet and steady. Charlie made good fires.

"I'll—we'll need your moon suit," Constance said after a few moments of silence. Charlie regarded her with a cold, hard expression. John looked blank. "It's a protective suit, boots and all," she said. "Sometimes there are toxic fumes, things firemen wouldn't want to get on their skin, much less breathe. It might come in handy tomorrow." To Charlie she said patiently, "Isn't that what you were thinking?"

Sometimes when she pulled things out of his head he hated it; sometimes it amused him; sometimes it left him feeling chilled, as if in the presence of a strange creature he could not fathom at all while she turned on him a look of complete understanding and awareness. That was when he hated it, he thought, when she knew him so completely and was so opaque to him. He shrugged.

"All right, then," she said, exactly as if he had answered. "The Molotov cocktail should have done some damage and evidently it didn't. I can't help but think it's because it didn't get to the source of the field. Do you suppose there's an intermediate space between the doorway and the transmitting mechanism? If there is, we could find that nothing we do outside the main place will be effective."

She looked at Charlie with that same unfathomable expression. She knew those were his thoughts, his assumptions.

She went on, "There has to be a space large enough for people. We know people have disappeared through the doorway and some of them came back out. So there has to be a space big enough for more than one person at a time. We know that. It could be that there's something like an airlock separating the doorway from the control room, or whatever it is. And to damage the control room the bomb has to get to it."

"The moon suit," John Loesser said, understanding now. "It has its own air supply, insulation?"

Constance nodded.

"I could do it," he whispered.

"So could I," Constance said.

"No! You're out of your ever-loving mind!" Charlie jerked up from his chair and attacked the fire, sent sparks flying up the chimney. He faced it and said angrily, "My job. You get that? Both of you? It's my job. You'd blow yourself up, either one of you."

"You'll just have to see to it that the bomb is idiot-proof," Constance said. "And instruct us. Nothing electrical about it. Or mechanical, probably. What's left?"

Charlie turned toward her, his knuckles white against the poker.

"You can't get within range," she said quietly. "You know that as well as I do. And it's going to take all three of us. Someone has to make sure that no motor is turned on while one of us is inside the thing. What if that happened? Would you get out again if the doorway closed down because electricity came on? We can't risk it. And someone has to help John get to the place. No accidents along the way. And remember, he'll be on skis for the first time; he'll need both hands for his poles. Someone's going to have to carry stuff, help him up when he falls down. Help him into the moon suit when it's time. You know you always needed help, someone to check it out. It's going to take all of us, Charlie."

"I won't let you go anywhere near it!"

"I'm immune," she said. "Exactly the way John is. It attacked me, gave me a fierce headache, a blinding headache for a few seconds, and then went away. I talked to Polly back in California and she said the same thing. We all know that some people within range weren't affected, some were. That part's okay."

"It's not okay!" he yelled at her. "You don't know a damn thing about what's behind that blackness! Neither does he! You think it's going to let someone go in and blow it up, just like that? You think it doesn't have defenses? It could double, triple the field effect, for all we know, as soon as someone gets near that door."

"It didn't, though," John said. "Remember, I was close enough to toss stuff through. Nothing changed. And you can use a flashlight. Mine was pretty small, but it didn't have any effect on it. I can go through, Charlie."

"Goddamn it, John!—"

"Carson," their guest said. "John Loesser died a long time ago. I'm through hiding behind him. Carson Danvers. It's time I finished something that began over six years ago."

"Let's check out the moon suit," Constance said, as if she had suggested they play Scrabble. "Someone's going to wear it eventually."

Charlie went to the basement storage room and returned with a suitcase. He opened it and pulled out the suit. He had not had it on in thirteen years or more, but it was in perfect condition. How they all hated the suits, he was thinking distantly, as he explained it to Carson Danvers. Turkey roasters. But only if the turkey didn't have enough sense to back up and get out in time. "It's awkward and cumbersome, but it protects against chemical fires, toxic fumes, even radiation up to a point and for a limited time. But you can't move much once it's on. Can't bend over very well. So you need help in getting into the boots, getting the seals right. And the air tank on the back is a bitch to manage without help. These straps can hold whatever you need in the front pouch. The charge will go there. You can't put it on until you're actually in the hotel, of course. You'd never reach it with the suit already on. And you can't see too well with the helmet in place, kind of like blinders on a horse. But you need the helmet, or the air won't work."

He explained the parts, how to regulate the air flow, how to grasp with the oversized gloves on, how to turn your head to get a wide-angle view of whatever was in front of you, and all the time he was doing this, he knew that Carson Danvers would not be the one to go in. That thing wouldn't let just anyone enter, only someone already carrying its signal, already primed. The honeybee with pollen. If a wasp tried to enter the beehive, it would be swarmed over and killed; only the bee with the right credentials would be allowed in. And he had the credentials to go through the door; the thing would recognize its own. The thing in his head wanted to go back home, wanted to take him home, and he wanted to go too. He would be allowed in; not Carson Danvers, not Constance, but he, Charlie, would be allowed in. It would be like going home.

☐ CHAPTER 18 ☐

JUD HENDRICKS, HERMAN KOHL, AND BOBBY Toluri were hanging out at the Lake Pike Diner, kidding around with La Belle, who was too old for them, but was a looker. A few other kids were there in other booths, and a couple of men at the counter, wearing parkas, dripping ice water from their boots. One was Jake Dorkins, the Dork, who taught algebra and coached basketball at the high school. The other was Ralph Wasilewski, just in from plowing Old Ferry Road.

Herman Kohl—who had a basketball scholarship to Penn State, if he kept out of jail, they liked to say—started to yell something at La Belle; Bobby Toluri punched him in the arm.

"Shut up and listen. You hear what Wasilewski's saying?"

At the moment he was saying nothing, having finished, and was now staring off in the misty, greasy, odorous miasma of the diner.

"Not a hell of a lot," Herman Kohn said.

"Yeah. What he was saying is that those guys in the four-by are holed up at Mel's camp. What the fuck for?"

"Poaching," Jud Hendricks said. He was the youngest of the three, still a junior; the other two were seniors. It wasn't too often that they let him hang out with them.

Bobby gave him a withering look, a warning that he might be sent packing if he didn't shape up. "They're army, dope. My old man knows stuff like that. He says they're army, they're army."

"Okay, they're army. Army can't poach?" Herman Kohl waved to La Belle and held up his Coke can. "Anyway, there's nothing up at Mel's except snow. Let them freeze their balls off. So what?"

Bobby was thinking, his forehead creased, his eyes narrow. "Look, first old man Tierney goes batty and shoots up the place. Right? Then Doc Gruening shoots his own head pretty damn near off. Right? Then the army moves in up at Mel's. Right? I bet they're testing a weapon or something up there."

Jud groaned and closed his eyes. "You're a nut. You know that? A real nut. Another conspiracy?"

"Maybe. What about Feldman? Lost in the woods! What a crock! He invented the woods around here."

"I read about some new weapons," Jud said. "They use superconductors, you know the stuff that has to be way below zero for electricity to flow through it. They could be testing something like that."

"Sure," Herman said. "Why bother going to the North Pole when you can go to New Jersey?"

"They'd pretend to be hunters. Why not? Did you see the van that went through this morning? Just like in *E.T.* I bet it was crammed with electronics."

They did not really believe any of it. They did not really believe there was a connection among the several instances of craziness that had hit, the deaths that had resulted. It was winter, after all, and Lake Pike in the winter drove people batty. Their basketball game had been called off for that night, and all three were on the team. But Marshfield High was still snowed in. The Marshmallows couldn't make it; they knew they'd get their asses whipped, the Lake Pike boys agreed, but it was an empty victory. They were bored. By now they were tired of the toboggans and sleds and ice skates. They drew closer together and tried to figure out a way to spy on the army. After a few moments, Bobby called, "Hey! Mr. Wasilewski, is Childer's Park Road open yet?"

"What for?" Wasilewski called back.

"Good toboggan runs up there."

"It's open." He returned to his conversation with the Dork and dismissed the restless high school kids.

"What then? Hike back up the mountain?"

"Shit no. We go down the back side of the mountain, across the valley, and then drag the toboggan to Mel's. We don't know anyone's there until we're nearly on top of them. Our plan was to toboggan down from Mel's on the road, only now the road's plowed and we're stuck. So they give us a ride to town. What's wrong with it?"

After another five minutes, they stood up and left the diner. All three of them were over six feet tall, Herman Kohl six feet seven. They were grinning broadly. At the counter Jake Dorkins, the Dork, watched them with unease. Bored kids spelled trouble, but what the hell could they get into with the whole damn county snowed in? Finally, he dismissed them too.

□ □ □

The drive had not been as bad as Constance had feared. There had been one stretch that required chains for about twenty-five miles; all the way traffic had been slow and cautious. She had concentrated on driving, keeping a wary lookout for cars out of control, for patches of ice. Charlie had maintained a brooding silence. Carson had said that when it was over, he probably would go to California, open a restaurant there, see Beatrice. He had sounded wistful and Constance had said something appropriate if not startling; then silence had returned. Suddenly Charlie broke it.

"Take the next right turn," he said.

Constance glanced at him; her hands tightened reflexively on the steering wheel. He was stony-faced, almost rigid, staring ahead. Gone, she thought, nearly crying out, except this was different somehow. She slowed down, searching for a road to the right.

Everything was prepared, she told herself. They had the suit, they had skis; Carson had proven he could move on them. They had the charge. A very simple-looking thing. Too simple? She shook her head slightly. Charlie said it was enough and he knew. Two-phase device, he called it. You pull the pin and that lets two chemicals mix. After about ten minutes they start a heat reaction that will reach eighteen hundred degrees and that sets off the plastique that acts like TNT but isn't TNT. Enough to blow up a bank vault. She made the turn off the state road. The secondary road was plowed, but hardly wide enough for two cars, and certainly not wide enough for a car and a truck, if a truck should appear.

Even if they were getting close, he couldn't feel *it* with the engine running, she wanted to explain to Charlie. He couldn't. It didn't work when the engine was running. She imagined the bank vault blowing up, pieces flying everywhere, showers of green bills. Her mind was skittering because she was so afraid, she told herself, and her mind skittered off again, this time to the image of a submarine exploding in the sea, with a shower of green and gold fish. That was wrong, too. The black door did not lead to anyplace on earth or in earth's seas. They had accepted that without discussion. The transmitter, the parent device, was in space somewhere. The door was a dimensional portal that led to space.

"The next left," Charlie said.

Not with the engine running! She slowed down again. She had studied the map, but now was confused. The last turn was not one she had planned; the coming turn was not on her mental map. On both sides of the road farmland had yielded to forests: black traceries of trees against a sullen gray sky, snow banked over five feet high making the narrow road a tunnel, pressed in on all sides with no retreat. No way to make a turn, to go the other way. Forward only, following the road that wound around hills, made turns too sharp, considering that there could be a truck coming. The hills had become steeper, higher; had become mountains.

On either side of the road there were occasional clearings in the trees, private roads or driveways that vanished in the hills. Few of them had been plowed out. Charlie was staring past her to the left of the road, his whole body stiff with tension. They passed a narrow, tortuous driveway that climbed up the side of a hill, and Charlie sagged.

"We've come too far. Find a place to turn around."

"Charlie, there wasn't any place to turn off back there."

"We'll have to dig it out. Won't take too long."

At the next driveway that had been opened, she turned carefully and retraced their way, past the next plowed drive, searching for the one Charlie knew was there. He caught her arm in a hard grip.

"There it is." He nodded at the opening in the trees. "Our driveway is on the north side of a valley. That last driveway is on the southern side of the same valley. Let us out here with the snow shovels and you take the car back up one of the open driveways and give us half an hour or so, then come back. You can't park on the road while we dig."

She stopped the Volvo and turned off the engine, then looked at Carson Danvers in the back seat. He had become almost as tense as Charlie. His scar was a bright red line along his cheekbone. He held his breath a second or two, then nodded.

"It's okay here," he said finally.

It was fifteen minutes before three. In two hours it would be getting dark. She said, "I'll come back at a quarter after three. Charlie, promise you won't go beyond the road here."

"Sure. We might not even be done yet. Let's get at it."

She knew he was not really seeing her, that he was simply impatient to get on with the job of digging. His eyes had a flat hard look that she had come to recognize over the years; he was looking inward at a landscape no one else would ever see.

The men got the shovels from the trunk and were already attacking the ridge of snow piled up by the plow, when she drove on. She turned again at the next opening, and when she passed them a minute or two later, neither looked up. Four miles farther down the road she came to the village of Lake Pike. There was a diner with steamy windows, a tiny Grand Union grocery store housed in a gray stone building, two churches, a gas station, a variety store. A typical lakeside village with a hotel at the far end, off the main street, presumably with a view of the water. She did not drive past the hotel for fear that Byron and Fred Foley were already in town. She stopped at the diner to have the thermos filled with coffee; they had drunk it all when they stopped to take off the chains earlier. The diner was overheated and loud with raucous teenagers and country rock music. A state trooper examined her as she waited for the thermos. His face was cherry-red, his hair carroty. She nodded politely, paid for her coffee, and hurried back to the car. Now she had drawn attention to herself, she thought angrily, and so what? She had a right to be out driving alone, had a right to want hot coffee, had a right to have three pairs of skis on her car that had no passengers. She drove out of town without glancing back at the diner. Four and a half miles to the driveway they were clearing. There had been virtually no traffic on the road earlier; there was a little now.

At least the stretch where she stopped was relatively straight. If a car did come, there was room for it to go around her. She got out and walked to where Charlie and Carson were finishing a passageway. It was wide enough, but just barely. Both men were red-faced and breathing hard.

"How deep is the snow?" she asked, nodding toward the driveway that was visible only because no trees grew on it.

"Maybe eight or nine inches," Carson said. "I went up a couple hundred feet; doesn't seem to get any deeper, and there aren't any drop-offs. It's okay as far as I went."

"There's coffee," Constance said, and pulled on her knit cap. "I'll have a look at the drive before I start in."

"You're going to drive?" Carson asked dubiously.

"She was born in a snowbank," Charlie said with a flash of his old amusement at his athletic, outdoorsy wife.

"Dad never got a son," she said to Carson. "So he decided his daughters would have to do.

I think I was skiing by the time I was three. Down Iron Mountain when I was six. I've been driving in snow all my life."

Thank God for the southern exposure, she thought a few minutes later, as she followed Carson's prints. And that it was warmer here than back home. No snow had melted in upstate New York since the first had fallen, but it looked as if this had melted off more than once. It was wet, heavy snow, maybe with ice under the top few inches. She stopped and looked around when she came to the end of the tracks. So far so good, she decided. She could make it up to this point. On one side the valley dipped slightly—not bad. On the other the hill started to rise—again, not bad. The curve had been gradual and by now the road was out of sight. Even if they parked here no one would see them. She made a soft sound of derision. They had already put up markers by clearing the driveway; their tracks would be enough.

When she got back to the car, the men had already put the chains on and stashed the shovels in the trunk; they were ready to go in. She took her place behind the wheel and started the engine again. She backed up first in order to make a wide turn and enter more or less straight. "The trick is," she said to Carson, grinning at him slightly in the rearview mirror, "to go very steadily, no accelerations or slowing down or sudden turns. Just go in slowly and keep going. Set?" He looked terrified. She glanced at Charlie who was again without expression. "Here we go," she said, easing forward; she turned, aimed at the snow canyon, and then felt the front wheels hit the resistance of snow.

No one spoke then. Ice, she thought distantly; she had been right. There was ice under there. The car swerved a little, not much, and then the chains dug in. She did not slow down. It really was not bad, she thought, feeling the car wheels find purchase, aware that when the front wheels spun on ice, the chains compensated. Not bad. Her father had taught her well.

Then she stopped. She had come to the end of the tracks, Carson's and hers.

"Why'd you stop?" Charlie demanded harshly.

"I need a trailblazer." She took a deep breath. "Listen, Charlie. I drive only if Carson goes ahead and signals that it's okay to keep going. And I don't mean the road. We sit in the car and wait for his signal. With the engine off."

Charlie knew she was right; there was no argument against her reasons. But he knew where *it* was. He could point to it now, go straight to it. That frightened him very much because he also knew he should not be able to sense it in the car with the engine purring away. Before he could make objections that would sound false even to him, Carson opened the back door.

"I'll go on ahead." He walked away, pulling on one of Charlie's knit ski caps.

Constance watched him, thinking he was a

good man, a very good man who deserved to go to California and open his gourmet restaurant and keep company with Beatrice until they decided to make it permanent. She hoped they would do that. Carson walked around a drift, tested the snow beside it to make sure she would have room to get through, then went on. She turned to speak to Charlie but he was gone again.

The black space, confined, close, airless, and still. This time he felt himself moving through it, not very far, not very fast, just moving, seeing little but aware of the nearness of the walls, aware of another abyss ahead.

A shudder passed through him and he felt Constance's hand on his arm. He blinked. "It's right over there," he said in a thick voice. "At the end of the valley."

"I can't see anything."

"I know. Let's get the skis off the car while we wait. They can stick out the rear window. God knows it can't get much colder in here than it is now."

They had to get closer, he thought, unfastening the skis from the rack. He had no idea how far away *it* was, only that it was over there. He could cross-country ski, but not well enough to carry the suitcase and manage two poles, and he knew he could not ski at all with the suit on. They had to get close enough for him to make it alone, no steep hills to negotiate, and then. . . . And then he would know what to do.

Constance had just opened the trunk to get

the suitcase out when she heard another car engine. "Charlie!"

He had stopped moving. "I hear."

Carson was not in sight. Charlie propped one pair of skis against the car and Constance closed the trunk lid. "I'm going to get us stuck," she said. "Stay clear." She ran past Charlie, got in behind the wheel and turned on the ignition. Charlie jumped back when she revved the engine and plowed into the snow with wheels spinning, digging in, hitting ice, then simply spinning again. A black car pulled up behind her. It looked misshapen with over-sized wheels and studded snow tires, a modified Buick that probably could go anywhere it damn chose.

A heavy man in a dark coat got out and came to Charlie. "What the hell are you doing in here? What's she trying to do?"

Constance stopped gunning the motor and got out. "We're stuck," she said brightly.

"You're trespassing. What are you doing in here?"

"We wanted to go skiing," Constance said. She looked accusingly at Charlie. "He said it was a good place. He used to come here all the time, he said. And now look at us, stuck."

"You dug through that snow bank to go skiing?" the man said in disbelief. "Come on. You're getting out of here."

"You the owner of this place?" Charlie asked then.

"Caretaker," the man said. "Out!"

With great patience, speaking the way a kindergarten teacher might talk to a backward child, Constance said, "We are stuck in the snow. My car won't come out. We can't leave. Will you please drive to town and call a tow truck for us. We will sit right here and wait. No skiing or anything."

The man walked to the front of the car, looked at the rear wheels. The Volvo was clearly stuck. He kicked the rear tire and scowled, then went back to his own car and spoke in an inaudible voice to a second man who had not got out. Now he did. He inspected the wheels and both men withdrew and consulted.

They both came back to Constance and Charlie. "We'll take you to our camp," the heavy one said. The other was lean-faced, and almost albino-pale. "We'll send a truck to pull your car out and deliver it to you at the camp. Come on."

"I don't think so," Charlie said. "We'll wait here for the truck."

The lean one reached into his pocket and pulled out a wallet with ID. "Buster, you'll do what we tell you. Police officers. Now move."

"Hold it a second," the other one said. "Who's with you?" He was looking at Carson's tracks.

"I was looking for a good place to park," Charlie murmured. "Out of the traffic, you know. Funny kind of ID you had there," he went on, studying the lean one. "Mind if I have a closer look?"

Now the heavy one withdrew his hand from his pocket. He had a gun in it. "Search them," he ordered.

The lean man was efficient and thorough. When he was finished, the other one said, "Mr. and Mrs. Meiklejohn, get in the car. Now."

Charlie walked to it, talking easily to Constance. "Actually they'll take us to Fred Foley. I was sure this road would lead us to him, but wrong. Can't win them all."

"You're looking for Foley?" the heavy man asked, clearly confused now.

"Yep. And Sid Levy. Wrong turn, though."

"You got that right. Come on, get in."

"Look, what's your name? FBI agent what?"

"Lovins. Mel Lovins. He's Jack Windekin."

"And I'm Charlie Meiklejohn, retired New York City Police force. I've been on this case with Fred and Sid from the beginning. Take my wife to your camp and I'll wait for a tow and join you. Is Fred up there yet?"

Charlie knew the instant he had gone too far. Lovins got mean again and snapped that no one stayed in this place, orders. For a second Charlie eyed him and his partner, thought about trying to run in foot-deep snow, thought about being tackled and dragged back, and he shrugged and got in the car. He was joined by Jack Windekin. Constance sat in front with Mel Lovins.

□ CHAPTER 19 □

CARSON WATCHED THE CAR BACK OUT. HE HAD heard nothing, but the actions had spoken eloquently. The FBI, army, police, whoever they were, were already trying to cordon off the area, not very successfully yet, but it would get tighter, he knew, remembering the entrances to the Old Town, the blockade, the patrols on the ridge. For a moment he felt a wild desire to jump up and down and wave his arms, go with them to some safe place, let the cops handle it all. The urge passed swiftly; the car was out of sight. Only then did he leave the clump of snow-shrouded brush he had been crouching behind. He had gone another two hundred yards or so without feeling the charged cob-webs, but even if he had doubted Charlie's certainty that this was the place, the bit of action he had just witnessed solidified his own conviction that this was it. He was sweating under the heavy clothes that Constance had insisted he put on.

Always before he had been able to drive up to the front door, take his gas can inside, do the job, and drive away. This time he didn't even know where the damn thing was yet. Briefly he cursed Constance for deliberately getting stuck, but then he realized that if she had not done that, they would have driven the car out, and with it the skis and the suitcase, and the bomb. Charlie had insisted that it was not a bomb, but rather a two-phase device, but to Carson it was a bomb. He and Constance had watched silently as Charlie explained how to activate it. Simply pull this ring all the way out, he had said, lifting the ring. No way it could accidentally come out. No electrical device needed, nothing mechanical. Sometimes you get fancy with wires and stuff only to have them melt too soon. He reached the Volvo, and, just as the two strange men had done, he examined the wheels and gave up on driving farther without help. Stuck. He looked inside and let out a sigh of relief when he saw the keys in the ignition. He took them out and opened the trunk and stood for a moment looking at the suitcase. It was not very heavy, not a burden to carry, but he knew he could not carry it and use the skis too. Constance had been right about that.

He took out the suitcase, tossed the keys to the front seat, and started to walk again. The road must lead to the hotel, he told himself, and it couldn't be very far, a mile and a half, no more than two. As soon as he was within view of it, he would consider cutting across the valley in a straight line, but until then he was better off on the road. In truth, he did not trust the valley, which widened as he went farther into it. It seemed that the snow was deeper in the clearing than here against the rising hill, and he was afraid there might be a brook somewhere under the snow. He could see himself falling into an icy stream, soaked through and through, resting, drifting into the comfortable sleep of hypothermia. And in the spring some kids would find the suitcase, open it, and pull the string . . .

□ □ □

The lower reaches of Childer's Park were where families went for picnics in the heat of summer; little kids played in the shallow stream that ran through a meadow. There was a pond that froze solid every winter, fine for ice skating. Up a bit higher was where the eight- to ten-year-old kids took their sleds, boys and girls. Higher than that was the turf of the junior high kids, all boys. No girls would risk the snowball fights, and fistfights, that broke out regularly among them. The highest part was reserved for the high school boys. The sled runs were long and somewhat dangerous, curving around drywalls hidden by snow, winding through stands of trees. Here the toboggan runs began, and they were the most dangerous of all. By the time the boys were old enough to try to join in the fun at the top of the mountain, they were also old enough for beer, for pot, whatever was making the rounds at the time. The cops cruised the road up there, and for the most part the boys tired of the snow games early in the season and were always searching for new ways to get the town cops out of the cruiser into the snow, whereupon the boys would leap on their long sleds or toboggans and flash down the slope. It was a game they played every year; the local police cooperated by yelling and sometimes giving chase, and more often getting back in the car to try to beat the boys to the bottom of the run in order to bawl them out and threaten them with charges everyone knew would never be pressed.

That afternoon there was a serious snowball fight, with the jocks holding off what seemed at times to be the rest of the high school population, but in reality was about a dozen other boys. Herman Kohl was bored with snowball fights, but Jud and Bobby were really into them, and he had to go along or get clobbered. In his mind he was planning their slide down the back of Childer's Park. No one ever went down that way, although it was as good as the front side, because they knew they would end up over four miles from town, and going down the front took them nearly to the elementary school. He had been over every inch of the ground with his father in hunting season, starting when he was twelve, and he knew exactly where the drywall was that would be their turning place, knew exactly how to get past the old Miller Hotel, coast through the valley, and halfway up the hill to Mel's camp. From there it would be a five-minute walk to the camp itself. A snowball hit him in the head and he turned to retaliate, but inside he was furious with himself for being in a fucking snowball fight. It seemed particularly childish that day when he had other things on his mind. This was kid stuff; he wanted to take on the whole fucking army.

□ □ □

Mel's camp was for hunters, and had never been meant for anything more than primitive shelter and a place to cook meals and eat them, and to play cards after a long day in the woods. There was a large common room with a plank table that could seat sixteen at a time, and four card tables with folding chairs. Other folding chairs were scattered around the room, some at the plank table, others apparently at random. The windows were niggardly in size, bare. Electric lights hung on cords from the ceiling, which was finished with rough boards. The walls were made of the same rough lumber. The floor was bare and echoing. There was a back door, to the kitchen evidently, and halls leading off from the central room. When Charlie and Constance entered the building, there were three men there. One was at a portable typewriter typing, two at the plank table. A coffee urn was on the end of the table.

Mel Lovins went to the table and spoke to one of the men, who got up and walked to Charlie and Constance. He was round-faced, nondescript, as bland-looking as a junior-high civics teacher. "Brooks Sussman," he said, extending his hand. "FBI."

Constance pulled off her ski cap and gloves angrily and slammed them down on one of the card tables. "Mr. Sussman," she said, "your associates have forced us to come with them at gunpoint. They forced us to abandon our car. I protest this kind of treatment and I want it on record. I don't know what in the world is going on here, but I just intended to go skiing and I was kidnapped."

Charlie blinked, then raised his eyebrow at Brooks Sussman, who appeared taken aback. Not my fault, Charlie seemed to be saying.

"Mrs. Meiklejohn, please just try to be patient until we get in touch with Agent Foley. They're trying to reach him now in his car." He looked at Charlie questioningly. "I thought you said you were in on this, have been from the start?"

"I am not a police officer," Constance snapped. "And I never have been, and whatever he's in on is his business. Where's the bathroom?"

Charlie spread his hands helplessly; after a

brief hesitation Sussman nodded toward the hall. "Down there." Constance marched off.

"She doesn't like guns," Charlie said. Weak, but he did not have a clue about what she was up to, what the act was for. He caught a look of sympathy that flashed across Sussman's face.

"Well, it's unfortunate that you missed this road and went in over there instead. If you know anything about any of this, you know more than I do right now. Our orders are to keep everyone out of the valley."

Oh, I know something about it, Charlie thought. On the short drive up to the camp he had felt as if he had circled *it* almost completely, that he could draw the coordinates to locate it with precision. What he lacked was the correct reference to calculate distance.

"How far are we from the hotel?" he asked.

Again Sussman hesitated. Then he shrugged and motioned Charlie to come to the table with him. "Just under two miles. We're plugging the various ways into it right now. Didn't expect anyone to dig through that bank, though."

A map was opened on the table, a topographical map with a red circle that stood out like a target. Sussman put his finger in the circle.

"There," he said. "We're here." He touched another place outside the circle. "You drove in about there." The spot he indicated was also outside the circle, about as far from it as the camp was.

Exactly how he had envisioned it, Charlie thought, gazing at the map. He wondered if

Carson had made his way into the red zone yet, and decided probably not; he was too inexpert on the skis. He had a lot of falling down to do on his way to the party.

A door slammed and there was the sound of boots stomping on bare wooden floors. Constance reappeared and cast a withering glance toward the table. She crossed the room, making a lot more noise than was necessary, moved a chair under one of the tables, straightened another one, continued past the table where Charlie and Sussman and the other two men watched her, and went into the kitchen.

"Maybe she'll find something to do in there," one of the men said almost meekly.

She came back and Charlie realized with near awe that she was casing the joint, looking for other exits, making a head count, right in front of them, openly, blatantly. At the same moment he was swept up in the other images that overrode what was actually before his eyes. Blackness, the too-small space, the other doorway that called, called . . .

"Mr. Meiklejohn? Hey, are you all right? Mr. Meiklejohn! What's wrong with him?"

He felt the hand on his arm and he was back, straining to see, facing away from the table, facing toward the hotel that was still calling him. Constance moved into his line of vision.

"He's very ill," she said coldly. "We think it could be smallpox." She kept moving, this time toward the second hall.

"Shit!" Sussman said under his breath. The look he gave Charlie was solicitous. "Maybe you'd better sit down. You want some coffee?"

"Coffee," Charlie said. "That sounds good. Actually it's a form of epilepsy, very mild. I hardly ever even fall down."

He had to talk to her, find out what she had learned, not make it obvious. How many agents were up here already, where were they? Two men entered the building together, breathing too hard, looking cold. Sussman motioned Charlie to the coffee urn and joined the two at the door, where they spoke in voices too low for Charlie to hear. Sussman cursed and motioned to a man at the table.

"Get your stuff on and go help them. Take Lovins with you. I'm going to the van a minute, see if they've raised Foley yet. Sit down, Meiklejohn. Just relax."

Help them do what? Charlie wondered bleakly, after Sussman left. Search the hotel in the valley? Set up spotlights? Find someone lost in the woods? He hoped it was none of those things. The coffee was bitter with an aftertaste of aluminum. He held the Styrofoam cup with both hands and tried to add up how many agents he had already seen. Seven, at least, and one in the van probably, and a couple more out there on patrol without a clue about what they were looking for or guarding against. Ten or more. Probably all armed. All antsy on a screwball assignment. He scowled at the coffee, not liking his addition at all, not liking the way

Constance was behaving, feeling the need to talk to her well up stronger and stronger, because he was afraid she had already made a plan and was tidying up details with all this stamping about, the bitch act that was almost too good.

Sussman returned and looked at Charlie curiously. "Foley wants you to hang around until he gets here, half an hour or so. He's on the road. He says you could tell me what the hell is going on, but you probably won't."

Charlie shrugged. "The hotel is haunted. I'd keep away from it and keep my men away from it if I were you."

"Shit!" Sussman said.

"Actually it's more like Dracula," Charlie said thoughtfully. And that seemed right to him. Dracula's sharp kiss on the neck claimed his victim for all time. He could call his victim home when he desired another kiss. That felt right. He drank the bitter coffee.

Sussman said in a level voice, "Foley also said that I could tell you what's going on here, that you might even have advice for us." It was obvious that this was hard for him, and also that he needed advice right now. "Look, Meiklejohn, we don't know what we're dealing with, that's for sure. One of my men has vanished in the area, not a sign of him all afternoon. Okay. We're marking trees, following that circle on the map, and we'll rope off the area. No one's to go in. You know how big that perimeter's going to be? Anyway, we'll do it.

But meanwhile I have a man missing out there. Do you know what's in that hotel?"

"No," Charlie said flatly. "And neither does anyone else."

Windekin, the pale man who had escorted them from the other side of the valley, entered the building, stamping his feet, blowing on his hands. "I drove the Volvo up after we got it pulled loose. Jamieson's in the truck at the end of the drive they dug out."

Sussman nodded, then saw Constance hurrying from the hall. "I want to see my car," she said. "If you've damaged it, you pay, you know. You can't just go around pulling a car like that with a truck. If you hurt the transmission . . . Give me my keys!"

Sussman sighed. "Let her look it over," he said, waving Jack Windekin back out. "You keep the keys," he added. "They're both staying here until Foley says otherwise."

Constance glanced at the men imperiously and swept up her cap and gloves from the table on her way out. "He'll tell you a fairy tale about the hotel," she said, and slammed the door behind her. Charlie sat down at the map table. Again, it was happening again, more and more often, with more power each time. He would *not* turn in that direction, he told himself even as he turned to look, tilted his head in a listening attitude.

Sussman swore and sat down. He hoped the bitch decided to clean the car or something.

Constance forced herself to breathe normally, forced herself not to run to the Volvo. Instead, she approached it with Windekin and examined the front end with great care. The gravel parking area had been cleared by the snowplow; there were four other cars in it, and the black van that had no markings or windows. No one was in sight anywhere outside. She frowned at the side of the car and said accusingly, "You drove it up here with the chains on!"

"Yes ma'am," Windekin said. He was stony-faced.

She looked inside. Three pairs of skis. Carson had decided not to try to ski in alone. She was not surprised. He was such a novice with snow; he thought he had a better chance walking in. Two miles, Sussman had said. Could Carson walk two miles through snow that might be up to his knees in some spots, up to his hips in others? She thought not. A Virginia boy, he had called himself. What did he know about snow? She continued around the car to the trunk and demanded the keys again.

"Sorry, ma'am," Windekin said. "I'll open it for you." He opened the trunk lid, and this time she could not prevent her sigh of relief. The suitcase was gone.

"Leave it open," she ordered. "I'm going to put away some of the stuff from the front." She moved the snow shovels to the rear of the trunk, cleared a space. The Volvo had a lot of space. She continued on around the car; now it was between her and the building, between her and the van. She opened the back door and pulled out her skis. Her father had given them to her when she turned eighteen and suddenly measured five feet ten. She put the poles on the snow beside the skis, and her gloves on the floor of the back seat. Ready. Windekin was watching her, looking slightly puzzled but saying nothing, too cold to protest. She took two other poles to the trunk, and he followed.

He never could explain exactly what happened next. He thought she was falling down and he reached out to help her, and then she clamped her hand on his wrist and pulled; as he started forward, her forearm caught him in the midriff. He doubled over and somehow his feet slipped and he ended up in the trunk of the car, winded, unable to call out, to move even, and the lid closed.

She closed it on the strap of one of the poles, just to make sure he had plenty of air when he began gasping in long painful breaths. Now she moved very fast, back to the rear seat to put on the skis, thrust her hands through the pole straps. She looked at the building and the van; nothing was moving, no one in sight, and then she left the parking area through the snow, heading toward the hotel.

□ □ □

They had fooled around too long at the top of Childer's Park, and then Jud had started to whine that if it got dark his mom wouldn't be willing to drive up for them to get the truck. And Bobby had started to chicken out. What if no one was at Mel's camp and they had to walk four miles to town dragging the fucking toboggan?

"You want to walk down, start walking. You going down with me, come on," Herman Kohl snapped. He held up the truck keys, made a show of thrusting them in his pocket. He started to pull the toboggan toward the back side of the mountain. "It's no different this way," he said without looking back at the other two. "Better even; faster." By the time he reached the best place to start they were with him, looking glum as they all surveyed the unbroken snow ahead. It wouldn't be faster, Herman knew; the other runs had turned to ice long ago, and this was fresh, deep snow, but it was steeper on this side and that would help.

Herman was the one with woods sense. He knew any patch of woods he had ever walked through, and he had been all over the hills here. He never thought consciously of what lay ahead, but as soon as a new feature came into view, he recognized it, like a clump of birch trees to the left. And the rotten oak that rattled brown leaves as they slid by under it. He knew to steer away from a clump that might have been snow-covered bushes, but was in fact a large erratic boulder, moved from somewhere else by the last glacier, out of place here in New Jersey. And it was great to break through the snow, to be the first ones ever to go down the back of Childer's Park. Tomorrow a dozen guys would want to try it, but he was the first. He saw four pine trees and made an adjustment in their direction. Jud was laughing just behind him, and now and then Bobby let out a whoop, and the three boys leaned this way and that and picked up speed, then slowed down again. They made a good team, worked well together on the toboggan.

They were coming up on the drywall. Herman could not have said what landmark alerted him, how he knew, but he did. The unmortared walls turned up here and there all over the hills, dangerous summer and winter. In the summer you might put your foot down on a snake snoozing away in the shade of a wall; in the winter you could get killed if a runner hit a wall. The snow drifted on one side usually, and barely covered the stones on the other, hiding them, but not cushioning a fall, acting as instant brakes that stopped a sled or a toboggan and sent the rider flying, often to smash into the wall itself. He started to make the sliding turn away from the wall that was not yet visible, when everything changed.

Herman was blinded by a sharp pain in his head that made him duck with his eyes closed. He heard Bobby yell something, and the front end of the toboggan hit the wall. Herman was thrown, and when he landed, he did not move for several minutes. He drew in a sobbing breath and tried to sit up. He was in a drift that had almost buried him. He struggled to get free; the headache was subsiding and he no longer was blind, but he couldn't make out where he was. Then he heard Bobby and Jud fighting up near the wall, and now he saw that he had been thrown over it, had rolled twenty feet or more down the hillside before the drifts stopped him. Jud was screaming shrilly, like a girl. Herman got to his knees in the snow and yelled at them both to cut it out, but it was not that kind of fight. He could see Bobby's back, Jud's arms flailing; the screams grew in intensity. He yelled hoarsely at them; at the same moment Bobby half lifted Jud, turned with him, and smashed his back against the wall. Jud's arms went limp and the screaming stopped abruptly. Herman yelled again, and this time Bobby lifted his head and turned slowly until he saw Herman. He did not move away from Jud, instead he picked up the boy's head between his hands and smashed the back of his head into the wall, then did it again, and again.

Herman threw up in the snow. "Jesus!" he whimpered. "Jesus, Jesus, Jesus." He was slipping down the hill, watching Bobby, who was still facing him, but with a look that was not human. "Jesus! Jesus!"

Bobby let Jud fall and got to his feet, watching Herman. He took a step toward him, moving as if he were blind, his arms swinging loosely at his sides. He tripped on the wall and plunged over it, landed face down in the snow. Herman struggled to his feet and tried to run.

He fell, got up, and pulled himself through the deep snow, fell again, struggled up again. Every time he looked back Bobby was stumbling through the snow after him, sometimes falling, sometimes rising, always coming after him.

"Jesus, Jesus!" Herman kept sobbing. "Oh, Jesus!" He was heading toward the old hotel in the valley, instinctively seeking the nearest shelter, a place to hide, to find a weapon in—a board, anything.

□ □ □

Carson Danvers had to think deliberately about every movement. Lift the left leg, drag it out of the snow, move it forward, put it down. The problem was that he was not able to lift his leg out of the snow; he was dragging it through instead, and it was a leaden weight. He was within range, and had been for a long time; they were all around him, pressing against his head, brushing his face. He staggered and caught himself against a tree and took several deep breaths. That did not help. A burning pain shot through his lower back when he pushed himself away from the tree after a minute. Both thighs seemed on fire. He heard himself laughing at the thought of walking into the hotel on fire; he took another deep breath. Lift the right leg. . . . Then he stopped again in bewilderment. Tracks. He looked at them hard, something large, breaking through the snow like a plow. Then he laughed again.

A Woozle! He was tracking a Woozle! The laughter was more like a sob than anything else. He had to rest a minute or two. The image of Gary swam before his eyes. Gary with his eyes shining in delight at Pooh and Piglet tracking the Woozle. He had to rest. He dragged the suitcase with him to a tree trunk where he could stop for a few minutes, rest. He sat down in the snow with his back against the tree, his knees drawn up to ease the pain. After a moment he put his head down on his knees. Just for a minute or two, he told himself. How long had he been wandering in circles tracking the Woozle? Elinor and he always took turns reading to Gary, each of them loving it possibly even more than the boy. *Winnie the Pooh* was their favorite. If he tried hard, he thought he could even remember the words, the sentences.

"One fine winter's day when Piglet was brushing away the snow . . ."

◻ CHAPTER 20 ◻

CONSTANCE KNEW CARSON WAS IGNORANT OF the treachery of snow, how it could trick the eyes, dazzle the senses; how it could drain energy and heat so insidiously that a person would not even be aware of fatigue until collapse was certain. Then, after the battle had tilted, one would crave rest, just a few minutes of rest, and those few minutes would ensure muscle stiffness and charley horses, and more rest would be required. She did not try to ski very fast, not on fresh snow that was unknown, through woods that were unknown. A rock, a stump, a log, any of them might suddenly appear, or worse, not appear, leaving no time to avoid the hazard. She was cautious.

She did not know how much of a head start

she had. Fifteen minutes? If she was lucky. Ten? Possibly. Unless they had a crack skier among them they wouldn't come that way. By the road? Again, possibly. They would not let Charlie take off after her, she hoped, prayed. Not Charlie. He couldn't catch her, but he might try, if they allowed it. He knew he had to stay out of range, but she no longer trusted his awareness of his own danger in competition with the strong pull the thing seemed to exert on him. When the trees thinned and she could see a good stretch ahead, she speeded up. She had to find Carson, find the suit and the device that Charlie insisted was not really a bomb. First she had to find Carson; down the hill, across the valley, somewhere on the other side of it he would still be struggling in the snow, trying to reach the hotel. Unless he had collapsed already. She speeded up again.

□ □ □

"I'll tell you a fairy tale," Charlie said to Sussman when the other images vanished. He was shivering.

He started to tell about the thing in Old West, disregarding Sussman's look of skepticism, which soon became one of baleful disbelief that he made no effort to soften.

"So why'd Foley tell me to keep away altogether? Why not take a generator down there and turn it on if that stops it?"

"Because the boys in white lab coats want to

study it," Charlie said with great weariness. This was what Carson had run into. No one could believe it who had not personally seen the effects. A fairy tale. An agent he had not seen before stuck his head in the door and called out.

"They found Hershman. They're bringing him in."

Sussman went to the door, Charlie at his side. They waited on the porch for two men supporting another one between them who was covered with snow. He moved like a zombie. Like poor Mrs. Eglin, who screamed and screamed, and then turned into a zombie. This one was not screaming. Charlie felt nausea and hatred well up together. A couple more men appeared, talking in low voices. They all looked cold, not dressed for treks through the snowy woods; they looked frightened. When they reached the building the two small groups had merged and they all entered together. Some went for coffee, with much foot-stamping. No one was talking above near whispers.

"What happened to him?" Sussman demanded, as the two holding up Hershman lowered him to a chair. He sat where they positioned him without movement. His face was vacant, his eyes dull. When he sat down, his hands dangled at his sides.

"We found him crawling in the snow," one of the agents said. His voice trembled. He turned and went to the table that had coffee.

"Jesus Christ!" Sussman stared at the casualty, then turned abruptly. "There are cots in there. For God's sake, put him to bed. We'll get a doctor."

"What was that banging?" asked one of the agents, averting his gaze from the two men who were leading the zombie into the hall.

Sussman glared at him. "What banging?"

He tilted his head, shrugged, and returned to the table to add sugar to his cup.

Suddenly Charlie saw again the seconds before Constance had slammed the door on her way out, striding across the room, sweeping up her cap and gloves. How long ago?

"Good God!" He tore across the room, out the door, hearing Sussman's curse, then hard steps pounding after him. He ran to the Volvo with several men close behind, one with his gun drawn, but now they could all hear the banging, and it came from the trunk of the car. Charlie was first to reach it. He saw the keys in the snow beside the rear tire, and he stepped on them, mashed them down into the snow, scuffed more snow over them as he hit the lid with his fist. There was an answering bang.

"Windekin," he said mildly, and stepped back out of the way. The agent who had already drawn his gun was right by him. He looked too young to be allowed to carry a gun, and too frightened. Charlie glanced inside the car; two pairs of skis. Then he looked at the snow and saw the tracks that vanished into the woods.

Someone found a crowbar and they forced the lid open, helped Windekin out. He had vivid red spots on his pale face. When he saw Charlie, he took a step toward him and nearly fell down. His legs were too cramped for him to walk alone.

"Where's the woman?" Sussman demanded.

Windekin shook his head. "She slugged me and shoved me in there. That's all I know."

"She's gone down the hill on skis," someone called, and they went to the side of the car and looked at the tracks.

"She's gone down there? What for?" Sussman glared at Charlie. At that moment a new car appeared on the driveway. Fred Foley, Byron Weston, and another man had arrived. Looking infinitely relieved, Sussman hurried over to speak to Foley.

Charlie went down on one knee to examine the wheel closest to the roadway; the chain had broken. He clucked softly and went to the wheel near the snow and looked at that one and shook his head sadly. He found and pocketed the keys he had buried in snow earlier, then got up and brushed himself. He sauntered over to Foley and Byron Weston.

". . . with a scar on his face. May be dangerous. I want him brought in, and I want him undamaged. Understand. Not a scratch."

"And the woman?"

Foley shrugged. "Bring me that man."

Charlie waved to Byron, who yelled, "Is Loesser down there? Charlie, he can't burn that hotel! Not this time! Is he around?"

Foley had got out of the car to talk to

Sussman; Byron Weston was still inside. The driver started toward the building. Sussman motioned to his men; they all trudged back to the hunting camp.

Charlie waved again to Byron, this time in farewell as the car left him in the parking area. The young agent was still with him, in the rear of the group heading back to shelter and warmth. Charlie snapped his fingers in exasperation, wheeled about, and hurried back to the Volvo. The young agent went with him. At the trunk of the Volvo Charlie leaned over, inspecting the lock. When the agent drew near, Charlie straightened up suddenly and hit him in the jaw. It was too fast for defense, too unexpected; the young man dropped. Charlie took the gun from his hand, got in the Volvo, started, and made a crunching turn in the parking area, throwing gravel. He raced down the plowed driveway, turned on the road at the end of it, and sped on toward the next driveway that he and Carson had dug out. He was afraid they would radio the truck there to drive in all the way and wait with the engine running until further orders. And if Constance had reached Carson already, if they had reached the hotel, had found the black door to hell, had gone through it, they would be trapped inside when the running motor closed down the mechanism.

The truck had backed into the space Charlie and Carson had opened. It cleared the banks but left no room for anyone to enter the driveway. Charlie stopped in front of it and got out, taking his keys with him. The driver opened the window of the truck as Charlie scrambled over the bank to approach the side door.

"Get that thing out of there!" the driver yelled.

"They're trying to reach you by radio," Charlie called back, passing the door on his way to the rear of the truck.

The driver stuck his head out of the window. "What?" Who?"

"Sussman. Call him now." Charlie waited until the head withdrew, then pulled out the agent's gun from his pocket and shot the left rear tire at very close range. There was a scream of outrage from the truck cab, which he ignored as he took aim at the right tire and shot it, then a second time just to be sure. He started to trot through the snow, following the tracks of the Volvo. The truck driver was yelling obscenities at him.

He had to slow down when he reached the spot where Constance had got the Volvo stuck. Now there were only the tracks that Carson had left, a multitude of tracks. One trip out to scout the way, then his return, then his departure a second time. Charlie could see where he had dragged the suitcase through the snow. Now he moved carefully as his fear mounted. Where did *it* start? When would he cross the line? He knew it was there, operative; he could feel it calling him stronger than ever. He knew that if he stepped into range it would claim him.

□ □ □

When Constance crossed the line on her skis, she nearly panicked with the suddeness of the sharp headache that struck. She swerved momentarily, then caught herself. The headache was blinding this time; it did not double her over in pain. She blinked. Exactly as Carson had described the sensation, charged cobwebs all around her head, brushing her face, pressing against her forehead. She continued to follow Carson's erratic trail through the woods. He had staggered here, had fallen, rested, had sat against the tree there. She found the suitcase; he had taken the suit out, abandoned the suitcase, too heavy to drag farther. And now the light was fading; if she did not find him soon, it would be too late. They would need a search party with lanterns, and that meant they would have to drive in and *it* would close the door.

After that it would be in Byron's hands, and his colleagues'. She thought again of the minuscule Martians trying to reason with the probe that swallowed and analyzed them as fast as they neared it, thought of ants trying to reason with a descending boot, thought of a man blowing up his television because he did not like the program, thought of Charlie going rigid, listening, hearing something she could not even imagine. She stiffened; gunshots! Three shots! Silence returned and she went forward again, and the next second she spotted Carson.

"I'm all right," he said thickly when she touched him. He tried to get to his feet, his motions very slow, as if he were drunk, or too recently roused from a deep sleep. He had the suit wrapped around his arm. The device was strapped to the front of it, accessible when the suit was on.

"Carson, get up. We're very near the meadow. It's not very far now. Just get up and walk, Carson." She took the suit as she talked. The flashlight, she thought, and felt in his pocket for it. "Carson, can you hear me? I'm leaving you. You have to get up and walk to the meadow, keep moving. I'll come back as soon as I can, but I won't be able to find you in the woods if it gets dark. Carson!"

He nodded, and let his head nod down to his chest. She pulled on him until he managed to stand up. "Follow my tracks, Carson. Just to the meadow. You can rest at the edge of the meadow. Can you hear me?"

"Follow," he said, and stumbled after her when she started to ski.

The meadow was very close; he had skirted it for a long time. She went straight through the woods toward it. When she looked back Carson was still moving—unsteadily, staggering, but moving in her direction. Very soon she was out of the woods, and no more then three hundred feet away from the building. There were tracks all around it.

Warily she drew closer, very watchful now, taking her time. She had come almost to the porch, and could make no sense at all out of the prints. People had stamped the snow, apparently heading toward the woods, only to double back. More than one, but she couldn't tell how many; the snow was too trampled. The porch extended across the entire front of the building, deep and free of snow. All prints ended, with only packed snow here and there to indicate that the people had crossed it more than once. Suddenly a figure ran from the building, screaming in terror.

He ran to her, clutching at her arms, although he stood much higher than she. A boy, she realized; he was only a boy.

"Bobby's crazy!" he sobbed, dragging her down. "Help! Help! Oh, Jesus!"

She wrenched free and released her skis, looking past him. "Get out of here," she snapped at him. "There's a man in the woods over there. He needs help. Follow my ski tracks and get him to the road. Get out!"

He kept grabbing her arms, her shoulders, sobbing in fear. She slapped him neatly, took his hand, and turned him in the direction she wanted him to take, all the while guarding the suit and the pull ring from his clutching hands. There was another scream, not his, and he sobbed louder, "Jesus! Jesus!" She gave him a hard push.

"Get out of here! Help that man!"

He lurched forward, then began to scramble through the snow. She did not watch him, kept her gaze instead on a crouching figure that was moving off the porch. "Dear God," she breathed. This had to be Bobby. The trampled snow now told the story. One tried to run away, Bobby came after him, and he sought refuge in the hotel, someplace where he could try to hide. Over and over. She moved carefully, sideways, and Bobby's head turned. She had become the target.

She knew the look of psychopathy. During her graduate years she had worked in many institutions, some for the criminally insane. They can't be reached, her instructor had said sadly, not when they are having an episode. No reason could penetrate. Their brains sent no signals of pain or fear, hunger, cold—any of the inhibiting checks on behavior that governed others. And Bobby was criminally insane, murderously insane.

She continued to move with caution, trying to get closer to the porch without breaking into a run. That could be disastrous. He moved with complete disregard for what lay ahead. If he stumbled and fell, he would simply rise and keep coming. If she could reach the porch, get inside, she could elude him, she felt certain. The frightened boy had dodged him; she knew she could, but first she had to get inside, stay out of reach of his great hands. She feared him in a way she never feared another person. Her aikido training had always served her well, but only with rational opponents who could realize that it was pointless to keep coming against her only to get thrown down again, perhaps suffer a broken bone the next time. He could have no such realization.

He was making a harsh noise deep in his throat. Not an attempt at speech, not anything she had ever heard, a noise so atavistic it made the hair on her scalp rise. She glanced at the hotel; the porch continued around the corner, a deep veranda for wicker chairs, where guests could rest at leisure and sip lemonade in the heat of the day. There were more stairs on the side. She edged in that direction. He followed, getting nearer, the animal sound growing louder. He would lunge, she knew, and then she would run. Not until then. She wanted to be closer to the sanctuary of the building first, but he was getting nearer. On the porch if he made a grab for her, she could handle it and flee, but here in the snow that was growing deeper with every step, even if she threw him, she would still be nearly helpless against his greater size.

She was within ten feet of the side steps when he screamed and rushed her. She plowed through the snow, then her foot caught on something covered in a drift and she fell down; he grabbed her by the ankle. She kicked out with all her strength and her boot hit him on the shoulder, sent him sprawling backward. She scrambled up the stairs and raced toward the door that had been forced open; she could hear him clambering up the steps. At the door she looked back and moaned. He was dragging the suit.

□ □ □

Charlie walked in dread. Distantly he heard the truck revving, then silence again. They must have driven it out to the road to allow a different vehicle to try to get through. He paused, listening, but could hear nothing. He walked on. Then he reached another drift, this one more like an avalanche that had swept down the hillside, into the valley proper. He tried to see past it and failed. It would stop a car, he decided, and felt a tension within him relax a little. Carson's footprints went around the drift, down the hillside, into the woods. He started after them, and stopped again. There was a tree limb crossing Carson's trail. The snow was trampled all around the area; Carson had found the branch, had dragged it here, and placed it very deliberately across the route he had taken. Charlie's mouth went dry as he considered it.

He heard someone calling him and looked about, settled for a mound of snow to duck behind. Not much protection, but better than out in the open. He sat down and examined the gun he had taken from the agent. A .45, good gun, three bullets gone.

"Charlie? You hear me?"

"I hear you, Fred."

"We're getting a jeep from town, Charlie, and we're taking it in there. And we don't want any trouble. You hear that?"

"Loud and clear. I won't let it pass, Fred." He could see for about fifty feet down the driveway where several men appeared slogging through the snow. "You can't get around the drift here, anyway," Charlie called. He could tell by the way they were looking around that they did not know yet where he was.

"Charlie, for God's sake, what are you trying to do?" Byron called. "Is Constance in there? You know the danger! Charlie, we can't let Loesser burn it out again! God knows when and where it'll turn up next."

Charlie knew all that. He did not respond this time. They were close enough now that they could locate him by his voice, close enough to see the mammoth drift that would block even a jeep. Of course, he thought, they didn't realize how near the line was. Could a jeep drive through the snow and cross it? He was afraid so.

"Charlie, give it up," Fred Foley yelled. "I've got men coming down the hill behind you. For Chrissake, just come on out and give it up!"

Charlie felt his stomach tighten. "Call them off, Fred. Not over there! They shouldn't be over there!"

The cluster of men moved toward him: Fred Foley, Byron Weston, a third man who was unknown. Charlie looked behind him at the hill, hoping Fred had been bluffing. He had not been. At least three men were slipping and sliding in the snow on the hill above the drift.

"Send them back!" he yelled. "Byron, tell him! They're within range if they come down there!"

Byron hesitated, started to reach out to touch Foley's arm, then drew back. One of the men on the hill screamed hoarsely and let go of a tree he had been using to ease himself down. He began to slide, yelling. A second man was doubled over, holding his head. The third one stopped in his tracks, then slowly, very carefully began to back up.

The man who had slid down the hill came into view, walking like a blind man in the direction of the hotel. Blood was shiny red on his face.

"Selene!" Foley yelled. "Selene!" He took a dozen steps that brought him close enough to talk in a normal voice to Charlie. "What's the matter with him?"

"Sometimes they are called in," Charlie said. "At least he's not homicidal. Sometimes they are."

Foley looked about almost wildly. Now he could see Charlie sitting with his back against the hill. Charlie waved the gun, then rested it on his knee. "Who's the new kid on the block?" he asked, motioning toward Byron and the other man.

"Michael Newhouse," the man said, joining Foley. "Physicist. Meiklejohn, we have to have the opportunity to study this phenomenon.

You're not an ignorant man. You should understand the importance of this thing." Too cool, too self-assured, almost movie-star good-looking, except for his dark eyes, which glittered and were too small.

"Charlie," Byron said imploringly, "don't make trouble. If Loesser burns it out, we'll just have to go to the next place it turns up. You know that. We can't let this opportunity escape us. You know that, too. We're going to bring in the jeep, and now that we know about where the range starts, it should be fairly easy to get the machine close enough to shut everything down long enough to get the area cleared. If Loesser's in there, we want him, Charlie. He's the only one who can go in and do the tests that Newhouse thinks might answer some questions. Think, Charlie, if it's an alien artifact, what that could mean to the world."

"What is that, Byron?" Charlie asked pleasantly, listening hard for the sound of another engine.

"Charlie! We have the tools to trace it back to its source, to communicate with them, to establish contact. It's the breakthrough every scientist on earth has been waiting for."

"What if it doesn't want to be probed and tested?" Charlie asked. "What if it has a defensive system your tests might trigger. You know what it does to people now. What if that's just a side effect of *its* tests?"

"Meiklejohn, believe me, we know how to take precautions," Newhouse said with a touch of irritation. "That's why we want this whole area cleared, to protect the innocent. We work with very dangerous materials all the time and to date our accident record is unblemished."

Charlie laughed. "What if poor old John Loesser doesn't want to be your errand boy? Volunteers? Would you volunteer to go in there, Newhouse?"

"Loesser will agree," Foley said. "You know what kind of prison term he'll get for all those fires?"

"You have proof?"

"We have your evidence," Foley said viciously. "Remember?"

Charlie shook his head. "I don't believe I ever did make a written report. Seemed little point to it, actually. And I do recall some speculative, rather idle conversation, but not much more than that."

Foley faced away with a disgusted look. "He'll cooperate," he said.

They all heard the jeep and no one moved as the sound came closer. Then Charlie raised the gun. "Fred, if it gets this far, tell him to stop, or I'll shoot the driver and the gas tank. You know I can do it, Fred."

Fred Foley studied him, expressionless. "What are you up to, Charlie? What the hell do you think you're doing?"

"Later. Just flag him down if he gets in this far."

Foley shook his head. "You son of a bitch! You know I won't."

Charlie knew. He had known Fred Foley for a very long time. Sussman might have agreed, not Fred. He sighed tiredly and stood up. They heard the safety being released. What the devil was Constance doing in there? And Carson? Why didn't something happen? There had been time enough, unless neither one had ever reached the damn hotel. Maybe she had taken a fall in the woods and lay unconscious? She could have broken a leg. What if she had been wrong about being immune? Too late. Too late for second-guessing her. She was in there by now, either immune or insane.

He would have stopped her if he could. Now all he could do was make certain no one turned on an engine, not until she was out of that goddamn place. If they trapped her inside that black door to hell, he would kill the lot of them. His hands were moist. He shifted the gun and wiped one, then the other. If she had got through the black door, the abyss, had pulled the ring, and then the jeep went through and the door slammed behind her, she would be there when the device went off. It could not be stopped once the reaction began. The three men watched him holding the gun steadily now. They waited for the jeep, listening to its laboring engine as it came through the snow.

Then he felt *it*. Not now, he wanted to cry out, aware of Foley and the others, but more aware of the call of the abyss. He could almost understand what it wanted of him, almost hear real words, almost name the sensations that swept him. He felt his head turning in spite of his efforts to resist, and from a great distance he could hear Foley speak.

"Jesus Christ! What's wrong with him?"

He started to move, one foot, the other, the gun forgotten, dangling as he felt himself drawn stronger than ever, a filing being taken to a magnet. He stumbled against the snow-drift, fell, and someone jumped on him, tried to get an arm around his throat. The shock of the snow on his face, the attack, made the summons fade; this reality took precedence. He half-rolled against the snow, enough to dislodge Foley. Charlie sank down against the drift and raised the gun.

"Back up," he grunted. "Just back the hell up."

Brushing snow away, Foley backed up, cursing. Charlie glanced at Byron and Newhouse. Neither had moved. Byron was staring at him with a shocked expression. "He's been affected by it!" he whispered. Then he turned frantically to Newhouse. "He's been affected. We're not in range here. If his wife's in there, and Loesser, they must have a plan to really destroy the source of the radiation this time, not just burn it out. We have to stop them!"

"How's Polly?" Charlie asked, and realized he had turned the gun to point it directly at Byron; it felt right aimed that way.

"I don't know. She's dropped out for the rest of the year. Listen, Charlie, tell us what they're up to. If you were attacked and survived, and

Loesser can go in and out at will, and maybe Constance, you must see that it's not as dangerous as we all thought before. We'll lick it."

"Tell that to Polly," Charlie said. "And Mike and poor Mrs. Eglin up at Orick, and the sheriff's men at Old West. Tell that son of a bitch wandering around in the woods, and the one they found crawling in the snow—" He stopped. The jeep was coming.

□ CHAPTER 21 □

CONSTANCE RAN ACROSS THE ROOM SHE HAD ENtered and ducked through an open doorway, where she stopped to listen. She could see the irregular entrance with pale light beyond, and then the boy's figure eclipsed it. His steps were heavy and loud on the bare floor. She did not move as he swung his body this way and that. Looking for her? Listening? His movements were not human; it was impossible to guess his intentions, if he even had intentions now. Again he made the hair-raising animal noise deep in his throat and lurched forward. He was still dragging the suit.

The hotel was very dark away from the lobby area. She could see nothing in the room behind her, and very little of the lobby that the boy was crossing, the insane noise echoing, reechoing until it seemed sourceless. He passed from her line of sight. Now, she thought, she probably could outrun him, get outside, get her skis. . . . The other boy must have tried repeatedly to get away, and each time this one had heard, had seen, had known, and had given chase. She bit her lip, listening for his receding steps. What if he caught the ring pull on a nail? Hearing him made her realize how vulnerable she would be if she moved. Soundlessly she took off her own boots. She nearly dropped them when there was a new noise. She peeked around the door frame and could see nothing. It sounded as if he were kicking a wall, maybe trying to kick it down, and his guttural voice rose to a near scream, dropped, rose. It was inhuman, full of pain and fury.

She closed her eyes hard and took a deep breath, then another. She knew she could get to the door without his hearing her. The other boy must have pounded like an elephant across the lobby each time he made a run for it. And then? She knew that was no good. She had to find the doorway to the alien mechanism. She had to stay alive, with a chance of escaping after the device had been delivered.

When she opened her eyes, only a second or two later, they had adjusted to the dimness enough for her to see that she was in a large room with boarded-up windows, completely bare. The strippers had been here. Hardwood flooring had been removed, exposing the rough underfloor. Paneling must have been peeled off the walls, leaving lathwork, with gaping holes in it. Pencil-thin lines of light revealed the outside wall and windows. She looked again into the main lobby where the boy was howling, and this time she could see a figure trying to climb the skeleton of a staircase. The strippers must have taken the stairs away. Hardwood, carved, whatever, they must have had value, and now there was no way for him to get to the second floor. She shuddered. He wanted to go home to *it* and he couldn't, so he howled his frustration. The realization struck her that she could not reach the doorway to the abyss either.

For an instant she knew there was no point in staying here, that the only sensible thing to do was run to the porch, put on her boots, find her skis, and get away. The boy was trying to climb a long narrow board that had been left standing when the stairs were removed. He got up a few feet only to slide back down, screaming. She could almost see Charlie in the bulky figure, and knew it might become Charlie if they didn't stop the thing here in this place.

Back stairs? Servant's stairs? There had to be service stairs, and they would be plain, not tempting to strippers. Silently she left her refuge and crept around the wall to a spot close to the entrance where she put her boots, to be picked up on her way out, she told herself. She began to search for back stairs. She had thrust the flashlight in her belt, and now took it out, but did not dare use it until she had crossed another room. The boy's cries were distant now. Another dining room? Another door. Another room, smaller, darker. The slivers of light coming through the boarded-up windows were growing paler. And the cobwebs were everywhere, brushing, pushing, trying to get in. She imagined them seeping through her eyes, entering her ears, her nostrils, her mouth. Shuddering, she stopped, forced herself to breathe deeply, then went on. Another room. Suddenly the boy's voice was close, and she drew back, afraid he had noticed her movements; then she realized that she had made a circuit of half the lower floor, unless she had missed part of it in the darkness. Had one of the rooms been a kitchen? She was almost certain she had not yet been in a kitchen; there would be signs even if everything had been taken out. Cabinets, a pantry, something would be there, and the back stairs would be nearby.

Many doors had been removed; a few still in place would not open, and the darkness grew deeper, windows smaller, with less light penetrating the gloom. Offices? She jerked her foot when a splinter dug in and she realized that she had not heard the boy's voice for several minutes. Had he fallen, hit his head? Made it to the top finally? Resting? She listened, then shook her head and went on to the next room. She did not believe he could move silently; he was not capable of thinking of the consequences of making noise, alerting her. But he might have glimpsed her light, she thought, although she was using it as sparingly as possible, guarding it with her cupped hand. She brushed invisible cobwebs away from her face, listened, crept across one room after another, through narrow halls, and at last she knew she was in the kitchen. There were cabinets—no sink, no appliances or table, but there were cabinets with doors ajar. She hurried across the space, through an opposite doorway, and found the back stairs, intact. The boy was still quiet, or tricks of architecture swallowed his voice. The thought struck her with sickening force that he might be handling the suit, tearing it apart, that he might have enough mind to wonder about the ring.

Her hands were shaking so hard, the spot of light danced on the stairs. "Stop it!" she said under her breath, and gripped the light with both hands until it steadied. She went up the stairs. Here were the bedrooms, an eight-foot-wide corridor, closed doors on both sides. The blackness was complete; her flashlight the only light. Somewhere near the center, Carson had said; that's where it always was. She started with the door to her left, opened it, shone the light around the walls, closed it again. Nothing but cobwebs, both real and invisible, charged cobwebs. The next door. The next. She crossed the hall to look inside the opposite room before moving farther down.

The light revealed the ruined walls, with their exposed plaster and lathwork and peeling wallpaper. Very pale slivers of light cut across each room, across closed closet doors, or sometimes doorless closets. She opened another door, began her quick sweep of light over the walls, and stopped. The light was absorbed by a blackness more intense than any she had ever seen. Before, the light touched a surface, reflected something back. But this time, it stopped dead. She caught her breath sharply. The light swerved; she brought it back and trained it along the outline of the black abyss. Too large for a closet door. A door connecting two rooms. She backed out into the hallway. She had closed each door after looking inside, but she left this one standing open. She made sure it was the only open door near the stairs, and then started back down. Now she had to get the suit away from the mad boy.

Constance made her way back to the lobby. She located the boy from the noises he was making, but she could not see him yet. Near the destroyed staircase was all she could tell, in a shadow that hid him thoroughly. The light coming through the broken door was almost gone, too pale to reveal the boy. But did he still have the suit? If he had dropped it, maybe she could creep in close enough to snatch it away and run.

She took a step into the lobby, the hall to the kitchen behind her, and then she aimed the light at the spot where the sounds of his breathing originated. When she turned on the flashlight, he was not there. She had to sweep the floor back and forth before she came to him, in a fetal position, sucking in great, choking gasps of air, the suit held like a blanket against his chest. As soon as the light was on him, he screamed and jumped up, clutching the suit. She turned and ran, and he followed, his boots thundering on the wooden floors. She did not dare enter any of the rooms along this hall; many of them did not have another exit and he was still coming. Over the thumping of his boots, and the hoarse, inarticulate sounds he made, she thought she could hear the air tank thumping also, and her heart pounded even harder. The suit would be useless without air, if the tank were damaged, which seemed likely.

She reached the kitchen and darted across it, crouched near the door on the far side, and waited. He came a second or two later, blundered into a wall, into a cabinet. He was barely visible in the failing light, no more than a great hulking shape. In despair she hung her head, trying to catch her breath. If only she could get close enough to hit him with the flashlight. Even as she thought it, she knew there was no point in it. She would need a sledgehammer to stop him. As a weapon the flashlight was useless, but suddenly she thought of how Candy, their cat, could not resist chasing a light, and she shone it against the far wall. His shape moved toward it. One of his hands tried to grab the beam, then smashed into the cabinet the light was on. She moved the light; he followed, futilely trying to snatch it. She turned it off and he bellowed.

Trying to make no sound, she edged along the wall to the nearest cabinet. She placed the flashlight on a shelf, aimed at the opposite wall, and then turned it on. He ran toward it, still dragging the suit, the air tank scraping the floor with every step he took. When he stopped at the spot of light, she started to crawl toward him. He banged his fist into the cabinet again and again, yelling, sobbing. If it didn't move soon, she knew, he would lose interest in it. She crawled faster until she could reach out and touch the suit. She did not try to take it from him, but found the air tank and let her hand slide around it, under the suit to the pouch strapped on the chest. She moved as cautiously as she could, but tried to hurry. Any second he might jerk away, go back to the lobby. Her fingers found the pouch, and she felt around it until she came to the cold metal of the ring. She pulled it.

He felt that and roared, kicked out. His foot caught her in the thigh; she stifled a scream and scrambled away. Her leg had gone numb. If he had groped for her then, he would have found her, but his brain was issuing no orders, reasoning nothing. When he heard her, he tried to smash her. If he saw her, he would follow. As soon as she was silent and invisible, he forgot her. He went back to the light, but only for a second this time. She could see the darkness of his shape moving away, heard his boots, his screams. She couldn't let him go back out there to the lobby, start his useless assault on the old stairs again. She forced herself up and hobbled to the cabinet that held the flashlight, reached it and took it out, waved the light in a circular pattern, then lowered the beam to the floor. He came after it.

She knew he would not let go of the suit. It was a pattern of behavior that some madness induced. A patient sometimes grasped an object from morning until night, until sleep relaxed the fingers enough for a nurse or doctor to take it away. She led him from the kitchen, playing the light on the floor, on the wall, on the open door. She led him to the stairs and started to back up them. He was coming faster now, spending less time trying to catch the spot of light, his animal noise louder. He would run over her, she realized, and swung the light around, shone it in his eyes. He screamed and kept coming. She turned and ran up the last dozen steps, ran to the open door, where he caught up with her and hit her on the side of the head with the back of his hand. He knocked her across the room, into the wall. She hung for a moment, then slid to the floor unconscious.

□ □ □

She stirred and moaned with her eyes closed. As soon as she cut off the sound, silence returned. When she opened her eyes a wave of nausea swept her. The light was still on, half-way across the room, shining at the hole where a baseboard had been. Groggily she crawled to it and picked it up. Still on her hands and knees, she hung her head trying to remember what it was she was supposed to do. Memory hit her and she snapped her head up. Pain followed so sharply it brought tears to her eyes. He was gone. She turned the light to the abyss, still there. How long? She had no way of knowing how long she had been unconscious. Steadying herself with one hand on the wall, she forced herself upright and started out, trying to hurry, but very aware that her leg was dragging, that she was mired in one spot, that there was no way she could negotiate a flight of stairs and get out of the hotel.

□ □ □

The jeep stopped twenty feet away from Foley. Two men climbed out; one remained behind the wheel. Foley looked from the jeep to Charlie. His face was set in hard lines, his voice grim. "It'll be dark very soon, Charlie. We're going in while there's still light."

"Someone will be hurt," Charlie said softly.

"Then someone will be hurt," Newhouse said in a clipped voice. "Send them in."

"Is that how it is?" Charlie asked Foley. He examined Newhouse with more interest. Foley waved to the man behind the wheel of the jeep, and Charlie raised the gun. "He'd better get out and look over the situation first, don't you agree? He might not be able to get around this drift."

"I'm tired of stalling," Newhouse said and, turning his back on Charlie, went to the jeep and got in. The driver shifted gears. Foley started to say something, but Charlie tightened his finger on the trigger. And then everything stopped.

It was like being caught in a hurricane, but without wind, or in an electrical storm without lightning. For a second there seemed to be no air, as if a giant vacuum had sucked them all in. Then the charged cobwebs were everywhere, pressing hard against everyone simultaneously, at the same time sucking them empty. Charlie dropped to his knees, both hands over his ears, as if what he experienced was pure sound. Foley fell down twitching. Byron staggered a few feet and fell face-first into the snowdrift. Newhouse clutched his head and screamed.

Carson Danvers and the boy were knocked down by the effect. When Carson began to stir, he thought he heard Gary sobbing. He crawled to him and cradled him in his arms, saying nonsense words over and over, rocking him. The boy sobbed against his chest. Not Gary, just a hurt kid, Carson thought finally, but he did not release him until they were both ready to stand up and start moving together.

When Charlie was able to move, Foley was pulling himself up. "Come on," Charlie cried hoarsely. He staggered to the jeep and dragged out the unconscious driver. On the other side, Foley hauled Newhouse out. Charlie drove around the snowdrift, the jeep tilting perilously, then back up to the driveway and through the snow around the side of the hill toward the hotel. Neither man spoke. Now there was a fierce glow in the sky, sparks were leaping up into the darkening air. Charlie drove too fast, the jeep skidded and slid and threatened to die altogether in too-deep snow, but he kept it going until they were in the meadow, and there the snow overwhelmed it. He stopped and stood on the seat, scanning the area around the hotel. And he saw her, sprawled in the snow. He left Foley and waded through the drifts to her.

She was conscious, but barely. He lifted her and then sat down, holding her in his arms while she shook. "Look at the mess you made," he said in her ear. "Warm?" The heat would drive them back in a minute or two; it was melting the snow around them already.

"Oh, Charlie," she cried, "there was a boy. A poor, mad boy! He took it in!"

"*Sh. Sh.* It's over. It's over."

He held her and watched the fire and waited for someone to come to get them. They would call it an earthquake, or a meteorite, or a gas explosion, or some damn thing. They were good at that. They would gather in the hurt, the dead, the destroyed who might live a long time and never know they were destroyed, and before long it would all be forgotten. But what if they had taken it to San Francisco, to Berkeley, or any place with a lot of people, what if they had triggered it there with their tests? He shook his head. He had known it was armed to defend itself if necessary; he had known it.

Foley joined them. "Well," he said heavily. "That's that, I guess. Let's go."

"She can't walk," Charlie said. "No shoes."

Constance wailed, "I lost my boots, and the skis my father gave me when I was eighteen! He was about eighteen." She put her head against his chest and wept. He held her and watched the leaping flames, the flares, the shower of sparks, one of the most beautiful sights on earth.

▫ Epilogue ▫

IN THE BEGINNING, ASSOCIATE KRI, SON OF KRI, often gazed at the glowing heavens, with the three pathways of stars that looked like ribbons, and his own lights pulsed in harmony with the gently pulsing lights from above. Those nights his shame drove him to renew his efforts to find the evil he had launched, the ugliness he had injected into such beauty. Each time he knew the probe had emerged from interspace he prayed that this time it would be destroyed.

Three times he had been offered the release of pardon and total annihilation; each time he had refused. From his laboratories had come the theories that propelled his people through the mysterious interspace and out to other star systems with myriad life forms. His solution to the multibody, space-time problem had proven correct, followed by his theory of subparticle transmission that haltingly, then with more and more assurance, allowed instant communication between any two or more defined points, and eventually the instant transmission of matter.

Space, he wrote, was not a smooth continuum, not a simple curve, or a plane, but was composed of many folds, often refolded, with forces never anticipated by the early explorers. The capsule he sought could have gone through an unknown number of folds, or could have emerged from interspace to follow the curves of infinite folds, back and forth in time, he theorized, with mathematics so complicated that no one of his people could comprehend his proofs.

Each time the fountain of lights with its hideous black heart appeared and disappeared, he pulsed the data into his computer, and possible trajectories were formulated, only to be discarded with new data, as new paths were hypothesized; some of these were not rejected. From a number that had been so large it had been meaningless, there were now fewer than a hundred possible courses that the cylinder might be traversing. In charting the emergence of the probe from interspace and back in again, he was also charting planetary systems, more than anyone had imagined, could imagine. No race, no confederation could explore them all;

one might as easily examine every grain of sand on an infinite beach.

His theories became even more abstract and abstruse; that no one read them any longer was a matter of indifference to him. The pursuit of knowledge was the only endeavor worthy of intelligence, he told himself now and again, and could not remember if he had made this up, or if he had heard it from someone else a long time ago. Eventually even the desire for knowledge faded, and for long periods he was motionless, a pale flicker the only indication that he still lived. He had been made a subject of study himself, and his observers reported that sometimes following his pale interludes, he almost blazed with an incandescence. No one knew how to interpret this. He no longer talked or wrote scientific papers. The observers also reported that sometimes after his pale interludes, he flared with the gaiety of laughter, and this left them uneasy. The masters would have put him to rest, but they did not dare. He had become a legend.

When it ended, only two observers were with him. For a long time the probe had presented its fountain of lights with the black lashing column at its heart and Associate Kri, son of Kri, had been observing it. This was his pattern when the probe emerged from interspace; he watched and pulsed data into the computer, and then faded back into his pale lethargy when the probe reentered interspace. This time something changed.

The fountain of lights with the unquiet black column that Associate Kri called the dark door of evil was glowing one second, then it flickered, dimmed, and faded out. The observers turned to Kri for an explanation, only to find him gone also.

He flared with laughter. Folds, he thought; of course, space did not fold by itself, one had to fold it. He had tried to explain this to the masters and they had not understood. He had told them in language made as plain as possible that at the moment of destruction of the cylinder, he would be able to locate it. And he had waited for that moment.

He folded space and interspace and time and stepped through to enter the cylinder. How little it had changed, he marveled, centered in the midst of the ever-rising, ever-falling torrent of light that ranged the spectrum of color. How beautiful it was! They had done their work well, better than they had known. Had they planned for it to be self-repairing? He did not know. But evidently it had that capability. There was a dead creature being probed by the photoscan. Useless, of course. Ah, he thought then, the black that he had called a door, really was aptly named. Another bipedal creature walked without grace through the darkness, dragging an object with it. This creature was alive, but senseless. He looked beyond it, and found himself outside the cylinder, surveying the world it had been probing. A lovely planet, with clouds, seas, obviously with an intelligent life form, since something here had destroyed the cylinder, or would destroy it momentarily. He turned his attention back to the interior of the cylinder, and suddenly realized that the creature that had entered was the destructive agent after all. He was carrying an explosive device. Kri knew he could fold space/time again, if he chose, and save himself, have enough time to learn everything there was to know about this planet, this creature with the explosive device, and he knew there was no reason for him to do so. Finally it was over. When the explosion came, Associate Kri, son of Kri, flared more brilliantly than even the mininova of the cylinder.